Passing Passions

Christopher Hammond

TSL Publications

First published in Great Britain in 2020
By TSL Publications, Rickmansworth

Copyright © 2020 Christopher Hammond

ISBN / 978-1-913294-81-6

The right of Christopher Hammond to be identified as the author of this work has been asserted by the author in accordance with the UK Copyright, Designs and Patents Act 1988.

All characters and events in this publication, other than those clearly in the public domain, are fictitious and any resemblance to actual persons, living or dead, is purely coincidental.

All rights reserved. No part of this publication may be reproduced, stored in a retrieval system or transmitted, in any form or by any means without the prior written permission of the publisher, nor be otherwise circulated in any form of binding or cover other than that in which it is published and without a similar condition being imposed on the subsequent buyer.

Cover image:
https://pixabay.com/photos/photo-album-album-photo-235603/
https://commons.wikimedia.org/wiki/File:Swanborough_Accomodation.jpg

May 1969 –

Queens Park, Brighton

It was the perfect spot. He was unseen and, according to his diminished expectations, he could see – just enough. The carefully tended lawns and flower beds of Queens Park sloped gently away from his secluded bench towards the duck pond and playground and, just beyond, to the house. All around was, so far, undisturbed on the early summer Sunday morning except by the weakest of breezes and the already strong sunlight. For as long as he could remember he had wished to be undisturbed and only to observe and learn. Now all he was able to do was watch and wait while every day he craved some small physical confirmation of the disturbance she had engendered in spirit.

    He had been compelled to do it. But sense that was supposed to be common told him that he had wasted too much of his last, precious term trying to find the house. There was no time to lose! There was no time for aimless wandering to the wrong destinations. There was no time to spend, in avoidable embarrassment, searching with the secretary to match the right first name to the right department; her co-operation and acceptance of his feeble excuse was little consolation. And, for what had passed as a final triumph, he had experienced the thrill of watching Caroline return home one day. He had found her house! He had observed Caroline's heavenly form for a few seconds from his vantage point in the park before she disappeared – the silver-golden back-combed hair, the big sunglasses, the white blouse, the leather waistcoat and the blue jeans. The uniform that he knew so well and the excitement of his hiding place made his heart race. He waited, and lowered his eyes occasionally to take in a paragraph of his newspaper – his cover. He was too self-conscious to give any passer-by the suspicion that he was in any way a voyeur. The pathetic surveillance had revealed his useless secret. Now, although he had no desire to believe it and although he sat no more than seventy yards from her, he was no closer than the day he had first seen her. Since then, he was once more forced to dwell on fantasy instead of fact. He pictured her walking out in the morning sun; he pictured himself emerging discreetly from his hiding; he pictured them meeting as if by chance ...

Michael, though, was not destined to be the slave of fantasy. It was true that in childhood and adolescence he believed it had singled him out as a plaything, to be led along fruitless and even frightening paths. He would sometimes ponder that he could be the only thing in the universe that existed, until it became a terrifying possibility. But Michael was too much a disciple of science for fantasy to turn his mind; a mind whose true haven, it thought, was in solid, physical reality.

As he sat on his pitiful park bench, it was not true depression and despair that gripped him. It was a nagging frustration at what he viewed as his own weakness and hesitation. As usual he blamed himself. There had been time and now there was so little – so little for the pursuit of two dreams. But dreams were useless, he told himself. His dictionary described the dream as an "insubstantial thing". Dreams were a jumble of disconnected thoughts which dissolved as soon as he woke up to reality. It was pointless to ponder and speculate about what might be. He had to escape from dreaming.

What did the look, the voice, even the feel of this less-than-handful of girls who had expressed at least temporary interest, make him aspire to? What if their attentions had not been ephemeral? Would he have reciprocated with undying devotion and, if called on, made the supposed ultimate sacrifice of love, and died for them? His thoughts had never strayed this far. In their different ways they remained objects of mystery and wonder. None, at that moment, was more mysterious than Caroline.

The fantasy of intellectual pre-eminence fought constantly with these other reveries. Anxiety tugged at him during each waking minute that was not spent in putting into order every equation and theory that he had been exposed to. Each part had to be memorised and repeated on demand in a coherent manner in response to the dreaded, unknown few questions in four weeks' time. But here he lingered in the park, observing and making no progress.

No one came from or went to the house, and few passed while he watched. His thoughts began to wander past it, down to Upper Rock Gardens. It possessed few discernible features reflecting its name but it had been the symbol, however imperfect, of first independence and many a thrilling expectation. Sweet memories were already obscuring the sour. Down further, Upper became Lower which then became Promenade – the Promenade made famous by past royalty, vintage cars, mods and rockers and, with luck, his own blues compositions. Countless and interminable, they had been hummed and had floated away into the sea mist, unplayed and very likely unplayable, whenever he had rambled back from coffee bar or pub alone. Down the road and under the Palace Pier Hotel he had first exposed a luckily half-converted audience to a rough guitar imitation of one of those vocal solos. And he had heard the first intoxicating sample of applause that he had always longed for. It had not been merely a diversion from the supposed rigours of study. It had been a part of the quest for recognition. The observer wished to be observed – but from a position of strength.

Weaknesses, only ever privately admitted, by one who had always sought solitude, had been ripe for exposure by room- or flat-mate. He hadn't been able to escape. First year Rock Gardens had initiated the uncovering and second year Hove had accentuated it. Spirits had sometimes fallen low in the depths of the basement in Norton Road. Relief had come in that period of occasional co-habitation in that bright, orderly, sweet-smelling flat – now full of strangers – also not a stone's throw from his bench. He recalled the glimpse of that other flat down in elegant Brunswick Square where he had been allowed to linger long enough to indulge in polite conversation with that certain other girl. It seemed right for her to reside in a cream-fronted Georgian terrace and have the best sea-view, even though she had expressed embarrassment at her good fortune. He was glad that she had never suggested visiting his grimy basement.

His brooding thoughts came full circle from Hove across the station and to his present, and perhaps final, refuge in Roundhill

Crescent, amongst the poorer, greyer and more densely packed terraces that huddled either side of the Lewes Road. The occupants of the Hove basement who had moved with him knew nothing, as yet, of his present tenuous attachment and his journeys from the Crescent to Queens Park. The steepness of the ascent provided him with some vestige of a labour to undergo in the pursuit of what, to a disinterested observer, would be called love. Michael had argued silently to himself as a boy and volubly but wanderingly to Bill, as a tiresome adolescent, about the meaning of the word. The concept of love had had no apparent scientific explanation but now the arguments had been suspended while the vigil continued.

That day, perhaps a month ago, he and Caroline had been close one evening, by chance at adjacent desks in the largely-deserted library. She had got up to go and in doing so had dropped some books. While gathering them up, a smile brightened her face. It was not overtly directed at him but he was convinced that it was not only an acknowledgement of his presence but a gesture of warmth. It was the first time he had noticed her but, like opposite charges, he was suddenly and acutely conscious of the attraction that their chance proximity afforded. For him at least, the electricity subsequently diminished neither with distance nor with time. It pulled him relentlessly and with increasing force but his wretched diffidence had held him back at each opportunity.

"You're an idiot," he told himself out loud but with some restraint, fearing to share a more colourful description of his incompetence with unseen passers-by. He kept further thoughts unspoken.

You stood next to her at the bus stop. You've sat at the same canteen table. And what about the time you walked past her with fat Frank in the library? He was only a casual acquaintance of hers – it was obvious. So why did she grab her books so suddenly and come over to talk to you both when she saw you walking away? She wanted to make contact with you. YOU, you idiot! And what did you do? Nothing! Bloody nothing! Each hesitation gives more time for some unscrupulous male, unlike you, to sweep her feet from the ground!

He could barely contemplate the possibility that one had already clinked wine glasses with her across a candle-lit table and had induced her to indulge in unthinkable after-dinner entertainment.

It was too much. For the moment, he had to leave. The cursory regard that he had been paying to the political tales in the pages of his mask of nonchalance was turning into fatigue as the morning temperature rose. He got grudgingly to his feet in preparation to return to other pressing obligations. But he had to make the detour because the direct way home seemed too direct, too final. He passed the duck pond and left the park a precarious twenty yards from the house. It still showed no outward sign of life, persuading him, for the time being, that there was little further reason to remain.

The heat of summer had always held some association with the advent or aftermath of the examination ritual. The success that had always appeared automatic hadn't instilled arrogance or boast. It had been gratefully received; but as the years passed the steady growth of competitive spirit within him was acknowledged and sacrificed to. The winning continued but it was no longer assumed to be his by right. The opponents, ever more numerous, were identified and their results at the time of reckoning listened to with increasing apprehension. Such was the anxiety born within the confinement of the classroom. Now he was no longer confined; the walls and protection had been removed, the rivals more numerous and less easy to identify, but just as ardently searched for. He was alone. He approached what he regarded as the final ceremony of initiation and the main competitor he faced was himself. He wondered why he was now left with so much doubt when he needed to be free of everything but self-belief. He had always been more than equal to the task; he could not fall short now, could he?

His hope had been that, by now, the great jigsaw of physics would be nearing completion in his mind. Instead, the pieces still lay uncomfortably scattered and even the frame of straight edges was unfinished. Was this confusion the stuff from which scientific eminence would spring? He received some crumbs of consolation from anonymous anecdotes of great men who had started modestly or from failure. The idea of permanent mediocrity after the triumph of childhood could not yet be faced; seventh in the final after doing so well in the heats was too improbable, wasn't it?

The origin of the desire for widespread glory didn't spring from conscious parental intervention. Mother and father equally were happy at the trophies acquired and would have remained so had they been less frequent. But, however obscure the mechanisms, Michael reasoned that some undefined, subconscious conspiracy between him and his parents was responsible for the need to shine. After only experiencing success in a small world, the acceptance of defeat, although in a larger one, was not easily made; but reasoning was ineffective in persuading him that obscurity and insignificance were not unworthy if the prize had been fought for honourably.

As he passed through the park gates, he turned to look once again at Caroline's house – then wished he had resisted the temptation. Seeing her again would have been wonderful if she had walked out alone. There were no exchanged smiles between her and the man, no holding of hands or placing of arms around waists, but his presence sent a wave of despair through Michael. Once more he, Michael, was someone of little or no consequence in the life of a girl, despite half-smiles in the library. He had not even been rejected – he was irrelevant. He fought the temptation to look back, and continued to walk, now devoid of hope.

From the park, the steep descent brought him to the cross roads beyond which the guest house string of Rock Gardens descended still further to the peaceful, shimmering sea. The signs of life from that street corner were sparse and marked by laziness. A bus struggled to the traffic lights at the top of Upper Rock Gardens and rested there in the late morning heat as if grateful for the red light and its trivial load of two passengers. When offered the green, its engine responded slowly at first but then the revs rose to an impressive crescendo and it was carried round the corner and onto more level ground towards Kemp Town. The buses had often broken what peace there had been in his mornings at Greycliffe Guest House, just across from where he stood. To be back there to start again was yet another futile wish. Two students left it at that moment and walked unhurriedly down the hill. A pang of useless envy passed through him as he thought of what he believed must be their present carefree state of mind. To him they still inhabited a world devoid of urgency and anxiety. If they were experiencing unrequited infatuation, it would not be complicated by the need to marshal mental powers to meet the imminent examination papers, in all their finality.

A middle-aged man in shirt-sleeves and waistcoat, a neighbour of Greycliffe, stood in his paved front garden and talked to an elderly woman on the other side of the railings. She moved off to a likely destination of worship to alleviate loneliness, to fill time or even to communicate with The Almighty. Left alone, the man seemed uncertain what to do. He turned momentarily to face his house but then decided to remain leaning on the railings to check on the infrequent mechanical and human traffic that passed by.

Perhaps I'm deluding myself but Caroline and her man didn't look right together ... he looks too old ... if he's a student, I've never seen him ... they look wrong ... Oh God! ... 1966-1969 ... I should now be resting in peace ... if only things had been ordered correctly, I would now be experiencing a period of calm contemplation of a syllabus mastered, and the imminent task of conveying such mastery would be faced with serenity. I would have the composure of the Greycliffe neighbour but with the added exhilaration of expected victory. Why have I been brought to my present dearth of certainty that I can achieve the things that I consider most precious? I can't yet think of leaving – of being turned away from this imperfect heaven. Someone who has such a desire to stay must find a way to do so – or must be found a way. Three years have transformed a previously unknown, to me, benign seaside resort into a maze, hardly any twist or turn of which seems to be without the recollection of high or low emotion. I have reacted to events sometimes in a way I don't want to remember. My imagined imperviousness to the vagaries of others has been shown to suffer from serious leaks. Dare I say I love this place? No! Never was a word more maligned, ambiguous, misrepresented or abused than love. All You Need Is Love ... I ask you! ... The Beatles – the authors of "Strawberry Fields", "Eleanor Rigby", "Drive My Car" and "Blackbird" – have just come up with this trite nonsense ... and everyone thinks it's wonderful ... life's more complicated than that ... All I know is that the seedy rows of guest houses, the odour of fish and vinegar, the hovering gulls, the smell of the sea, the dingy, musty flats from Kemp Town to Hove are now the precious backdrop of my life. All the world might be a stage but this small piece is all I want. Every character on this stage and every corner and back-street of it conjures up countless musical phrases that are engraved on my mind. Those exciting moments of scientific study beneath the lonely lamp in a darkened library have made me want more. A cold-hearted academic would pronounce that, at this time, I do not need a Caroline. But still I seem to. How can she just be pushed into my life and then withdrawn from it without contact? I cannot so easily be abandoned by her and all that surrounds us! ... can I? ...

The memories and idea of imminent loss continued to trouble him as he strayed further from the homeward route – down Rock Gardens and into St James' Street. At the junction with the broad avenue of The Steyne he felt obliged to turn and make his way towards the shared home that lay just off the Lewes Road. He could not squander more time. He would be able to fit in some relativity before going off to practise with Steve and Jeff. Yes, relativity remained a decidedly grey area, his knowledge of which at that moment would not withstand the rigours of close questioning. Energy could not yet be equated comfortably with mass and that seemed to be only the start. Lectures had provided too little enlightenment. He still had faith that a reasonable period of quiet, painstaking study could clear the mists of ignorance but he wasn't sure that the time left was reasonable.

... *Maybe a two-one wouldn't be a disaster* ...

The notion struck him as if for the first time as he passed the junction of Lewes Road and Elm Grove where he had started his morning's ascent to the private place of Sunday morning worship.

... *But a first is the real prize to be grasped! ... I can't think about a mediocre pass ... that'll mean kissing academia and Caroline, and both figuratively, farewell* ...

29, Roundhill Crescent – 30 minutes later

"Y're a bairk! Y'know that?" Tony employed his fake Liverpool accent as he looked over Jim's shoulder. "Y've missed x-squared out o't'denominator; no wonder y're answer's twenty times too bloody big!" Tony's voice had slid across to Yorkshire.

A pained smile brought additional wrinkles to Jim's prematurely weather-beaten features. But the glance that he cast across the room at Michael signified that he was not unduly troubled by Tony's discovery of his error. It was more common for the roles to be reversed. Tony didn't share the desires of Jim and Michael for academic eminence. He either never had been searching for or had been made, by an unremarkable studentship, indifferent to the acquisition of a badge of qualification. Michael had, unaccountably, found some sort of common bond with Jim and Tony during the first year and had shared flats thereafter. Although without animosity, the Greycliffe fraternity had become mere acquaintances.

"Well, anyone can make a mistake – even me," Jim retorted in his real Lancashire. "It's wonderful. I've almost finished this rotten thing." It was uncharacteristic of Jim to spend any part of Sunday in scholarly contemplation, if it could be called that. His present labours had been prompted by an irritated tutor who had laid down a final deadline for submission of a dissertation long overdue. But Jim and Michael had shared from early days some sort of desire to be accepted as intellectuals – to one day rub shoulders and join in informal debate in some Senior Common Room.

"Y' don't look well, Michael. Jim lad, doesn't he look ill?"

"You do look a bit pale," agreed Jim, "You're not sickening for something or in love are you?"

"I'm as well as can be expected – I'm just not getting enough sun." Michael was determined to keep the real reason for his morning's walk a close secret and he hoped that he hadn't betrayed anything in reaction to Jim's random but fairly accurate remark. He also had no confidence in his state of mental stability. He pondered with trepidation about that guy he had known in the second-year who had become so depressed he was never seen again. Apparently it had been about a girl.

"It's creeping finals disease," said Tony, reverting to his real New Malden voice.

"Well, I've got a touch of it too, but I wouldn't tell you," said Jim, still with an expression between pain and pleasure.

"I didn't notice – but then you always look ill," said Tony.

"I don't always look bloody ill." Jim's show of hurt was unconvincing.

"It's all that Double Diamond and smoke," Tony continued undeflected. "Michael shouldn't look like you. What about all that running he does – and he never gets drunk."

Michael took some quiet pleasure at being singled out as someone with peculiarly healthy habits. He was less pleased by the fact that he not only apparently looked ill but privately regarded his mental and physical health to be on the verge of collapse.

"Look who's talking – and you should have creeping finals lurgy if anyone has," said Jim, "When did you last pick up a physics book? You are now supposed to be engaged in a pastime called revision."

Jim ignored the attempted riposte by Tony as he directed his face characteristically towards the ceiling as though about to bay like a wolf. The action immediately preceded a pulmonary heave culminating in a short, sharp cough. Tony's opinions remained firm.

"There you are. Just think, only two and a half years ago your lungs were still pure and virginal."

"You don't appreciate the pleasures of tobacco ... Oh God!" Jim was obviously about to divert the focus of conversation away from himself. "Four bloody weeks left – it's 'orrible. What am I going to do if I don't get a first? I'll have to get a job! I'm still thrown by bloody Prof. Boyle telling me, bless his heart, I'd probably need a *good* first to do theoretical nuclear physics. Isn't a medium first any good – or even a poor first, for God's sake? Do you know, he actually said that with steady, plodding work, anyone should be able to get a first."

"Oh well, that's alright then," said Michael attempting to joke, not sure that even he had plodded for long enough and in the right direction.

"What am I going to do if I *do* get a first?" said Tony. "All my plans will be ruined – everyone will start expecting so much of me. Did you ask Boyle what prospects you have if you try and cram it all into a month?"

"No comment," said Jim.

"I'll bet you get a first." Tony looked at Michael with mock malice in his face, "You're always in the library these days."

"How would you know?" said Jim.

"It's not doing me much damn good. Half of it still isn't making any sense," said Michael.

"Only half! There we are – bound to get a first, I'd say," continued Tony.

It was true, Michael was often in the library; but it was no longer a refuge for quiet contemplation. His reading was now beginning to be feverish. He thought back to his first tour. It was just like the afternoons he had spent at Foyles. He could wander and browse in the books without time limit. Every now and again he could not resist the long-standing habit of smelling between the pages. He had pulled out a volume entitled *Introduction to Nuclear Physics* and settled into an armchair by a window. The place was too unfamiliar for him to feel at home but it was where he wanted to be. Undisturbed and in comfort, he would be able to indulge himself – first paddle in the shallows of chapter one and eventually cover his shoulders in the deeper waters where nasty equations lurked. He saw no obstacles. It was all here waiting for him to devour it, although he would not openly admit as much. He wanted to digest and assimilate it all, make it part of him. He felt he could do it simply because he was Michael Burgess.

Now, Michael would have been thankful if he had a fraction of the confidence that Tony gave voice to. He had created some façade of assurance and competence that was, embarrassingly, beginning to be believed by others. At Roundhill Crescent his abilities were hardly questioned because the discussions were rarely directed at the mysteries of physics. Michael had unwittingly spent years in the careful construction of what passed for pride in his own abilities, which had grown into something that at first seemed essential but was now something of a liability. This edifice had seemed strong, impregnable, but it had really been vulnerable and dismantled too easily. He longed to be able to respond to personal verbal assault with a firm declaration of the particular critic's own shortcomings. But too often he placed unjustified weight on criticism, as though it were all useful in the quest for self-perfection, for the careful sculpting of the inner idol.

Bill, his friend of many years' standing back home, was an example of someone who had no such idol. He was content in the sure knowledge that whatever he did, someone else, somewhere, could and would do it better. Michael had been frustrated in his many attempts to instil some measure of a feeling of superiority in Bill. He had been exasperated but secretly envious of the absence of pressure that Bill's assumption of incompetence gave him. He had wanted Bill to believe in the power and uniqueness of self, but it had been an easy creed to follow in those days when there seemed to be little else but domestic adoration and scholastic success. Now it was being more and more replaced by a wretched belief in uncertainty.

"Don't expect any sort of degree and then you won't be disappointed," continued Tony.

"That's the distillation of your philosophy of life is it?" replied Jim, "It's not exactly compatible with my pursuit of the great unknowns of physics – puzzles just waiting to have the darkness lifted from them by my intellectual acumen."

"Sounds awfully good," said an unimpressed Tony, "but who, in their right mind is going to be convinced that you're the right man for this mind-blowing task. You can't even get your project in on time."

"Great physicists can't be constrained by trivial things like dissertation deadlines," said a temporarily arrogant Jim.

"No, but trivial physicists can be. You realise that after another year of this, your main limitation, if it isn't now, will be financial, don't you?" said Tony.

"Don't worry, I'm broke already. You know that very well."

"… And the shiny exterior of research will soon become tarnished by worries about cash deficits."

"Oh, God, there speaks a true philistine," said Jim with an exaggerated sigh, "Michael and I are not listening to you. And anyway, this useless conversation is not helping me to finish this rotten … I mean superb dissertation."

"Any bits of the paper you don't want, Mike," said Tony, suddenly seeking new diversions from his apparently anti-intellectual discourse.

"You can have it all. I'm going back down to have a look at one or two things."

"Ooh, goodie, throw it over."

Michael finished his coffee, his words lightly concealing the fact that he was still intent on another hour of relativity before whatever might turn out to be lunch. Tony wasn't deceived.

"Oh no, he never stops working. I told you, Jim, he's bound for a first."

"Don't keep saying it. If you do it might not happen," said Michael as he attempted to show an air of calm in his slow descent of the threadbare stair carpet to his room. He was not unhappy about being singled out as the resident bookworm; it endowed him with some sort of distinction within the group without removing what he believed to be reasonable popularity. If only his efforts were proving more fruitful.

Well before he had sighted the seafront on that first day, his fear had been of the inability to be a part of a circle. The circle he had wished for was, and had remained, ill-defined. For one who claimed a desire for the solitary life, he was unaccountably anxious about rejection. This stemmed from the tiresomely practical apprehension of being without humour, or being the butt of it, or possessing no attraction for girls or, worst of all, of being thought of as without intellect. Now, there was only apprehension about physics. Any other had been rapidly transformed into an inescapable resignation from anything that might have passed for romance.

... *Who was that strange guy with Caroline? ... Does it really matter now? ... It's only physics that matters now, isn't it? ... oh hell! ...*

He asked himself these questions as he sat down once more at his paltry desk, with a reluctance brought on by the perception of mountains that remained to be conquered. Three years, a thousand days, was all it had been from when he had first experienced that all-consuming tension at the sight of the grey waves beneath the grey sky. The old Ford, containing his parents and Bill, had made its slow, uncertain way along the front. There had been the short relief of a stop at the Lyons corner cafe, the last interlude before he had to find and enter his new home.

... *Can all that time have passed since the four of us stood outside the recessed, glass-panelled front door of Greycliffe, with its lace curtain and "No Vacancies" notice making a show of privacy, waiting for the aggressive sound of the bell to be answered? ...*

October 1966 –

The Brighton Guest House

"Hello, I'm Michael Burgess." Michael's first words with a Brighton resident prompted an uninviting response. Mrs Higgs, the landlady of Greycliffe Guest House, met his hopeful grin for an instant with a stony look and then diverted her eyes. She appeared to have a momentary desire to study the gaudy red flowers that patterned the wallpaper of her hall.

"Come in," she said firmly but without any kind of emotion, and stood to one side. As Michael passed her and stepped into the dimly-lit hall she gave him a second, fleeting, faintly suspicious glance and then turned her full attention on his unsuspecting parents. "You haven't brought much nice weather with you, have you?"

Mr Burgess's reply was, as ever, politely cheerful, "No, you're right there. It is a bit grim."

Grim was the fitting adjective for both the sky and the jaw of Mrs Higgs in its determination to tolerate no nonsense from any student. The jaw jutted from beneath tight, thin lips and the piercing grey eyes, enclosed by expensive spectacle frames, darted to and fro rapidly. An impartial music-hall comedian could have easily accommodated her into his act but her humorous aspects were not at that moment readily apparent to Michael. Neither music-hall nor landladies had featured prominently in his life and so he had no expectations of or grounds for disappointment in Mrs Higgs. Now he at least knew there was little to lose, judging by the first moments of their meeting, but he was uncomfortable at being regarded suspiciously by anyone. He saw himself as being above suspicion, as being someone with whom others should only meet with friendliness and openness. He had spent his young life trying to avoid conflict.

"He'll be in room 6 on the second floor." The statement, made to Michael's parents, was firm and final as Mrs Higgs led the procession through the hall, past a highly polished and obtrusive gong and up creaky stairs covered in sombre but impeccably hoovered maroon carpet, "You'll be with a Mr Griffiths." At these words Michael was momentarily disappointed but then quickly resigned to the arrangements that had been made for him. Official documents had informed him of shared accommodation but he was hopeful that either a mistake had been made or that another single room had been found in response to his initially stated preference. He wasn't one to complain and he decided that just to be in this new world was paramount and a shared room in Mrs Higgs' emporium was sufficient. He would take it.

The initial conversation was not marked by its fluency. "Well, he's got a nice room." His mother offered this compliment to Mrs Higgs on his behalf, although none of the newcomers were convinced about its veracity. Michael stiffened at the words, which converted him into an object of, rather than a participant in, the attempted discussion. He wanted to introduce some element of dissent but his charitableness made him join in the subsequent murmurs of agreement. The maroon bed covers matched the dullness of the stair carpet and the second-hand furniture was probably never meant to be admired, even at first-hand. The view from room 6, at that moment, consisted of the upper windows opposite, to the far left the tiniest hint of sea and, below, the roof of a double-decker straining up the hill.

"Many others turned up yet?" Mr Burgess asked the question that Michael was about to. He was grateful for the early arrival which afforded him essential solitary breathing space before he had to confront new and permanent associates. The question had been posed in Michael's mind more from the point of view of one who wished to delay such confrontation until it was unavoidable.

"Well, there's one bloke – he's a strange one if ever I saw it. Came on his own dressed in some sort of army jacket, hardly opened his mouth and wore sunglasses all the time – and look at the weather!"

The description made Michael conscious of his own sartorial sobriety and mode of arrival, a feeling emphasised by his father's words.

"Yes, I'm sure you'll get all sorts. We've just had a stroll around the University and it's quite entertaining to see some of the fashions."

The comments inspired a general mood of what passed for joviality amongst the non-students present and the initiation of remarks about student attire, length of hair and the apparently dubious distinction between the sexes. Michael's dress sense remained far above scruffy and even marginally above casual. Bill at last entered the conversation with characteristic honesty.

"Yes, Mike looks pretty smart for a student."

"Maybe I do now but just think – I can change from smart to scruffy without anybody being concerned about it. You, on the other hand, are confined in a commercial strait-jacket of respectability."

"How dare you call me respectable," said Bill as ironic smiles passed between him and Michael. In spite of Michael's mild counter-attack he had no desire to resemble a refuse-collector or a foreign legionnaire or even, based on some middle-aged observations, Jesus himself. If necessary, he would adjust his vestments to avoid jeopardising his social acceptance. After a brief reaffirmation, on the part of Mrs Higgs, of the virtues of smartness, he was glad that she reverted to business.

"I serve breakfast from 7:30 to 9:00. I always make sure that they have a good breakfast inside them before they go out."

This attempted show of motherliness by Mrs Higgs was not in keeping with Michael's first impressions. Its reality was further diminished by the furtive glances she gave him. Reaching into her housecoat pocket, she handed him two keys.

"This is the one for the front door and this is the one to your room. Alright?" The words were spoken as if to a partial imbecile, or so Michael thought, "Don't lose them, will you?"

Mrs Burgess was pleased to be in accord with Mrs Higgs on the last imperative. Michael was irritated that his thoughts remained unspoken.

... I will not be viewed as a potentially naughty schoolboy. I am a dignified adult. I am, and always have been beyond the suspicion of anyone. Especially someone like you Mrs Higgs. I am Michael Burgess. I will not be classified as just another adolescent ...

Bill easily found humour in personal disparagement, where Michael had never been able to. If Bill were able to stay here in Room 6 with him, existence would be as perfect as sharing a room would allow. Their origins and childhood achievements had been so dissimilar but they had discovered so much similarity in their ideals. Both had visions but, unlike Bill, Michael had expectations of making them a reality and a vehicle for recognition, if not glory. Bill, with a dead mother and unknown father, and brought up by a kindly aunt and uncle, had said any achievement was a bonus; but Michael wasn't content with narrow victories in the third division.

Michael would have been happy for Bill to stay and talk endlessly about music and art and the great mysteries of the opposite sex; to continue the rambling conversations that were often marked by ignorance, but which inspired unscheduled future quests for enlightenment. Bill, the elder by three years, had usually been the initiator. His difficult life had nurtured self-help and independence. He had been many years ahead in earning money and putting it to his own use. He had wandered far on foot and bicycle to, as he put it quite genuinely, commune with nature. He had bought the obscure blues LPs, the Charles Atlas body-building course, the second-hand encyclopaedias. He had been the first to venture into London to art galleries. He was an enthusiast but a dabbler. Michael was the one who picked up, mentally or physically, what he had brought in and tried to mould it into a representation of self-improvement.

Bill had bought the guitar in a characteristic moment of passion and impetuosity but had been too exasperated by its reluctance to yield a recognisable melody to him in the first hour. Bill had been the first to talk of Segovia but had quickly dispensed with ideas of emulation and was almost relieved to remain an observer and listener. Michael had bought the guitar from Bill at what could only be described as a knock-down price that had taken no effort to knock down.

"Well, we'd better get the rest of the stuff out of the car and then we'll have to be making tracks."

Michael experienced a sudden surge of excitement at his father's words, as though he had not been expecting the eventual parting to take place. He was to be left to his own devices, to journey, to fly unassisted into the unknown! But hadn't it always been like that, he asked himself? He knew what the answer was. He couldn't remember when he had last sought parental help for anything academic. But now he would lack someone immediately at hand who could offer unstinting praise.

The guitar, in its plastic case, was lifted from the boot along with a supplementary small suitcase. Michael would have felt less self-conscious if he could have said the goodbyes while holding onto the guitar but he felt it would be considered too casual, and left it leaning against the suitcase, an incongruous still-life in the centre of the pavement. The parting remarks that nobody in the awkward group wanted to utter began unpromisingly for Michael.

"You'll be alright, won't you?" Mrs Burgess asked the unanswerable question.

"I'm not going to be on the other side of the world – only in Brighton, Mum."

The verbal agreement that this retort of Michael prompted in Mr Burgess and Bill did little to arrest his mother's anxiety.

"I know, it's just that you haven't been away from home before like this – I can't help it."

The words came forth with inadvertently and excruciatingly poor timing. Two girls of student age, dress and demeanour passed close by. Michael hoped either that they had not heard the conversation, which was unlikely, or that he would not suffer the misfortune of ever meeting them again.

"So long, Mike, keep in touch," Bill offered his hand. The handshake was probably the first they had ever made; it had an unwelcome formality and seemed to signify a finality in the relationship they had enjoyed. Bill was heading for what Michael saw as the slippery slope of engagement and marriage and was worried that their discussions might not take place again, even at odd times, in splendid seclusion. Yet Michael had every intention of keeping in touch. He wanted to enter this new world but could never leave the old one behind. He preferred to envisage himself as a foreign correspondent, observing and reporting on a strange country but keeping himself back from full integration.

Having surmounted the difficulty of the last-minute hesitations, kisses and handshakes, Michael experienced with guilty relief the final scraps of conversation through the open window of the car.

"Anyway, give us a ring later on this afternoon. We'll be back home in a couple of hours. You can reverse the charges – the firm won't notice it," said his father. After a few decades, Mr Burgess had earned the meagre concession of a company telephone but bragging about it would never cross his mind.

Michael knew he should not have done, but he looked forward to giving the inevitably banal and predictable first despatch from the South Coast. Within seconds of starting up, the Ford Prefect was out of sight. The width of Upper Rock Gardens had made it easy to perform the U-turn and it hadn't even had to wait at the lights before the left turn down and a last wave.

The thrill of, at last, being left alone in unfamiliar territory temporarily overwhelmed all other preoccupations. Unfettered exploration was his self-imposed mandate. The seaside location, which had before today seemed inconsequential to him, now assumed a new aura of excitement and mystery. He gazed down the road towards the sea now barely perceptible in the mist and steadily darkening afternoon. He had only ever seen the purportedly famous front on television when bank holidays came round, to show record crowds, record high or low temperatures or fighting gangs of teenagers. It was not a place he would have chosen as a new home; it was not Cambridge. But he had surprised himself by the ability to overcome the disappointment.

He thought of that day in January last. The melting of previously fallen snow had been abruptly curtailed by a viciously penetrating cold. Every soul venturing out cowered against the merciless wind but his group of presumed hopefuls had been led round by a brave, enthusiastic young woman, perhaps already in her third year, and for Michael the exhilaration had been at least as great as for a combined guided tour of the Pyramids and the Taj Mahal. He had, however, not been optimistic, especially in view of the statements emphasising the low probability of entry, and he was down to his second choice.

... Cambridge entrance was casually swept aside ... because I was told there would be too little time to cover the syllabus after A-levels ... God, I was dumbstruck but took it without complaint – just like me! Why had I put down Bristol in first place? ... They just want very high grades ... which I've got except for that damn pure maths ... and we all got low grades in that ... I can't be blamed for that can I? ...

It had already been dark outside, on that arctic January day, when his interview had eventually commenced in the cramped portakabin office, lit only by an anglepoise, of an amiable but barely intelligible Italian. His fears of an oral physics examination had not materialised; in fact, his interviewer could hardly have ascertained whether he knew what physics was. He even managed to read and become a little incensed at some of the report from his school which lay on the desk; it forecast a "very good" degree, but perhaps not a first. Everything seemed to have been worked out before he had arrived, but he had not been expecting the words "unconditional entry" that the tutor had eventually uttered; Michael almost wondered if the accent had fooled him and was on the point of asking for a repetition but subsequent smiles and handshake reassured him. A ten-minute chat with a nice Italian about nothing in particular had changed his life as much as anything ever had.

Outside in the darkness he had jogged and staggered ecstatically through the snow and wind, which seemed no longer cold, towards the waiting car.

"I'm in!" he had almost shouted as he leapt in, still in a state of shock about what he had been told.

"That's fantastic. I knew you'd do it!" He and his father had driven off in a warm state of collective triumph.

As he picked up his guitar and turned back to enter Greycliffe, he comforted himself with statistical reports of the nine anonymous hopeful students who failed to get the place he now had. The popularity of this University was unsurpassed, it had been said. He was content. He had arrived!

The Guest House – Later that evening

Michael's room-mate, Owen Griffiths, had turned out not to be a six-foot five-inch scrum-cruncher, as he had half-imagined, but a slim, athletic Welshman. Michael considered them to be as compatible as could reasonably have been hoped for. The two had been grammar school pupils, both liked athletics, both played the guitar and both were science students. The only blemish that Michael could see in Owen was a love of rugby, albeit as a swift fly-half rather than someone who would screw your head off. There was no instinctive bond that Michael had found with Bill, but he did not envisage a year marked by clashes of character or outlook on life. Initial conversation was desultory rather than fluent, with Owen constantly complaining about the non-appearance of a trunk that had been sent separately. For now, Michael had no reason for dissatisfaction.

Mrs Higgs had announced, in her so-called welcome, that there would be tea and sandwiches in the lounge at 6 o'clock, ostensibly for the newcomers to get to know one another. Despite the tranquillity that still pervaded Greycliffe when Michael and Owen descended to the tea party, the room was surprisingly full. The event was not like a stand-up cocktail reception which could be entered anonymously, but full in the sense that almost all available chairs, of varying height and forming an approximate circle, were occupied. Neither Michael's nor Owen's confidence quite ran to a firm self-introduction to all assembled. They murmured "hellos" in the direction of Mrs Higgs by whom they were then introduced with, thought Michael, commendable grasp of their names and places of origin, except that her use of his Christian name he considered inappropriately affectionate. He made a quick glance around the room, for that was all he felt capable of at the time. It told him both that the mysterious sunglassed individual was not there and that the dress of nobody present had been touched by the same, quasi-military influence. There was a good smattering of ties, hardly-worn jackets and Michael's beard appeared to be unique. He was amazed that the previously deathly hush of Greycliffe had suddenly produced this crowd.

"God, you must be an artist!"

These were the first words directed at him. They came from a tubby youth sporting strikingly blond hair and thick-rimmed glasses. The momentary surprise at being singled out from the gathering with such a blunt comment was rapidly followed by a surge of satisfaction. Without engineering it in any way, he had suddenly and simultaneously acquired a form of distinction and been forced into a conversation. He was also pleased to negate the supposition.

"No, I'm doing physics."

"I don't believe it! You've got English Lit. written all over you – hah, that's a joke! Call me Con, by the way. My real name's Clive Oliver Norman Burtenshaw. I don't care much for any of them so the acronym's the best compromise." Michael was grateful for the definition of acronym.

Con's remarks seemed to catalyse tentative exchanges of names, details of origin and immediate reasons for their presence in Brighton, but the general mood was one of bewildered individuals being asked to do something faintly unnatural and being reluctant to comply. The proceedings hung precariously on the edge of conversational paralysis until relief came temporarily in the unlikely guise of Mrs Higgs. In spite of a practically untraceable glimmer of a smile, she tried to stimulate some sort of verbal interchange.

"Well, I suppose you're all looking forward to your student life – probably the first time some of you have been away from home."

There were some suppressed murmurs of agreement, but they were such as might greet a sergeant major asking new recruits if they were going to enjoy tomorrow's square-bashing.

"As long as they don't give us too much work to do." Gareth, Con's room-mate – an individual who did exude some self-confidence, was the first to project his voice across the room.

"Well, you won't get anywhere if you don't work hard. I can tell you that." Mrs Higgs was undoubtedly recalling all the hard work she believed she had completed in her life. Michael momentarily pictured her on hands and knees, scrubbing floors and dreaming of her guest house by the sea. She continued with her logical train of thought, apparently unimpressed by the attempted joke, and firm in her beliefs, "You must have done some work to get to university."

"No, it was just natural genius," Gareth's banter almost amused even Mrs Higgs, but at the same time, Michael thought, it was a poorly concealed boast.

"Oh, listen to him!" she invited the assembly, but managed only to extract a few scattered smiles. It was going to take something more dramatic to dislodge the firmness of the entrenched expressions of intractable unease across the room. Con continued to attempt to enliven what Michael now regarded as their side.

"Do I *have* to share a room with this natural genius?" Con's smile was full of foreboding but Michael slightly envied the way he was already able to make even pretended rude remarks about someone he barely knew. Michael would not for a long time, if ever, address Owen in a similar fashion. It transpired that a majority of the assembly had attended fee-paying schools, Con and Gareth included. They made remarks about having covered some of the first year maths syllabus already, which sparked that well-known feeling of impending competition in Michael.

Although the level of apparent anxiety among these mutual strangers, gathered in the unfamiliar and unlikely surroundings of a Brighton guest house in October 1966, eventually began to fall, it was an inescapable conclusion that the allure of coffee and sandwiches was about to fade and die. Many had probably thought of an appropriate murder weapon but it was Gareth who produced it.

"Anyone fancy going to the pub?" he asked nobody in particular. The suggestion was met by audible relief and what passed for a crescendo of voices in agreement. Gareth was courtesy personified as he thanked Mrs Higgs for her catering; Michael, along with a fraction of the others, followed suit.

Mrs Higgs seemed resigned to the temporary loss of her new clientele.

"Don't have too much, will you. You've got to be bright and early tomorrow."

The obvious route, down Upper Rock Gardens and right into St James' Street toward the town centre, was followed.

"Might as well go to the first one we see," Gareth called back over his shoulder as he strode out.

"I think this is a case of the uninitiated following the overconfident. Heaven preserve us from natural leaders." Owen smiled, and Michael warmed to his words.

Within five minutes, they came upon The Royal Oak, whose red cockerel had announced its presence from a distance, and filed into the Public Bar. The public was there in copious amounts. The Royal Oak was as full as it could practically be. Asphyxiation seemed to be a distinct possibility due both to the high density of individuals attempting to get air and the only slightly lower density of those contaminating that air with tobacco smoke.

"Let me get the first round," said Gareth, forcefully making a path towards a bar around which could just be discerned a few obvious regulars, who had presumably installed themselves when the evening was still in its infancy, and the premises spacious. They were outnumbered, by an order of magnitude or two, by equally obvious students. These ranged from the fairly cleanly cut to the fairly grubbily uncut but such a gathering at such a date served to identify them with a high degree of certainty. The substantial proportion of young women was also indicative of the nature of the evening's patrons. Michael scanned their faces with intense interest, a survey facilitated by the state of mild confusion and the buzz of a hundred conversations bouncing around the dimly-lit room. The one or two pretty faces arrested him for a few moments but not knowing where their owners' lodgings or seats of learning were located, his interest remained both academic and cursory. At that moment in The Royal Oak he was content to contemplate the destination of the following day.

The more immediate destination of the bar was finally reached by Gareth with his followers arranged in a less than tightly knit group a short way behind. Michael's height forced him to bend slightly to inform Gareth of his order.

"A lager, if you don't mind." Michael thought he ought to omit the lime he had taken on his previous infrequent public house visits.

"Pint?"

"Why not – thanks."

The rest uniformly chose bitter.

The locals sat or leaned protectively around their bar either silently or participating in snatches of inaudible conversation with each other or with the three hard-pressed individuals behind it. They must have experienced such invasions before and would do so again. If they had come for relief of loneliness, their hopes had every chance of being fulfilled. Those with aspirations of quiet drinking had either abandoned them some time ago or left in search of an off-licence. Michael found himself next to a short, thin-faced man whose initially glazed expression betrayed neither annoyance at nor pleasure in his surroundings.

"I can tell, y'know, I can tell – you're one o' these students – eh?" The man stumbled through the sentence, his Scottish accent dwelling for some time on the first syllable of student. Michael was not confident of this being the start of an intellectual conversation, but he entered into it with as good a spirit as he could muster.

"Yes, that's right – you guessed it."

The man nodded and his face re-arranged itself into a lop-sided smile.

"Jesus Christ, they're packin' em in – eh? F..." The final word faded as the man swayed towards his beer on the counter but failed to lift it. He swayed back towards Michael.

"Y" know. I could tell these students a thing or two. I've studied life – I tell y' – eh? ... Mind, I've studied a book or two – eh? There's not much y' can tell me! Christ, they're packin' em in tonight! Hissory – it's all there – I'm a student o' hissory – it's all there – power, money and sex ..." he broke off, into a chuckle at some apparently private joke and dragged on his stub of a cigarette.

Michael's discomfort at being the sole recipient of this attempted monologue went from mild to moderate when the man took a more personal tone.

"I can tell, y'know ... I can tell you've no experience o' life ... all you students ... same." He lowered his voice and came closer, "I'll bet, y'know ... I'll bet y've never done it!" Another chuckle ensued.

"Well, I never discuss my secrets," said Michael, maintaining the semblance of a brave face.

"Arrr, whassa discuss. No – I can tell in y'r face – y've no experience, student."

Michael looked quickly around hoping that the Scottish philosopher was the only individual with these amazing powers of perception.

"No, you go to it, student ... you know what I mean ..." The chuckle continued, accompanied by an elbow nudge.

"One lager, Michael," Gareth reached out with the welcome relief which was enhanced when the man suddenly decided to shake Michael's soft hand with his roughened one.

"Well, good luck to y', student – go to it – eh?"

"I'll see what I can do."

The next chuckle and barward swing appeared to signal the end of the conversation. Michael was grateful but considered that his erstwhile standards had slipped so far that the final advice the man had given did have some attraction. A shift in Michael's position occasioned by further movement of individuals towards the bar put enough bodies between himself and the Scotsman to prohibit further exchanges – he hoped for the rest of the evening.

He was once more in reasonable proximity to the Greycliffe contingent. These erstwhile solitary souls had been conveyed from the semi-frozen state of Mrs Higgs' front room and were now being thawed out by continual jostling with bodies of a higher social temperature. The ambient noise was a frenzied mixture of low buzz, sudden outbursts of male and female laughter from individuals or groups, grunts, and sounds resembling the lowing of cattle and baying of hounds. He caught a snatch of nearby chatter between a young man and two girls. The man's face, which didn't appear to have ever needed a razor, was crowned by hair permed into a mass of tight curls. He was clothed in a manner approaching the anonymous sunglassed inmate of Greycliffe. Otherwise, his openness of face and fluency of speech were in direct contrast. The girls were overtly more conventional. Michael categorised the young man as a relatively veteran student, despite his looks, until he heard his confession:

"I wonder how many of us first years wonder what the hell we're doing here ..."

The development of the theme was lost to Michael, due to another general rise in volume from the crowd. He was irritated, but only transiently so, by such frivolous regard for something that had been causing him increasing excitement and expectation. He was also, again, perturbed by his own conventionality and the fact that he was nowhere near to expounding his views to any female audience. Any annoyance was greatly moderated when he noticed that both girls frequently looked around the room, perhaps for means of escape, even though the young man kept on talking. He was further strengthened by the conviction that he, Michael, knew precisely what he was doing there.

The anxieties that had reached their climax that morning, and had created the nucleus of tension in his stomach with tentacles reaching to most other parts of him, was, at that moment, a vague memory. Doubts about intellectual recognition by future teachers and the social acknowledgement by other students, even the female section, were slowly but magically being pushed to the back of his consciousness. The transformation in his life in the space of twelve hours had been extreme. The day had begun with almost total uncertainty. Now, without noticeable effort and nearly three pints of lager, he basked in the heat of the local within a circle which, whether ideal or not and although barely formed, represented some sort of acceptance. His contemplation was interrupted, predictably, by Gareth.

"Con and I thought we ought to go on somewhere for a bite to eat. I doubt whether the pies here will be edible."

"Er ... yeah, sounds like a good idea."

Michael attempted a large gulp at the quarter pint or so left in his glass. The mouthful was larger than he was used to. By the time he had swallowed it he had to gasp for air. He tried as hard as he could to appear to finish the rest of his drink in a leisurely fashion and, although full of barely containable gas, placed the glass in triumph on the bar. The unfamiliar influence of the beer began to make him wistful and blissfully optimistic.

... How could I have done better? Why did I ever think of pursuing the fantasy of my own room in a quiet house at a manageable distance from others? ... And this isn't going to be a continuation of the diligent conformity of school, Michael ... This is not the start of steady accumulation of qualification for respectable employment. You've got the whole of three years ... Three years, Michael, to turn you from a shy, unknown teenager into a scientific star! ... The whole of three years!

May 1969 –

Caroline

Two and a half weeks – eighteen days ... oh my God, eighteen days ... but it's twenty-five to the last one ... the final final ... It's no use counting the days ... Keep calm, you can do it ... you know you can ... you've always come out on top ... haven't you?

Michael could not contemplate the prospect of departure – of leaving a micro-world that had pulled him in and wrapped him up in a comfort blanket of aspirations to explore the mysteries of the cosmos and, along the way, meet a girl who liked him as much as he liked her.

... so many scientific mysteries remain just that ... are there too many for me to go on, as I so ardently desire? Will I ever be accepted even as a promising scientist, let alone a great one? ... And why do I still want to be near to, even to live with, that elusive girl? ... Of course, Bill always goes on about the mating instinct ... as though the process of procreation were paramount ... I have no experience of mating as yet ... and, on recent experience, possibly never will ... but I plough on with the wild notion that I might someday occupy the thoughts of some young lady for at least a portion of her waking hours ... why does a pretty face bring these fantasies to the fore? ... Why do young men constantly succumb to the allure of a pretty face? ... I'm nearly a scientist. I want to know. How can neatly positioned eyes, nose, mouth and cheeks and a smooth skin assume such importance and have such power? ... A pretty head on a pretty body does not necessarily coincide with sympathy or understanding or kindness or cleverness or even health ... does it? ... does it? ... And if they're unkind or downright unpleasant some men will still cling on ... Sarah was kind, but was there ever anything more for me? ... and Angie ... oh, I can't think about her anymore ... and now Caroline ... even if I do amuse her in some remote way, she leads another life ... What on earth ... ?

Michael's mind had roamed through these random musings as he alighted from the bus and walked through Falmer House and up to the library. What caused him, mentally and physically, to stop in his tracks was the sight of Caroline's strange man talking to Richard Woods. Richard and Michael were the only boys from their school to have made it to Sussex in the 1966 intake. Richard had never assumed the role of friend as far as Michael was concerned. There seemed to be a semi-permanent sneer in his words and manner which Michael had never been able to accept or reciprocate.

... why did it have to be bloody Woods who followed me down to Brighton? ... still I suppose I've been able to steer clear of him most of the time ... except for those gut-wrenching episodes that I've tried to forget ... he's doing something like sociology I think ... whatever that is ...

Despite his misgivings, Michael had to stop Woods when he parted from his conversation.

"Hello, Dick. Revision going OK?"

"Good God! It's not like you to think of my well-being, Mike." A broad smile creased Richard Woods' face despite the unpromising reply. "If you must know, I think I'm steadily accumulating enough ammunition to get me an upper second – at least."

"Oh well, if you say so." Michael managed to generate and maintain his own smile. "Er ... who was that guy you were just talking to?"

"Who – Alan Mercer? He's a lecturer in European Studies. I grace his seminars from time to time. Why? Don't fancy him do you?"

"No, I do not fancy him. You know very well that I do have a passing interest in female students."

"Well, you could still fancy him."

"Look ... it's just that ..." Michael faltered in his attempt to say what it was "just". He couldn't think of a benign excuse and decided to keep Woods in the dark. "Oh, well ... it's a private matter ..."

"I say – intriguing or what? I didn't associate you with any sort of subterfuge."

"It's not as exciting as that, Dick." Michael made to walk on.

"If you say so." Woods looked back at him with a puzzled expression that made Michael wish he hadn't asked.

The steps up to the library had never seemed so steep. He knew he would head to the French section but he wondered why.

... a senior lecturer! ... having some sort of liaison with a student! ... is that legal? ... maybe he was giving her extra tuition that day? ... but on a Sunday!? ... tuition in what? ... and by the look of them it wasn't a fun tutorial ... oh, God ... what's going on? ... oh hell, she's here again! ... she doesn't know you're not reading French ... you're reading physics, so bloody read! ... or go and say you're desperate about her ... one or the other ... am I desperate? ... Michael doesn't get desperate does he? ... does the lecturer double as a lover? ... Oh hell I hate that word! ...

Caroline removed the knitted bag from her shoulder. He didn't worry that she hadn't given him a glance as she sat down at her desk. A week or so ago he had begun to imagine her as being sent to complete the romantic picture; the triumph of his finals and their undivided devotion. He still refused to see this as impossible, despite the spectre of the senior lecturer.

... I'm not asking for the world am I? Why can't we share this small corner of it ... just the two of us? For ever encompassed by the gently sloping meadows beyond the library walls, the long shadows of late afternoon splashed across them ...

Segre's *Atomic Physics* lay heavy on his compartmentalised desk, opened at a well-worn chapter which he thought of as central to his understanding. He shut the book and tried to scribble a version of the words and equations that he had just read.

... Yes! It's better! It's coming ... but I'm still missing a few bits ... the steps from equations 3 to 4 aren't clear damn it! ... I've got to get away ... I can't sit near her ... I can't talk to her ...

A miserable, third-rate approach formed in his mind. The invitation was written on a page torn from his notebook. He knew the coat so well, the cream-coloured mac with the wide collar. Few garments remained in the basement cloakroom. One or two were similar to hers but he was certain of his target. The pounding in his chest was strong as he slipped the paper deeply into the pocket and glanced furtively around to make sure he was unobserved. Some kind of serenity possessed him as he bounded down the library steps considering himself released from weeks of mental oppression. Waiting for buses was unthinkable. He strode, in happy, peaceful delusion, across the park in the direction of town, avoiding the main road until there was no other path.

"Working late again I see. God, your brain must be so full of physics! No wonder you're smiling to yourself," said Tony, the unexpected, solitary occupier of the lounge at Roundhill Crescent. "The others have gone to the pub but I thought for once, you won't believe this, that I'd stay behind and emulate your good self."

"Don't be fooled by me. I'm putting the hours in but not necessarily the physics. I just couldn't concentrate tonight – so I gave up."

"You look quite pleased about it."

"Any anxieties I might have about finals seemed to lift a bit tonight. There are other things in life."

"Now you're going all philosophical. I should watch that if I were you. Coffee? Tony passed into the adjoining greasy-linoed kitchen, "What do you suppose these other things are then?" His voice echoed as Michael slumped into an armchair from which a haze of dust ascended.

"What about wine, women and song?" said Michael without thinking.

"Sounds alright for starters. Which order are you going to take them in?"

"That would be telling."

"Alright, tell me then. You're already well into song, shall we say, so we can forget that; and – no, don't tell me – you're not going to start drinking like everyone else? No, I can't see it," said Tony, handing Michael a mug of instant, slumping into an opposite chair and eyeing him steadily. "But ... you've occasionally been associated with a member of the opposite sex. Could you be venturing in that direction again – bad time to try it, if I may say so."

"Venturing would be putting it rather strongly."

"Ah-ha! Interesting."

"Are you really interested?"

"Oh yes, even me."

"I ... might be ... in love ... I suppose." Michael had not had the slightest intention of uttering such words but they had just come out. Perhaps it was that Tony had made a similar pronouncement in the distant past.

"You're not serious ... yes, you are aren't you?" said Tony apparently even more interested.

"No, forget I said love. All I can say is that something's happened. I was sitting near her by chance one day a few weeks ago in the library and I suddenly felt there was something amazingly special about her. Up to that time I'd never seen her before. Never."

"Don't tell me you haven't been working all this time and just having secret meetings for God's sake!"

"Oh, I've been trying to study alright – but she does have certain distractive powers. I ... I haven't even spoken to her yet."

"A few weeks eh? Speaking from experience, which, as you are aware, is on the limited side, you're going to have to make some move or you'll go bloody mad. In my tragic case, I knew her a bit to start with so it was easier – at least to make an initial sortie. You've got a more difficult job."

"I have ... done something ... this evening ... quite crazy really."

"Are you going to let me in on this insane act?"

"I don't know. I'm surprised I told you anything."

"Oh come on, you can't leave me in suspenders now. We all like a bit of sexual intrigue."

"Is that what this is? ... I wrote her a note and put it in her pocket. I asked her to meet me tomorrow night." Michael closed his eyes and smiled in a resigned manner. The response from Tony was more encouraging than he could have dared hope.

"Might work – who knows. Stranger things have been attempted. She does know who you are, by the way?"

"I know she does. Look, for a while we'd been exchanging glances – smiles. And then one day in the library I was walking along with Frank Morton – you know him – and she was filling out some book withdrawal slips. As soon as she saw us she stopped everything she was doing, grabbed all the books, nearly dropped them and rushed over to us."

"So?"

"So she said, 'hello, Frank,' and they exchanged a few boring sentences as we walked along and then off she went. But she kept looking at me."

"So Frank Morton didn't even introduce you?"

"Not a word."

"Miserable bugger! And you didn't find out all about her?"

"You know me – but I did get her name – Caroline. And she's reading French I think."

"Mm ... Still, maybe she's dying to get into bed with him."

"What?" exclaimed Michael, "Frank Morton? You *are* talking about the woman I think I might be in ... er ..."

"Some fat blokes have got a lot of pulling power."

"No, I know love is supposed to be blind but I'm not taking that seriously. I was convinced that she wanted to speak to me, to be near me – and I'm not talking about going to bed. It hasn't crossed my mind ... much."

"This *does* sound serious."

"You er ... will keep it to yourself, won't you?"

"Oh no, I want to tell everyone ... don't worry your pretty little head – model of discretion me. Where are you meeting her?"

"That *would* be telling."

The upstairs bar of the King and Queen was, on the face of it, no place for secret or secretive liaisons, although if moved to, one could probably yell the most lurid of intimacies without anybody noticing. Michael's eyes scanned the long, brightly-lit room like the beams of some forlorn lighthouse, restlessly rotating, afraid that they would miss someone who might be waiting but who might not wait for long. He sipped briefly and intermittently at his beer but he still wasn't a dedicated drinker and this was no time for serious drinking. Business in the bar was booming to such an extent that he was continually in fear that she was waiting in some niche, at some table that he had missed, despite his vigilance. He didn't know it would be like this; it was not a place he frequented; it was almost a random choice. That first night at the Royal Oak had contained a similarly compressed mass of humanity, but then there had been nothing to search for in desperation, just everything to observe – as though an outsider. Then, time had not been slipping away but lay endlessly ahead. The letter's appointed time had now been surpassed by half-an-hour but Michael had no thoughts of abandoning his post. With glass eventually recharged, after several fruitless and half-hearted attempts to catch eyes behind the bar, his own continued to scan.

The memory drifted into the back of his mind of when he had once before been under this roof. Another room had accommodated some long defunct blues club. Peter Green and his band had been on. Michael had told Bill about it; Bill appreciated Peter Green. He had seen him at the Ricky Tick in Windsor. A guy called Jeremy – he couldn't remember the surname – played slide guitar and they had talked excitedly about the soaring slide up the fingerboard that followed the rap on the drums and led in the thumping dotted rhythm of the ensemble ...

Du-um, dee-dum, dee-dum, dee-dum, dee-da-da ...

Bill was often moved to break out into a vocal representation and an accompaniment on his ever-make-believe guitar. Michael preferred just to carry the sound in his head. Neither would ever grow tired of reminiscing about such musical gems, as they regarded them. Michael's electric guitar was no longer make-believe. He had his group, he had made his demo, he had Rod Wyatt but at this moment wished that he didn't. After that impromptu, chaotic gig back in Windsor, Rod had walked up and given him a card, saying he worked for CBS Records and that "he liked the band and particularly his voice". Even bass-guitarist Jeff, a school associate rather than friend and now in his Sussex band, was raised to a reasonable level of uncharacteristic enthusiasm by this. Michael's first thoughts of imminent pop-star eminence were mixed with scepticism. He asked himself, "what was this Wyatt guy doing at a run-of-the-mill teenage dance?" Subsequent meetings had revealed that this was an independent venture of Rod Wyatt's, who might or might not have been employed by the said recording company. His persistence might have been welcome for a young man in a dead-end job but had rapidly diminishing appeal for Michael.

... Oh Christ! Wyatt's coming down tomorrow for another get-together as he calls it ... I'm going to have to cut it short! I've just got to! ... I want to be left alone – with Caroline ... and physics of course ...

"What's this, drinking on your own? That'll never do. Ha, ha!" The words, spoken at near to point-blank range from behind his shoulder startled him in the most unpleasant of ways. At that moment, the sudden materialisation of Rod Wyatt was marginally more unwelcome than the appearance of Banquo's ghost before Macbeth. The only consolation was that Michael hadn't yet murdered him.

... I don't deserve this! ... not me ... not kind Michael Burgess ...

"Oh ... Rod! ... what the hell are you? ... how are you? ... No, I'm ... just taking a short break before going back to do a bit more studying, you know ..."

"What, at half past nine? You are a glutton for it and no mistake."

"Well that's what I'm down here for eh?"

"Yeah ... oh, this is Cliff; one of my partners in crime, so to speak – in the record business that is."

Cliff towered even over Michael, a medallion glinting crudely against the copious hairs of his tank of a chest. He produced the most grudging of smiles, behind a stubbled chin, and the most crushing of handshakes as he and Wyatt squeezed against the already over-burdened bar.

"I know we're meeting tomorrow and that but I thought we could do with a little sea air so we came down this evening," said Wyatt. "What a coincidence, bumping into you like this, eh?"

"Oh ... actually I was supposed to meet a friend for a drink but they haven't turned up yet," stammered Michael.

"Great voice Mike's got, Cliff. When I first heard him, I thought, yeah, we could do something with that voice."

The idea of unspecified friends of Rod Wyatt "doing something" with his voice made Michael come as close to anger as he ever did. The rage, though, was thwarted and modified into a pang of regret that he had ever bought an electric guitar in the first place.

"I've spent my whole life singing with my voice. I don't think anyone's going to make it much better," said Michael.

"Don't be so sure," said Wyatt, Michael thought somewhat threateningly, "I know people in the business who've brought on some artistes right from nothing, isn't that right, Cliff?"

"Never spoke a truer word, Rod."

"I know your talents, Mike, but let's face it, there's always room for improvement ..."

... There's room for improvement in nuclear theory, relativity, quantum mechanics, stellar structure, statistical mechanics ... do you want me to go on!? ...

It was there! Suddenly it was there! The cream-coloured mac, worn by a girl with blonde hair – and she was leaving!

"Excuse me ..." said Michael jumping from his stool and leaving Rod Wyatt suspended in mid-sentence.

In his unprecedented desperation he evoked annoyed looks as he forced a path through the mass of barely movable bodies. The girl was already half way down the stairs and he had not even reached the top.

... She's been waiting while I was preoccupied with that fuc ... bloody Rod Wyatt and now she's given up – but I'll catch her, don't worry ...

Anguish and triumph clashed inside his head and then both collapsed into disbelief as the girl, at the foot of the stairs, turned to look up. Her eyes happened to meet his for a split second but it was just by chance. She was not looking for him, and he was not looking for her. He couldn't comprehend why he had been subjected to such cruel fate, as though some mischievous spirit was playing around with him. The girl had looked so much like Caroline to his over-enthusiastic imagination but the resemblance had been transitory and illusory. She was not going to come; perhaps she would never have come.

The desire to carry on walking down the stairs, out of the King and Queen and back to his room was almost impossible to overcome, but it was not like him to appear unpredictable, eccentric or illogical, even in front of Rod Wyatt. He forced himself to go back to his place by the bar and dredge up an unconvincing explanation.

"I was sure it was my friend. He looked as though he'd missed me ... but it wasn't him."

"You were in a bit of a hurry, my old son. Not been stood up have you?" said Wyatt, passing a sideways smile to Cliff. "Don't chase buses or women my dad used to say. You'll only make a fool of yourself and there'll be another one along in a minute."

"I'm not chasing anyone and I'm not hanging around in pubs waiting for women to turn up," announced Michael, unsmiling, and with as much conviction as he could.

"Sounds pretty firm on that, eh Cliff?"

"Look ... I'd better get back. I've got a lot of studying to do. It's only two and a bit weeks to the final exams now."

"No peace for the wicked, eh? I wonder what you've done to deserve it? Anyway, I'll see you tomorrow at three – same place."

"I've ... yeah, OK, see you then," said Michael on the verge of a refusal to comply with Rod Wyatt's plans.

With a further imprint of Cliff's fingers around his hand, he walked out into the bath of warm, still, summer air; perfect air for taking while wandering entwined in mutual affection with some girl, a girl who had never existed. He thought, uselessly, of ambling along promenades or through lanes where memories had been cleansed of past malevolence; the air was perfect for stopping, concealed in a side street to place lips lightly, longingly together. This fantasy had to stop, it should never have started, he told himself bitterly. The words of that song had come close to thrilling him in those first few weeks, and he hardly ever paid attention to words – but they had conjured a fantasy of wrapping that someone in a warm embrace ...

Reach out ... I'll be there ...

... The first lines don't apply to me even now? ... do they? ... I have to go on ... my hope is not gone ... Would I shelter someone with love? ... what does that mean? ... perhaps that's all too serious for me ... but I would like that "hand to hold" ... Oh, I'm so divided, so bloody cut up and pulled in different ways. How did I ever think I could shut myself away here and get drunk on physics? How? ... It was bound to start as soon as I hit the south coast ... A long time ago, it had been a game that even I was drawn into ... now it's no game...it's destructive ... confidence-dismantling ... time-wasting ... still the blue jeans and the back-combed blonde hair is trying to ensnare me ...

Three years back, there was apprehension but no anguish. Back then, it all seemed so different. Time was never wasted, even lingering to daydream of plans for the next cup of coffee. Back then, mystical dark streets were filled with the mists of October and the clouds of hot breath mingled in the still, cold air ...

October 1966 –

Sarah

More than a month of Michael's first university term had passed as he sat one foggy day on his own, glancing to and fro across the snack bar in the area known as the Junior Common Room, or JCR. His mind was changing down a few gears in the aftermath of a Dr Rodwell tutorial. So far these had not been too severe trials of intellectual strength but he never treated them nonchalantly. He wanted Jack Rodwell, his personal tutor, to have a good opinion of him.

Dr Rodwell's room was in the so-called second phase of the Mathematics and Physics building. Like tales of Spanish hotels, that he had only heard second-hand, this was far from being finished. The negotiation of a path of rickety planks between piles of sand and cement had to be undergone before entering a dusty ground floor corridor. Cables looped precariously from the ceiling and in the middle distance, the sound of an electric drill could be heard echoing.

In their first one-to-one meeting, Michael had found his tutor to be an untidy looking man behind an untidy desk, but he was relieved to meet a teacher who espoused informality and spoke to him like an adult. Given time, Michael thought that he could even divulge aspirations and anxieties to Jack Rodwell. Even in the course of this brief conversation, Michael could not resist stating a fragment of personal conviction.

"There's always a goodly fraction here who never wanted to be students in the first place and it's a waste of effort pushing them," Rodwell had said.

"I'm not one of them. I've been thinking about university for a long time. In fact, I'd like to be in your position."

"Grief, no student's ever quite put it like that."

Michael was afraid he had overstepped the mark.

"So you're determined to be an academic, or whatever it is that I am."

"Strange perhaps ... but it seems to me like the only thing worth being ... to use your brain to unravel the universe around you ... untainted by thoughts of how much money you're going to get out of it – or whatever ... sorry, sounds completely unrealistic."

"If ever, now is the time in your life when you can allow yourself to be unrealistic, Michael."

The more prosaic routine of putting pen to paper in attempted response to the weekly set of problems was now in motion. Michael's chosen subject was one of the most appropriate for perpetuating his school life. The disciples were set tasks by the teacher who already knew what the answers were. In physics there was certainty – there was right and there was wrong, wasn't there? In contrast, a good proportion of the snack bar population were now beginning, perhaps had done so for some time, to realise that their chosen path was not nearly so confined. They were Arts students. There was doubt, uncertainty and conjecture in everything they read, but it did not reside purely in their own shortcomings. They had free rein, if they had a mind, for supposition, surmise, intuition or even guesswork. In contrast, he viewed what he had set his heart on studying had arisen from centuries of inspired but painstaking logical thought. He knew that he was a long way from contributing to it, but he liked to imagine a time when the scientific world would be inspired by his own insights.

As he worked to the end of his tea and jam doughnut, he basked in the current lonely spell. It was then that Nigel, a fellow member of Rodwell tutorials, appeared. His scrawny frame and puzzled countenance did not at first mark him out as a rival physicist. But he, annoyingly, seemed to generate too many right answers. And suddenly he changed the course of Michael's life, unwittingly and dramatically.

"Hello there. Getting over the Rodwell hour?" said Nigel coming up behind a Michael whose first reaction was to plan an escape.

He had rarely approached Michael in this way but, unaccountably, he could not have chosen a better time to do it. Nigel's companion caused Michael's heart to bounce around his ribcage like a demented parrot.

"Oh, this is Sarah," said Nigel with astounding nonchalance verging on boredom.

Michael's follow-up reaction was to announce that he did not believe what Nigel had just said and done. The words didn't materialise.

"Hi..." was all he managed to get out as the girl with the blonde hair, tied in their regulation bunches, and in the familiar expensive-looking grey fur coat, now being slipped from her shoulders, sat down at his table.

The long, slowly-moving queue at registration, a couple of weeks before, would have been tedious but for the opportunity to study the girl, now identified as Sarah. She was some fifteen places ahead of him. Because of this, he had no need to perform the conspicuous act of turning round every now and then. She was far enough away and in a position which allowed him to examine her in safety. For him, she stood out as though covered in red paint. In the line of individuals variously army-surplus-jacketed, sandaled and sockless, Jesus-bearded, mini-skirted (some precariously so), necklaced (male or female) or broadly conventionally attired, she was on the far, although seemingly exclusive, side of the last group. The grey fur coat could even once have been alive but she wore it without ostentation. The length of her skirt, revealed briefly as her coat fell open, could have left him trying to imagine the shape of her thighs, but thighs were still a long way from his mind. It was her face which dominated his thoughts. It was too angelic, too pure. She was beyond his reach – it was immediately obvious to him. If he was ever destined to become acquainted with her, he was certain that there was no chance of her interest being aroused by him. Her face was and would remain effectively light years beyond his touch and certainly beyond his lips.

From that first sighting, she had materialised and vanished like a ghost on rare occasions during his wanderings between tutorial, library and snack bar. He had caught fleeting glimpses of her in the distance. She had appeared from and disappeared into the mists of those dark October evenings as he stared ineffectually. She had been other-worldly. Now she sat in stunning solidity not a yard from him and directed words straight at him!

"Hello ... hope you don't mind us joining you."

"No, not at all ... no," he said.

... What are you saying? How could you conceivably think that I want you to sit anywhere else in the universe? You don't know how long I've been waiting for you to sit just where you are sitting at this moment! ...

Another reaction then suddenly came hurtling up and crashed into the previous ones.

... Is this ... Sarah ... nice name! ... Nigel's girlfriend? ... Does he take her to cinemas and hold hands with her? Have his hands ever been anywhere else? ... If so, the world is a much more peculiar place than I thought ... I suppose I can't blame him but how on earth did he manage it? ... if he did ...

"We're both members of the Roman Catholic Society," said Nigel, as if he had read Michael's mind. At least it was some explanation for why they were together but Michael still could not rule out any nefarious behaviour.

"You're one of these clever scientists are you, Michael?"

... Her sweet face smiled at me! ... Her lips spoke my name! ... Wait a minute ... what are you thinking? I thought you wanted to be above the temptations of pretty faces ... it's bound to lead to embarrassment and ridicule ...

"Yes, that's right. They were having problems here unravelling the mysteries of the universe so they got Nigel and me in to help them out." Michael's attempted joke succeeded in making Sarah laugh, at least briefly. Even Nigel forced out a transient smile.

... Why on earth am I trying to make jokes? ... just calm down! ...

"I could never make sense of chemistry and physics and that sort of thing. I think the teachers gave up on me at an early stage," said Sarah.

... she doesn't just speak, does she ... it's sort of just above a whisper ... and the words and laughter float through the air ... like petals being caught by a summer breeze ... are you crazy? ... calm down, Michael!

"What are you reading?" he asked.

"Rather too much at the moment."

... and she's got a sense of humour! ...

"No, art history actually – at least that's what I intend to do. This term we have a required reading list of literature, politics, philosophy – all sorts of things – a bit hair-raising really."

"It sounds it," said Nigel sombrely. "They're probably running a physics course on *how* to read."

"Oh, Nigel, you are funny."

... *No, he's not that funny* ...

"We just have to try and remember something about what Planck or Heisenberg or Einstein said."

... *You don't seem to have much trouble, Nigel old son* ...

"These famous scientists all seem to be German, don't they?" said Sarah.

"Not a bit of it," said Michael trying to be clever but with as mild a riposte as anyone could manage. "Most of the great scientific discoveries were made in the British Isles."

"Oh, and you two are going to carry on the tradition, are you?"

"Well, at least Nigel is – but I'll be there if he needs me," said Michael without really seeing any attraction in such scientific collaboration.

"Are you staying in one of the guest houses?"

... *She wants to know where I live!* ...

"Yes, I'm in a jolly place called Greycliffe – at the top of Upper Rock Gardens."

... *Don't give her the number!* ...

"Sounds like something out of a Bronte novel," said Sarah.

"Not quite as romantic I'm afraid. The landlady has a grim determination not to smile and her husband's got a dreadful cough – particularly at breakfast time. Sounds like a deep-sea diver being strangled."

"Makes Craig House seem positively heavenly," she laughed breathily, "We're down in Burlington Street, Kemptown. Our landlady's quite sweet really."

... *You've got that have you? Craig House, Burlington Street, Kemptown ... forget it and you die!* ...

As Sarah spoke with her crystal clear enunciation, Michael conjured a picture of the possible origins within which her voice had been nurtured.

... *Father's a baronet probably ... mother's undoubtedly a pillar of the Women's Institute ... it would be rather nice to hold your hand ... I know I never will. This is as near to you as I'll get – and that's a bonus ... This is hopeless! I've got to get a grip on myself ... anyway, we've probably got nothing in common ... except being here ...*

Sarah's home, he discovered while trying not to sound probing, was, appropriately, in Surrey – near Guildford. He couldn't remember whether Nigel was from Broadstairs or Basingstoke. Her interest in art had already taken her to Florence and she said that she had been on the verge of going there that very week as a volunteer to help in the clean-up after the devastating flood. This event was news to Michael; he was suddenly ashamed at being so out of touch. Then she asked him directly: "wasn't it a blessing that the David was undamaged?" He attempted to be effusive in his agreement. He would have dearly loved to offer her his viewpoint on the said statue, but he could only just about remember having heard of it. He was sure that it was Bill who had told him about it. Bill always went into raptures about the great artists, although even he had never seen David in the flesh, or rather in the stone, either. The two of them had only recently managed to cross the channel on a cosily packaged holiday. It was an adventure at the time but Michael feared he would be increasingly likely now to be bumping into stalwarts who had yak-trekked across the Himalayan foothills or braved hairy spiders in the jungles of Borneo.

"Do you know Florence at all?" Sarah asked Michael.

"I'm ... afraid not, no. I hope I can soon. It sounds wonderful ... so what happens at the Roman Catholic Society?" he said, trying unnecessarily to steer the conversation away from the narrowness of his artistic horizons.

"Well, I suppose you could call it a discussion group, with visiting speakers – that sort of thing. You're not a prospective member then?"

... I'd love to say yes ... could I fake my religion? ...

"No. I'm a nominal member of the good old Church of England – but I did spend years singing in a church choir. Can't interest you in the Choral Society can I?"

"My music teacher was convinced I was tone deaf," said Sarah, "so perhaps I'll have to decline your offer."

... damn it! ... oh God, please don't say you do want to join, Nigel ...

The conversation progressed haltingly with Michael trying his hardest not to make too many jokes or direct too many questions at Sarah, but he began to feel that maybe these would be the only questions he was ever destined to ask her. This meeting had been little short of miraculous but he had no confidence that it would ever recur. It was one of those random events. In his mind it would leave him with no grounds for phoning her up or knocking on her door, even if he could summon the courage. And still, in the back of his mind was the irritation that the invisible, indefinable force was causing him to be anxious about such things. His emotions provided a fine example of contradiction. One strand required aloofness and detachment while another constantly looked for lips to kiss and waists for arms to be placed around. In the girl who sat on the other side of the table, the latter had found all it could hope for, but as the cups emptied and the brevity of the encounter became ever more apparent, it became more powerless to exert its influence. Even if Nigel had suddenly vanished, there would have been no crude attempt to seek a second meeting. Michael would wait and hope for further miracles. He was able to do nothing else.

"Well, I ought to go to the library." Sarah's statement made the future bleaker for Michael, a future only slightly lightened by the departure of Nigel in another direction. Michael accompanied Sarah, he hoped without overt signs of subterfuge, from the snack bar right to the top of the library steps but could then find no good excuse for following her into the history section. Cheery and transient farewells preceded a sombre meander towards physics where he decided to console himself with another look at Schiff's *Quantum Mechanics*.

... Mm ... no easier than the last time I looked at it ... still, keep going ... immerse yourself in wave functions ... that's the stuff for the troops! ... treat the allure of these sweet features with caution ... you'll only end up sliding down the slope into the mire of lost dignity ... remember that cousin of yours years ago who was described in hushed tones as having "got herself into trouble" ... how great you felt not to be involved in that sort of entanglement ... how fantastic it was – is – for physics and music to be the centre of your life with no capacity for emotional injury ... oh God! ... you know you're on a knife edge ... a few more inducements and you know your idiotic arm would want to encompass her girlish frame, your stupid lips would consider it the summit of privilege to press themselves against hers ... it's OK, you're safe – one meeting was more than credible ...

The second incredible meeting took place a week or so later. She appeared, as before, through the early evening fog – part of a straggling bus queue, some of whose members stood half in the road with thumbs raised hopefully. Sarah stood prettily and neatly on the pavement. Although he was a latecomer and she in the midst of the queue, he was astounded as she turned and made a concessionary smile at him, a smile that somehow induced his brainless legs, although diffidently, to walk towards her and his heart to pound with the athletic effort.

"Hello, studying late today?" he asked tentatively.

"No, I've been to a meeting," she replied shyly. His natural diplomacy prohibited him from immediately enquiring further.

"I've been to another dramatic Choral Society get-together."

"Oh, are they always dramatic?"

"No, sorry, just my joke. But they can be quite uplifting – especially when everyone hits the right note."

"You know I think you tend to exaggerate a bit," she said with a laugh in her voice that made his head swim rather pleasantly.

"Sorry, I don't mean to be so flippant. Actually it's marvellous being in a choir when things are going well. It's very exciting to hear voices harmonising, even amateur voices."

"Yes, I'm sure it must be," she said with polite enthusiasm.

They filled the following pause by clearing throats and looking up the road towards Lewes hoping for the big headlights to shine out through the fog.

"Er ... what kind of meeting have you been to?" he said.

"Well ... I hope your views aren't too diametrically opposed ... the Conservative Association actually."

"I ... don't think I'm going to ostracise you for that."

"Oh good. Only, Conservatives do seem to be a bit of an oddity in a place like this."

... I am relieved it wasn't the Marxist Club ...

"You can't believe all you read in the papers. I'm afraid I don't have awfully fixed ideas in any direction – don't tell anyone." He felt able to confess as much to her. "I think my parents always vote Labour but I waver a bit. In fact I'm a very passionate waverer."

She laughed. "Perhaps I can persuade you to join us then."

... just show me the application forms ... you've got a new Conservative! ...

"Well, I ... Tuesday nights are a bit taken up with the choir I'm afraid. Put me down as a possible. Good grief! Is this a bus I see before me?" Michael hoped that the approaching vehicle would either not be too crowded and yield up two adjacent seats or be so packed that a modest amount of squeezing together wouldn't be considered out of order. The preference for seats was satisfied and Michael sat down still somewhat in disbelief. His incredulity was steadily enhanced by the notable ease with which comments and questions started to flow between them.

... Is she actually enjoying talking to me? ... I feel as though I'm relaxing ... No, don't relax too much! ... you'll tell too many boring jokes ... a girl of my own age seems to want to talk to me ... is she aware of her looks ... must be ... oh dear! ... would I have cowered at the back of the queue if she'd not been pretty? ... I can't help it ... I didn't manufacture my hormones ... anyway, here I am ...

The bus too quickly reached its destination and he followed her off with tension rising exponentially. The inner pressure finally forced the words out of him.

... It's now or never ... I think I'm going to do it ... oh help! ...

"Er ... would you like a coffee?"

... You didn't actually say that did you? ...

"Mm, that would be nice."

... She didn't actually say that did she? ...

"How about over there?"

He had passed the café many times but never thought it would rise to such prominence in his student career. Someone or something had situated it perfectly for him. It was what he considered appropriately respectable for her. The Pool Valley Coffee Bar might have furnished him with some kudos at being observed in her company but The Pavilion Parlour held only the slimmest of chances that her attentions would be diluted by friends bumped into or her gentle voice obliterated by juke box emanations. A week before, the machine had played something that had hammered continuously in his head as he walked along the front at night. The bass ostinato, overlaid with those rich organ chords, had induced him to make a purchase, which he now announced without a thought as to its relevance.

"Er ... it's called 'Gimme Some Lovin'," he said with some hesitation and with a marked effort not to make it sound like a request.

Let me in, baby, I don't know what you got ...

... do you know what you've got, Sarah? ... do you look in the mirror and think: "I look very nice" ... surely not ... conceit and vanity doesn't fit with you ... surely you think surface features have little meaning ... it's just that you are nice to look at ... and why do these songs keep mentioning a baby ... some American colloquialism I suppose ... I would never dream of calling you baby, Sarah ... and I would never say "let me in" ... it sounds so blatant ... and let me in to what? ... the songwriter seems to think he's made it ... have I made it? ... have we made it? ... probably never will ... what does he mean by "it" anyway? ... drinking coffee is hardly making it ... I would never ask any girl bluntly to give me some loving ... whatever that means ... I've never thought about these song lyrics before ... they never meant much ... they still don't ... if "loving" just means intercourse that could hardly be more irrelevant at the moment ...

He considered that it would have been easy for her to decline his offer, with plausible excuses of an essay to finish or a tutorial to prepare for. He did not look upon the interruption of her evening as an achievement, let alone a triumph, but he relaxed more than he had expected. By the time the waitress had delivered their coffee, he realised that they were talking with something approaching ease. There was no shame in his history, but Michael glossed over details when hearing of her private schooling, her home in a Surrey village, which he imagined as spaciously impressive, and her father's job in the Ministry of Defence. Lieutenant-Colonel sounded rather grander than his father's rise to lance-corporal. Yachting at Cowes was also something he had never participated in. He hardly knew where it was. If pressed, he would have felt uncomfortable, as he had done long before, of not being able to offer any examples of Burgess ancestors who had come anywhere near the gates of academia or who had not been mere cogs in the wheels of industry. She did not press, and he was relieved that she was far from boastful. They knew, without saying, that they were both fortunate to have undergone no privations or struggles in life and to have devoted families. Some dispassionate sociologist, such as Woods, would have placed Michael in the working-class category and Sarah several rungs higher. Michael never thought of placing himself in any class – ever.

When asked of her plans, she appeared to have no great ambitions. She said she would work as hard as she could but that she just felt privileged to be where she was and study something she found very interesting, if not totally absorbing. The last few weeks, and particularly this evening, had made Michael's blighted hopes of Cambridge fade to insignificance, but he was bold enough to suggest a desire to be, at least, a well-known figure in physics. She smilingly pointed out that such a standing would be accompanied by endless lecture-giving, committee meetings and evermore expectations from peers. He laughed off the fact that he had not given this any thought.

Michael admonished himself for offering a second coffee, but the refusal was polite. He found it difficult to come to terms with the fact that he was handling that fur coat as he helped her on with it, and tried his best not to even brush her shoulder with his hand.

"This is a nice coat," he said.

"Thanks. It's not real though, you'll probably be pleased to know."

"Even better."

As they walked out into Castle Square, the renewed intensity of the cold made her hug the coat round herself. The effort required to prevent himself from putting his arm round her, drained some more fuel from his batteries but it was a small price to pay for the most enchanting cup of coffee he had ever drunk. Coffee bars were really coming on in his life.

"Oh, there's my bus," she said suddenly.

"Do you mind if I'm lazy and ride as far as Rock Gardens?" he gasped hopefully as they half ran to the stop.

"No, of course not."

Rock Gardens was too near. It was reached too soon for him to propose another meeting. He was Michael Burgess after all, but as he and his spirits descended from the bus, he convinced himself that parting assurances that they would "see each other around" had been accompanied by some hopefulness in her eyes. The road was the steeper both because he was truthfully not optimistic about "being seen around" and because there was no Bill at the top of Upper Rock Gardens to whom he could recount the evening's stupendous coffee bar event.

May 1969 –

Richard Woods

Michael was once more drinking coffee and, this time, attempting to look inconspicuous by sitting in the corner of the student snack bar with his head in a book. The desire for concealment was unpromising considering the large number of empty tables. His aim, when he had finished drinking and considering the future, was to run as quickly as he could into the library and hide in the physics section. The French quarter would never be approached again.

… how can I come face-to-face, or anywhere near Caroline, after I deposited that stupid note … which she obviously threw away immediately … I don't believe it! … not Woods again … he's seen me … is he suddenly following me around? …

"Mike! You look a bit of a lonely soul in the corner." Woods established himself with coffee at Michael's table.

"No, I'm trying to clear my mind before tackling the rigours of atomic theory."

"I'll believe you … by the way, I'm still intrigued by your interest in Alan Mercer."

"Oh, not him again. I did say it was private. Are you looking for a sociology project or something?"

"No thanks. Come on, Mike, old school friends can share a few secrets. Knowledge of your private world might just cheer up this dreary period of revision."

Michael knew he was not going to get rid of Woods very easily by keeping him guessing. After all, he hadn't done anything shameful – very far from it.

"Well if you really must know ..."

"I must."

"I'm interested in a girl ..."

"Aren't we all, old chap ... is that it?"

"But this particular girl is ... I think ... going around with this ... Alan Mercer character."

"What, you do mean a student?"

"That's right."

"Jesus Christ! What do you mean 'going around'?"

"I happened to see them leave her house together."

"What, you were doing some spying were you?"

"No I was not. I often go for a walk in Queen's Park and they just ... appeared ..."

"Really ... I suppose lecturers having it off with students isn't exactly cricket. Mind you, looking around, as I do, I couldn't exactly blame them. Who is she?"

"Her name is Caroline Selwyn."

"Funnily enough, I have come across her – academically, not physically unfortunately. She volunteered to be interviewed for some project I was doing. Strange girl, though. Not a very good subject – I felt she wasn't revealing everything about her background. Bit of a cock-teaser actually."

"Quite what ... do you mean by that, Dick?"

"Oh, come on, Burgess, you must have heard the expression. She's quite nice looking, but she's got an aloofness about her. You feel she's the sort that might lead you on and promise all sorts of delights, and then drop you like the proverbial hot brick."

It was an added burden on Michael's already overloaded brain to listen to this casual demolition of his cherished vision of the girl. He tried to console himself with his lack of faith in what Woods ever told him, and his perception of Woods as chronically insensitive.

"You can pursue her if you must, of course." Woods continued, "But to avoid disappointment ... well, you know ... and if she's already screwing with old Alan ..."

"Yes, thanks for reminding me. I'll think about it."

... I can't think about it ...

Michael did not want to think about what might or might not be going on. He felt he had to hold on to some belief in innocence and purity and simplicity. Woods next remark made these seemingly elusive ideals come flooding back.

"I wonder what happened to that Sarah? She was a bit of alright. Haven't seen her around much – must be dedicated to deep final study, although I never saw her as an academic."

"Maybe you saw her more than I did ... no, I don't want to know any details."

"You're not getting any. But I have to say, you did impress me by getting her to go with you to that Christmas Ball."

December 1966 –

Invitation to The Ball

"I ... was wondering if you'd like to come to the Christmas Ball ... with me, you know ... ?"

"Oh ... Michael! ... That's very kind ... I'd love to."

... This cannot be happening; this is unbelievable; I've arrived – again! Yes, yes yes! I've done it ... perhaps I've made it? ... I can't imagine how, but it's happened! ... Ha, haaaaaaa! ...

Michael fought manfully to remain outwardly calm as these thoughts played a sort of mental bagatelle inside his skull. The first term was now travelling beyond the bounds of wild dreams. He was being paid to become totally immersed in the atomic physics that before he could only toy with – and he was beginning to understand it; and what was more, Sarah, the prettiest girl he had ever come across, had accepted his big invitation. And Eric, Jack and Ginger would be playing! His natural reaction, to assume that something would go wrong to mar this perfection, was, at this moment being gently suffocated.

He had not expected to be taken seriously. There was no detectable hesitation; no other suitor to make her think and falter for even a second. Astonishment made it difficult for him to continue the conversation.

"... oh, great ... only ... I wasn't sure you'd be er ... interested ... they've got a good group playing ... one of the best ... Cream ... with Eric Clapton ... I don't know if you've heard of them ..."

"I think so, yes. Anyway, I trust your tastes."

He had spotted Sarah on her own in a corner of the JCR, by the towering window. The sloping seats of the multi-coloured reclining chairs made the fashionable shortness of most skirts arresting in the extreme. The quantity of thigh that Sarah revealed was appropriately modest and Michael was more than sufficiently arrested if not remanded in custody, but after quickly noting it, he filed it away in some mental cabinet and made no further observations. He had been contemplating such a proposal but the suddenness of the opportunity and execution took his own breath away, if not hers. He now, foolishly, pictured himself in a new world where boldness had displaced hesitation.

"It's a couple of weeks yet so I can get the tickets before my money runs out."

"Oh, I must help you with ..."

"No, don't worry ... my invitation."

"That's very kind of you. I might have to get a new dress."

He was continually hopeful that he could extract some academic or philosophical gems that might possibly be lurking in his subconscious, but he marvelled at the fact the she still gave no indication of boredom with his conversation. He was happy to suggest no more definite plans until the time came to whisk her away to the Ball. His mark had been made. It was reserved but, as he was continually hearing in maths tutorials, it was both necessary and sufficient – for now.

When, two weeks later, he took off on foot from Greycliffe in the direction of Kemp Town and the hallowed guest house which accommodated Sarah, he suddenly realised that the mode of eventual conveyance to the Ball had not been considered. He would have to phone for a taxi, wouldn't he?

Room 6 at Greycliffe had been even more a hub of activity than usual that evening. Both Owen and Michael had secured partners for the Christmas Ball and each had spent some time soaking in his ration of hottish water apportioned by Mrs Higgs. The spartan echo-chamber of a bathroom, with its slightly-less-than-adequate heater, was not conducive to lying and luxuriating but Michael underwent the ritual with sparks of excitement shooting through his body. Owen had found his girl through circumstances very different to Michael. She had, a week or so before, been what was referred to as a blind date. Michael had only the vaguest of notions of ever coming across the concept.

"It's a bit complicated see, but a girlfriend of one of my rugby mates mentioned that a friend of hers wasn't having much luck meeting people and was prepared to go out on a blind date for an evening." Owen had explained, "I was worried what she'd look like if she'd been having so much trouble. You know, like back ends of buses came to mind. Anyway, as it turned out she wasn't at all bad looking and quite good fun so I asked her along to this do."

Although his own date was not exactly "blind", Michael still knew little about her, or how she might react to his prolonged company. Before he had left Greycliffe, he had, for some reassurance, been compelled to put his new record on again. It spoke about a girl – but then they all did. She didn't correspond especially to the one he was about to meet, but he wished to impose some association. The resonant voices, proclaiming *Good Vibrations*, seemed to come from the half-deserted streets that he had trudged in the dark evenings of the recent past.

... Do those Beach Boys really spend their time surfing with beautiful blonde girls in colourful clothes ... Sarah might sometimes wear colourful clothes ... and her voice is gentle ... but sunlight? ha! ... the words don't make much sense ... what the hell are "good vibrations"? ... It's not about a girl ... it's a sound ... evocative – that's a good word Bill uses ... somehow amplifying everything that's happening ... she smiles softly, I suppose, but how do I know she's kind? ... so far she has been ... but that's not very far ...

Michael walked along Upper St James' Street realising that his journey was shorter than he would have wished. He assumed, illogically, that more of a delay would engender more calm, promote more confidence, in his ability to lead and be protective. No clear plans came about as he walked. He merely contemplated the individuals he had left behind in the sombre rooms and staircases of his guest house. Pity inappropriately conveyed what he felt, and he was too charitable to be smug, but there was happiness in being included in this surprisingly small minority from Greycliffe who could this evening describe themselves as escorts. Con and Gareth had made the excuse of a party they preferred to go to.

The turning into Burlington Street was agonisingly imminent. When he got there, he stopped on the opposite side of the road for a few seconds, took a deep breath of cold air and looked down the street towards the promenade and the now invisible sea. Burlington Street suited her. It was narrow and secluded and the buildings had what passed for elegance, while Rock Gardens was a broad thoroughfare for throbbing double-deckers and some dwellings that had seen better days. Burlington Street might in some circumstances have been described as inviting but that hardly began to describe his feelings about Craig House half way down on the left.

Before he knew what was happening, his finger was first on the bell push and was then being withdrawn sharply as the unexpectedly shrill note echoed into the hall beyond. The door was opened wide almost immediately by a breathless girl, the pallor of whose skin was in extreme contrast to the darkness of her hair and dress. The first impression of terminal anaemia was quickly dispelled by the vivacity of her manner and her subsequent rapid ascent of the stairs, clinging to the hem of her long gown.

"Sorry to dash!" she gasped, "I've got a crisis with my dress. I was just borrowing some cotton from the landlady and happened to be nearest the door. Sarah's in room 4 ... just up here on the second floor ... oh my God, this would have to happen now ..."

The girl continued her athletic feat of stair-climbing towards some dizzying altitude, muttering to herself as she went.

"Right ... thanks." Michael's words were barely heeded. He caught enough of a glimpse of the girl to be temporarily stopped in his tracks by the extent to which her neckline plunged but the brief leer was swept aside with derision as he met Sarah on her way down. They both stopped. His heart was suddenly forced to try and triple its resting rate. The hair that he had only ever seen tied in its girlish side bunches had been liberated and fell onto shoulders that he had never dared think would ever be revealed to him. They were uncovered, in his eyes, to the perfect degree, fringed by lace that had no need to descend for further revelation of any forbidden fruit. Far in the back of his mind there were the whispers urging him to taste but they were overwhelmed by the cries of wonder at this innocent youthfulness. It was a paradox that the ball gown had turned the woman, as she had to be described, back into the girl that he desired most. He could not believe that this was all for him, but neither was it credible that she had dressed to display herself to the world and to say: "this is what beauty is like – I am beyond your reach." He saw no guile in her.

Her smile both dazzled him and restored some of his confidence, calming his beleaguered heart. At least this smile was exclusively his. There was no one else on the stairs to share it.

"Hi, Michael! I thought it might be you. I'm almost ready, come up."

... Almost ready!? ... you mean it gets better? ...

He followed, quite content that there was no indication or compulsion to kiss on the cheek.

"Oh, just hang on a minute ... Cathy, are you decent?" said Sarah hesitating outside her door. "Can Michael come in?"

"He can. I'm as decent as I ever will be," said a philosophical and clearly Irish Cathy who sat staring into a dressing table mirror applying what she described as the finishing touches to a great work of art. The room was so different from the one he had just left. The trappings of femininity and the subtly perfumed air softened what could have been merely utilitarian. Apart from his thoughts of Sarah, he immediately felt at home in such a room. The withdrawn young man felt an ease among girls that he had never felt among boys.

"Michael, how are you?" said Cathy in her soft accent at his reflection in the mirror, "If you'd been ten minutes earlier you'd have seen the bare canvas, which, I might say, is not the most wondrous sight."

"Oh, just listen to her," said Sarah, "She looks gorgeous, doesn't she?"

"She does ... you both do," he said, for the present glad to have escaped trying to say directly to Sarah how she looked and making it sound totally inept.

"There, Sarah my love, we have a fan club of at least one. Actually," Cathy lowered her voice and looked at Michael, "I've a suspicion her fan club's a lot bigger. Makes you sick. She's so pretty she doesn't need all this make-up. But you might have noticed that already, Michael."

"Er ..." said Michael.

"Oh honestly, Cathy. You do talk nonsense – and you're embarrassing Michael."

"Perhaps we ought to get a taxi," continued Michael almost mechanically.

"Now there's a man with initiative," said Cathy, "Would you book one for four and we'll share the fare, that is when my beau turns up – that's B E A U."

"Um ... there are some directories down in the hall. I'll show you," said Sarah.

Michael followed her down the stairs to yet another new venture. He had never ordered a taxi in his life. The house was becoming more and more active, with men arriving and couples leaving. The phone was attached to the wall under the stairs concealed from the main part of the hall. He hoped he would have the right change.

"Can I leave it to you?" said Sarah, giving him a slightly guilty smile.

He was glad to be left alone. The directory had several pages of advertisements for taxis, from Shoreham to Eastbourne and up to East Grinstead and what looked like hundreds for Brighton. He picked a number at random and, with trepidation and held breath, dialled. Having stuttered out his intended journey, the frown on his face dissolved as the voice at the other end, polite to a fault and frequently calling him "sir", told him that: "yes, they would have a vehicle free in fifteen minutes – would that be alright?". The relief and triumph that propelled him back up to room 4 were met by stunned astonishment.

"Well, well, well. Look who it isn't! Fancy seeing you in a lady's bedroom." The amalgamation of smile and sneer that Richard

Woods created with such expertise was turned on Michael with all its brilliance.

"Good God, what the hell are you ... ?" Michael began spontaneously giving himself a mental pinch and asking himself again whether Woods really was standing in front of him.

"What am I doing here? Same as you, old son, I should think. You do look pretty, Mike."

"I wish I could say the same about you." Michael wondered how such a reply could have come out but he kept smiling.

"Now ... correct me if I'm wrong," said Cathy looking in turn at the men and a confused Sarah, "but do I get the impression that you two have a sort of passing acquaintance?"

"Unfortunately we've passed each other millions of times I should think," said Richard Woods. "As Bertie Wooster would say: we were at school together."

"What an amazing coincidence," said Sarah, "What a ... lovely surprise."

The two men concurred politely but each with his own proportion of irony. After the first jolt of astonishment, the coincidence didn't strike Michael as especially bizarre but his sudden drop in vitality stemmed from the uncertainty of how long he would have to spend in Woods' company that evening. The presence of Sarah was too wonderful to be thought of as a consolation but the presence of Woods was, in no small measure, a dark obstacle.

"I hear you were in the process of booking a cab, Mike. How efficient of you," said Woods.

"It'll be here in fifteen minutes – so the man said."

"Oh they always say things like that. I suppose we'll just have to be patient," said Woods.

... Trust you to deflate my ego just when it was beginning to expand ... and trust me for allowing you to ...

Michael struggled mentally to treat the notion of Woods' past being littered with taxi cab bookings as a complete fabrication.

"Well, folks, I've reached the finished product. I'm ready," said Cathy, spinning round from her mirror and beaming at the assembly. She had the sort of self-assurance that Michael saw neither in himself nor Sarah. In a way, that enhanced Sarah in his eyes, but he could not deny the instant appeal that Cathy possessed. Woods had obviously fallen for it. Years of experience seemed to be lurking behind her easy manner but where had that come from? She looked, and was probably, no older than Sarah.

"Let's wait down in the lounge," said Sarah, picking up the grey fur coat from the back of a chair. Michael was quick to take it from her and help her into it. She still did not realise how the sight of that coat had so entranced him from the first day, the coat that he could spot from half a mile on a dark night.

"We haven't got a little bar downstairs, have we?" asked Woods.

"We have not, you're right. This is not an Irish guest house, unfortunately. You'll have to be patient, my dear," said Cathy grabbing him by the arm and leading him down the stairs. Michael was amazed how anyone would want to hold Woods' arm in such a manner, call him "dear" and seem to regard it as amusement.

December 1966 –

Going to The Ball

When the taxi arrived, Michael decided to show a measure of self-sacrifice and leadership. He let Woods jump in the back with Sarah and Cathy. From his spacious vantage point beside the driver, Michael began to settle into something approaching the thrill and expectation that he had felt before the appearance of Woods.

... Having a chauffeur is something I could get used to ... this is the first time I've taken a girl to a dance ... what a bloody debut! ...

Once more, Michael felt a peculiar surge of commiseration for all those left back in the fog of the town and who were not being sped along towards a scintillating evening with a beautiful girl. But then, he wondered whether he wanted such speed. There was no morning traffic to obstruct progress and allow him to gather thoughts. The multi-colours illuminating the window of the refectory that were suddenly there behind the trees, were, to him, not signals from some cosy club in which he could hide, but more –

spotlights under which he would be expected to sparkle. As Michael debated with himself about the size of tip, Woods surprised him by handing the driver some money and asking him to keep the change. Offers of recompense were waved away with vague suggestions of drinks being bought at some later time. Michael permitted himself to place a hand lightly on Sarah's shoulder as she stepped from the car but he quickly removed it as they walked side by side across the moated quadrangle, contenting himself with the intermittent, accidental touching of arms. Some time back he had entertained visions of ambling across an ancient Cambridge quad, but now this was the only place he wanted to be.

"Very nice, old chap. How *do* you do it?" said Woods as he and Michael stood waiting for the girls, who seemed to have had to disappear simultaneously into the ladies' cloakroom.

"I didn't *do* anything really. We met by accident and I just asked her if she'd like to come along tonight," said Michael trying to neutralise Woods' curiosity.

"Mmm ... some accident! You sound very blasé about it."

"Actually, I really came tonight to listen to Eric Clapton."

"Ha ... ha."

"She's a good Catholic girl by the way."

"I've heard that before. That demure exterior could easily be hiding a hot little arse you know."

Visions of the said posterior did, for maybe a millisecond, try to insinuate themselves in the pleasure centres of Michael's brain, but loyalty to Sarah and disloyalty to Woods combined to crush them. His reply was mollified by Woods' generosity with the taxi.

"I ... don't think there's anything she's trying to hide, Richard," he said, smiling and glancing around for possible listeners. "She's ... just a nice girl."

"You don't sound as though you're interested. Given half a chance I certainly wouldn't mind ... ah, ladies!" Woods changed the subject and tone of his voice with expert ease as Cathy and Sarah reappeared, "How about a little drink?"

The dense smoke haze hung in the air of the Students' Union Bar. Below it, the absurd density of bodies was squeezed, on the face of it, too close for comfort but, presumably, for the very purpose of seeking comfort. The throng was safe. The crackle and buzz of disjointed phrases provided the background upon which real conversation would not or could not be placed. Michael was at that moment attracted by the huddle, by not having to work too hard, by not being too exposed. It temporarily alleviated the sudden fear that the dialogue he and Sarah had previously, for some reason, managed to maintain without effort, would soon lapse. The presence of Cathy was something he was grateful for, although he couldn't bring himself to say the same about Woods. In his desire to be alone with Sarah, to not have to share her, to be the sole recipient of her thoughts, expressed with the reservation and naïvety that so invigorated him, he had paid no heed to the possibility of their meetings becoming habitual. He had started with the notion that intermittent, innocent liaisons would be sufficient, but Cathy's perception of Sarah's burgeoning fan club loomed large and disturbingly.

"Well, what are we having? Sarah?" Woods spoke while Michael was making plans to.

"Um … Dubonnet please."

"Cathy?"

"Half o' Guinness. I'll brave it. Although it doesn't taste like it does back home."

"Mike?"

"Lager – but I'll get them."

"You can get the next one – come and give me a hand with them."

Michael looked for a path through the multitude that would allow him to overtake Woods but his push didn't amount to the shove imparted by Woods and he was left trailing. Even the production of a banknote was waved away.

"It'll leave you with more to get your little girl drunk," said Woods.

"Oh, so that's the object of the evening is it?"

"There's no harm in getting her loosened up. She's a bit reserved it seems to me – somehow childlike. I know she makes me a bit stiff."

"I'll treat that remark …"

"With the contempt it deserves. I know – only jesting old chap."

Woods slipped into his customary role of attracting attention, this time of those manning the ramparts behind the counter. They seemed to be in perpetual motion between pump and optic, already mopping brows and wearing expressions of exasperation, with T-shirts liberally streaked in hard-earned perspiration. Michael surveyed the invading hordes. Looking at them again, how unlike the cosiness of the Royal Oak it was. There were men, and even boys, fitted into their evening attire with the aplomb of would-be playboys – Woods was one. There were others who were besuited under clear sufferance. Michael sought inclusion in the first category but the second-hand suit did not compare favourably with those that sported silken trimming. A fraction of the male fraternity was known to him; observation of that ill-fitted proportion allowed him some mild amusement. The size of the unknown remainder puzzled him and gave him visions of some hidden army of intellectual bon viveurs who only ever surfaced for such occasions.

But the girls! From those who could be uncharitably described as plain to those who came close to Sarah, they stunned him with their cosmetic ingenuity. Locks of hair, which were used to falling in uncontrolled and hastily brushed profusion onto shoulders clad in dowdy sweaters, had been marshalled and intertwined into elegant sculpture. Napes of necks that too rarely saw the light of day curved captivatingly. Eyes that had, willingly or unwillingly, grown tired in the act of devouring the appointed volumes or had dutifully stared, glazed over, at the scribbling in the early morning lecture, had been shaded and outlined and lashed into fantastic, sparkling shapes, with cheekbones heightened as never before. Jewellery dripped from ear-lobes and lay alluringly against throats. Breasts of acquaintances that he had not tried to observe, or had not realised even existed, had been raised startlingly from their secret hiding places and held together by some magical force. He had never seen the cleft so purposefully revealed to such an extent by so many in a public gathering. Cleavage was hardly yet in his vocabulary. The dances he had experienced, that one hand could easily count, had been strictly and youthfully high-necked. Any speculation of other attributes that lay concealed beneath the floor-length dresses, if it would have occurred to him at all, were postponed by a nudge from Woods.

"Here, grab these."

"Oh ... right."

This time it was Michael's opportunity to lead. He forged ahead and, with commendable dexterity, avoided spilling one drop of the Dubonnet that he guarded, even at the expense of several splashes of his lager. He delivered his charge into Sarah's delicate fingers and treated himself to a smile directed straight at her and returned with directness.

"Oh, Michael, you are kind," she said as his head swam in response.

"You have to thank Richard I'm afraid. Don't worry, I'll get you another before the evening's out."

He couldn't help it. The stimulus of what surrounded him and pressed in on all sides made his thoughts turn. There was no way out. He unfettered his imagination for a few moments to think about a certain bosom.

... why are we boys so fascinated by girls' breasts? ... this is nothing short of a scientific question ... to which I have no clear answer ... but something excites me about it ... them ... what is it? ... deeply concealed memories of being fed as a baby? ... but girls don't feel the same ... do they? ... perhaps it's a case of being drawn to 'something you've got that I haven't' ... does this work both ways, as it were? ... oh, no ... I mustn't be seen to look ...

For a long time, her face had obscured everything else but when he had eventually found himself looking below her high neckline, making sure she was not aware of it, it was as though a discovery of something totally unexpected was being made. The childlike features seemed to him strangely incompatible with whatever was making her dress curve out and in, although more modestly than many in the vicinity, including Cathy. Michael was sure that she would not have reverted to cotton wool and the idea that it was really all Sarah intensified the thrill of looking at her more than he thought it should have done. There was hope that a gentle kiss on her lips, before he was much older, would not disappoint her, but he was sure that knowledge of even a fleeting desire to apply his lips anywhere else would. He was still trying to dismiss the temptations that arose as being unbecoming in him and, when looked at objectively, as being based on absurd trivialities. With this in mind, he floated back into the fantasy of The Ball with Cinderella at his side – the kind of Cinderella who had stirred a little boy's passions at pantomimes long past, before he had known why. He wondered whether he knew any better now.

"So where is it that the Guinness tastes better, Cathy?" Michael asked after they had sipped in response to Woods' overdone toast to a good evening.

"The dear old Emerald Isle – County Cork to be precise. I'm actually what they call an overseas student. I come from the land of poets and scholars – not including myself in that of course."

"But you've at least started to be a scholar by coming here," suggested Michael.

"Well I managed to pass exams in the only couple of subjects I liked – English and History. Still I suppose our history is rather ingrained in us – based on hatred of the English that is." She laughed, but Michael sensed that this was no joke.

"Oh really?" said Michael, surprised that anyone could hate the English.

"Well, once I've savoured the last few drops of this stout, which isn't bad, even though it's English, I'm keen to hit the dance floor," said Cathy, "Come on, Mr Woods, drink up."

"What a demanding woman you are," said Woods, who surprised Michael with his acquiescence.

"Oh, look, I'm a bit slow. You two go ahead – we'll see you later," said Sarah.

Michael's urge to kiss Sarah was infused with renewed passion by her excuse to break with what he saw as the overpowering presence of Woods. If Sarah was feeling the same way, she didn't show it.

"He's quite a character isn't he?" she said as Cathy and Woods passed through the bar door to become intermingled with the ever-moving crowd outside.

"Mm ... that could mean a lot of things ... oh, there's a couple of seats, shall we grab them?"

They sat down at the corner of a table occupied by another group, the male fraction of which gave Sarah at least two surreptitious glances and raised Michael's morale by at least two substantial notches.

"No, I mean," continued Michael, "when somebody's described as a character it usually signifies that they draw attention to themselves by, say, being provocative or, metaphorically or in reality, making a bit of a noise. But it doesn't mean that someone who doesn't do that hasn't got a very rich personality – underneath as it were."

"You mean someone like you?"

"Ah ... well, let's not make this personal ... oh dear, you've seen through my dull exterior."

"Now would I let someone dull take me out?"

"Certainly not."

"From a woman's point of view, he's rather lively – OK he does make provocative statements, but he's fun to be with."

"What Woods? He's about as funny as a road accident."

"Now, Michael, that's enough."

Michael felt a peculiar enjoyment at being gently reprimanded.

"I suppose his good looks wouldn't do much for you," Sarah continued.

"Good looks? What Woods?"

"I thought you'd rise to that."

His enthusiasm for her suggested move to the dance floor was genuine but his misgivings went unsaid and, he hoped, undetected. Jumping around to the beat of a record in total privacy was a pastime that he had often indulged in, even though he regarded it as teetering on the edge of the ludicrously juvenile. Now, he would have to be carefully controlled. The urge to shield her delicate ears from the onslaught of the amplification, and to enwrap her supposedly fragile body, was resisted, but he watched her nervously. They began to move, without close mutual scrutiny, looking to left and right in preference to straight ahead. He didn't want to make her feel observed or judged, and looking into her eyes without words passing between them would have hastened an intimacy that he, and he guessed she, was not yet ready for. Then, he was surprised, if not taken aback, by the sight of Owen, in a far corner, indulging in a long kiss with his blind date. He could not imagine how they had achieved such intimacy in such a short time. Michael was not envious. He preferred Sarah to regard him as attractive but restrained – not as one whose priority was to lock lips at the earliest opportunity.

Some relief of his tension came when he noticed Cathy and Woods across the floor. Woods, seemingly in the throes of some orgasmic convulsion, looked pleasingly fatuous. Cathy, on the other hand, while performing a very exaggerated version of Sarah's dancing, looked gloriously balanced. If the influence of Sarah had not been so strong, he could have looked upon her as desirable.

How sweet it is to be loved by you ...

... it would be stretching things to breaking point to imagine I'm "loved" in some way ... and do I need the shelter of your arms, Sarah? ... I suppose it would be pleasant but ... I do want to thank you for coming to this dance ... perhaps you couldn't think of anything better ...

A problem suddenly presented itself to Michael as the bouncy, dotted rhythm was terminated and a form of adagio begun. It was too soon to retire from the floor and they could not remain detached and look anything other than out of place. He placed his right hand as gently as he could on her waist and she raised her hand to clasp his. She smiled at him and then looked down. He was careful to maintain a respectable gap between their chests; it was enough to feel, for the first time, the warmth of her body with one hand and the moisture of her palm with the other. He believed himself content in such detachment, even as he looked across the floor at Cathy whose chest and cheek were surprisingly already firmly pressed against those of Woods. He mused that someone whom Cathy was inclined to embrace in such a fashion could not be all bad, but he couldn't immediately put his finger on the good. At the end of the slow song, he let go of Sarah's hand but held onto her waist for as long as he considered acceptable.

Then, an acute rush of boldness and an idea of inevitability filled his head as they moved along the semi-darkness of the corridor towards another bar. As their arms happened to touch, he felt for her hand and his heart pounded as she let him hold it. The act was not accomplished without some effort. He didn't want her to feel that she was somehow attached to him in any permanent way, or to give any interested onlookers such an impression. He was amazed that she seemed to want her hand to be held; that she didn't want him to continue in his assumed role of benign bodyguard.

"I'm sorry if I've been a bit slow in saying it but ... er ... you do look rather lovely tonight ... well, you always do, that is ... but ... particularly tonight." He made what he hoped was the private pronouncement after a fortifying gulp of Newcastle Amber. She blushed, looked down for a second and then up into his eyes, "You're very kind. You do too. No!" She stifled a laugh by placing her hand to her mouth, "Not lovely ... oh dear, you know what I mean."

"I ... think so."

The relief of their laughter was like the injection of a strong dose of whatever drug was currently fashionable, if either of them had known, or been interested in, what that was.

Michael was surprised again, despite the coffee bar episode, that he was able to talk to Sarah almost as easily as he did to Bill. He had never conversed with a girl in such a way before. He hardly knew her and he was, as ever, cautious about words he used and topics he ventured into, but he was bold enough to silently conclude that she liked him. He was certain that he liked her and he rejected stupid, pointless dreams of anything more.

When it was time for the main group to appear, he took her hand and led her to what he considered a safe distance from the stage. There, he let her hand go, not wishing her to feel entrapped. While they had been away, the now familiar, to him, heavy black cabinets had been piled one on another, endorsed in brilliant white by Mr Marshall – the stamp of universal approval. They were surmounted by their companion gold-fronted boxes that glinted in the spotlights and waited silently to empower their owners out of all proportion at the flick of a wrist.

"'Scuse me, folks." The Scottish accented voice, not talking to anyone in particular, came from close behind them. Michael and Sarah turned to be confronted by a man holding up a bass guitar like a sword from which the onlookers drew back dutifully.

... Heavens, if it isn't Jack! – and Eric and Ginger! ... what the hell has Eric done with his hair? ... Is that a bubble cut? – looks ridiculous ... Of course, I know their numbers well, Sarah – I know every note of their first

LP ... another of the records I've bought recently ... Bill and I stood right next to the stage at the Ricky Tick in Windsor ... I wouldn't sink as low as hero worship and only grudgingly as far as admiration but the sound does inspire me ... I'm thinking of getting an electric guitar you know ... but you don't want to hear all this do you? ...

A wild-eyed and wild-haired Ginger Baker located himself behind an array of drums and cymbals that Michael was not convinced would or could all be utilised. His hidden left foot thumped the bass drum causing Sarah to start visibly and Michael to hide his surprise by placing a protective arm lightly around her waist.

The driving beat and guitar arpeggios, so familiar to Michael, began. Despite the recited allure of cars and cigars, Jack Bruce screamed that he was only happy when playing his guitar. The mute audience remained stationary and mesmerised. There was unspoken agreement that this wasn't the sort of thing you danced to. The guitar solo started with a few familiar bars but then broke away into avenues unheard of. Michael was anticipating remembered phrases, that he could even have sung to forcefully right there and then, but the meandering improvisation left him stranded.

... I've only ever played written notes or chords ... but I could improvise couldn't I? ... I could learn to ... even some of Bach's stuff is like improvising – so they say ... did Eric Clapton play the guitar for several hours and forget to eat like I'd heard? ... did he do that? ... would I ever do that? ... I've been born into three meals a day convention ... like Sarah probably ... there must be other ways to stardom than through drug-aided starvation ... there must be ...

With Cream's last number still ringing in their ears, they sat once more in the upstairs bar and Michael savoured the first drink a girl had bought him. The increasingly demented looking bar staff, now paddling in some muddy mixed beer concoction, served solace to a persistently arid clientele. A tall young man with curly hair placed his order by calling over the heads of one or two disgruntled customers who thought that they had worked for and earned priority.

"Scotch and soda if you wouldn't mind," he said with unstoppable confidence, "Darling, what are you having – same again?"

... darling ... the word's nice but he makes it sound false ... I don't think I could ever call Sarah "darling" ...

Darling was a girl Michael knew of from her photographs, but he wasn't sure which of the twins of some Cabinet Minister she was. They were similarly physically decorative; he thought almost unfairly so since they seemed to have so many other things going for them – a bit of fame, more money than him, and perhaps higher than average intellect.

... she's probably not doing physics though ... so that's alright ... and she's actually not quite as pretty as Sarah ... so there ... this darling guy – Piers Fourget isn't he called? ... lots of brains I suppose ... oodles of self-belief ... he's "known" – he "runs things" ... perhaps really I'd like his bravado ... bet Sarah wouldn't really go for him though ... obviously much more drawn to someone shy and unobtrusive like me ... I can't stay like that all the time though ... I've got to think bigger ... would Piers' girlfriend go out with me? ... an aspiring working-class physicist? ... suppose not ... I don't want to be "classed" ... but I don't think I could discuss politics and philosophy well enough ... but Sarah doesn't make me feel inadequate ... and her father's nearly a Field Marshal as well ... probably ...

Whether by accident or design, Cathy and Woods had approached Michael and Sarah and proposed they join them for dinner. Michael's silent reaction was mixed, if not torn apart. The added company might make Sarah less bored by him, but then he would have to endure another hour of Woods.

... Woods would have to appear tonight of all nights! ... Christ! Bloody Woods of all people ... if I was at university in Vladivostok he'd have found me ... but Cathy's nice ... she'll make it lively ...

"I suppose this isn't too dreadful for the price," said Woods, his tone mellowed by more than partial inebriation. "What d'y' say, Sarah?"

"I think whoever was responsible has done extremely well. I'd hate to have to organise all this."

"Me too," said Cathy. "But saying something's not too dreadful is quite a compliment from Richard. Has he been drinking, do you think?"

"Me? Drunk? Never! I'm just feeling content and mellow. Who wouldn't be eh? – dining with beautiful women, supping the fruit of the vine, looking out on a future landscape of intellectual challenge – ha! – I could even swallow a draft of nostalgia with Michael here."

"Oh no, not nostalgia. Please!" Cathy's protestation failed to curb the topic as they slipped into stories of schooldays. As Michael had expected, those of Cathy and Woods contained many more dubious activities than his and Sarah's, but he was taken aback by Sarah's shamefaced confession that she had drunk too much and been sick at a parental party. Michael worried that she might be heading the same way as a new bottle was tilted towards her glass.

"Oh, Richard, really I shouldn't," she said. "You remember we arts students have got a bl... wretched long essay to do by Monday."

"Now steady on, Sarah, mind your language," said Woods, "I shall be awfully hurt if you don't all join me. Come on, we'll all feel more relaxed tomorrow. We haven't had much."

"Oh, Sarah, if I could only tell you some parties I've been to – which I won't – at least not here!" said Cathy.

"Spoilsport," said Woods, "Yes, many a morning has been greeted with my head vibrating to the gentle throb of the steam hammer. Mike seems to be keeping his past to himself. But there again, as I said, he's as straight as a die. Oh, I'm feeling rather relaxed I have to say. I could recline in your arms, Cathy." He attempted a mock sideways lean against her arm.

"The only reclining you'll do tonight is in bed – your own that is – and on your own," said Cathy.

"Did I say anything? ..." said Woods.

Before the four had left their table, Michael's thoughts had been of engineering a separation of the couples. The evening had been spellbinding even with Woods present, but he felt that he deserved now to be alone with Sarah until he could deliver her safely to her door. The alarming three in favour, one abstention for a short exchange of partners, however, was not to be resisted. Cathy grabbed Michael's hand and pulled him towards the centre of the floor.

... surely Sarah can't be dying to dance with Woods ... I don't mind a dance with Cathy but two at the most ... please ... I've now had some practice at dancing, dining and drinking with Sarah – and holding her hand to boot! ... and now we're being kept apart by Woods! ...

"It's OK, Michael, I won't allow her to be carried off into the night," shouted Cathy above the rising throb of the music. "Relax a bit!"

"Oh hell, I don't look that possessive do I?" he said. "It's another dirty word – like ambition."

Cathy's last order was easy for him to obey; he didn't want to let her down.

... How can I be impervious to such magnetism? ... so she doesn't have Sarah's features ... but she's not bad ... not bad? ... how can you talk about a girl like that, Michael? ... but her body pulsates in some way ... her dark eyes look at me without guile ... perhaps with Sarah I feel safe ... too safe? ...

The beat slowed and Cathy unhesitatingly stepped forward, silently but gently demanding to be held as close as was reasonable in the circumstances. The irresistible, although rapid, downward glance at the milky smoothness of the fraction of her breasts that had been allowed exposure began a brief sortie into self-forbidden territory, a transient incursion that afforded him a new perspective on feminine appeal. It would have been so easy and was suddenly so tempting to lift her chin and kiss her with passion but it was impossible for him – especially in public. She provided exquisite consolation as the music finished, by placing a surprisingly wet kiss against his cheek and saying: "Thanks, Michael, you're a gentleman. Let's go and rescue Sarah."

"We've come to claim and be claimed," she said as they walked up to the other two. Michael's eyes were intently focussed on Woods' hand that had been placed on Sarah's bare shoulder. He had not dared look at how closely Woods had pressed himself against her in the slow dance. Now that they had been returned to each other, Michael knew he could not fairly be reprimanded for holding closely, kissing cheek or even mouth, but still he refrained. His aspirations were concentrated on the not-too-distant moment of parting.

... It must happen then ... I just know it's going to happen! ... at last ... would you believe it? ...

Sarah's suggestion that they catch the next coach was met with an acquiescence that he hoped didn't appear too ready. Even Eric and his band were now fading into the background. They climbed into the half-light and half-emptiness of the throbbing coach; Michael looked round for familiar faces and was pleased to find none. He willed it to move off as they sat with the ringing in his ears accentuated in the sudden silence and fatigue of inaction; above all, he willed Cathy and Woods to catch a later excursion. Any attempt to place his arm around Sarah's shoulder would have risked exposure to ridicule for him and a stiff neck for her, given the volume of overcoat involved. The compromise of his hand placed on hers was, he thought, more comfortable and sensuous as well as being discreet. The erstwhile anonymous, distant, unattainable young lady now laid her golden head gently against his shoulder and pressed her arm against his, causing him to catch his breath and marvel at the random crossing of paths.

Relaxation became liberation as the coach began to crunch its way out across the gravel towards the Lewes Road leaving the dinner companions and Eric, Jack and Ginger behind. Making conversation was no longer mandatory in his mind. Touching her hand and feeling the softness of the false grey fur occupied him sufficiently.

His hand dug deep into its folds and pulled her closely, and now fearlessly, to him as they strode along the deserted, windswept sea-front, their faces specked by raindrops. They laughed at trivialities and even at Woods.

Few of the windows of Burlington Street were lit. Michael's imagined, socially-impoverished, pitiable community had retired to their dull slumber hours before, with their guest house signs swaying in the wind. On the pavement opposite Craig House two other obvious Ball-goers stood with arms and lips enfolded and hadn't moved appreciably while Michael and Sarah walked up to her house.

"I've had such a wonderful time, Michael. Thank you. It couldn't have been better ..." said Sarah awkwardly, as though she had been preparing the speech.

"You took the words right out of my mouth ..." He was not prepared to say any more. Gently, but now without hesitation, he pressed his body and lips against hers. For the first time that evening he was conscious of a physical stirring other than the beating of his heart and he moved his hips backwards with as much subtlety as he could.

"Oh, Michael ..." she said as their lips parted. The kiss was a flash compared with the steady glow on the other side of the road but he was too amazed that it had taken place to worry, even though he had anticipated it. With what passed for impetuosity in him, he kissed her even more quickly once again. He could have tried to fool himself that the whispered utterance of his name was a sign of devotion and longing but self-delusion did not prevail. He considered the two words to mean that Michael's kissing was quite passionate enough this evening and should be curtailed before Michael became too engrossed. He was content.

He kept hold of her hand as they stepped away from each other and her pretty smile provided him with enough reassurance that his amorous attentions had not been seen as over-indulgence.

"I hope your essay won't spoil tomorrow too much ..."

... Oh dear, I just want to curl up on a sofa with you ... how about tomorrow evening? ... after you've done your essay ...

She stepped up to her door, searching for the key in her bag.

"I'll try not to think about the essay ... bye ... and thank you again ..." she whispered in the way he believed only she could. "See you ..."

Sarah closed the door, excluding him from the warm, inappropriately red glow of her hallway, now dimmed for the lateness of the hour. He turned and walked off as slowly as he could without attracting accusations of loitering. The over-loud laughter of the other couple, who had now managed to unravel themselves, bounced along the street and emphasised his sudden loneliness. But the emptiness was softened by what he saw as triumph, not of conquering someone but being smiled upon by them.

... To enclose her in a cloak of protectiveness is so enticing ... but I've got to resist such temptation ... it's so early ... I mustn't stifle her ... that's what they say ... there is time ... but I can't have been drawn into this web of desire for it to be just pulled apart can I? ... the chance coming-together can't be as randomly and indiscriminately broken ... why should it be? ... I'll give it a few days, then I'll make contact again ... it'll be easier now won't it? ...

The echoing, harmonic phrases had made their mark. "Good Vibrations" and a distant undercurrent of "Gimme Some Lovin" were still reverberating inside his head.

... Am I picking up good vibrations? ... what are they? ... who knows? ... she is giving me some sort of excitation there's no doubt ... the songwriter sounds like a physicist ...

The face that had looked back at him could alone have captivated, but the rise and fall of the notes, however coincidental, and the lyrics, however banal and unconnected, would enhance, almost painfully, that captivation in solitary moments of the future. A second glimpse of the crimson carpet and red-embossed wallpaper of Craig House, as she had gone back in, had set for ever the background of the portrait. The brief meeting and departure at the quaint guest house, huddled with its neighbours under the black December sky, had been awarded by his subconscious the status of turning point, of something that could never be repeated and which had to be recorded, encapsulated and frozen in all its poignant, hypnotic detail. But his conscious thoughts dwelt as usual on uncertainty and self-criticism.

... It's crazy isn't it? ... it would generally be referred to as infatuation ... an obsession of someone who isn't thinking straight ... does abstinence make the heart grow fonder? ... they would say, those unknown sensible people, that I should concentrate on my studies ... not dwell on trivialities like prettiness and girliness ... physics has all but gone out of the window recently ... I can't let it go ... I can't let her go ... just like that ... can I? ...

Christmas 1966 –

Windsor, two weeks later

"Good to see Cream again, eh Mike? On form were they?"

"Yeah, not bad at all."

"Sounds like you're going to have some good dances down there in Brighton."

"It's a good start. But in this case I'd've preferred just to stand around the stage and listen. Like we did at the Ricky Tick."

"Those were the days. So you did have someone to dance with?"

"Yeah, I ... took a girl ..."

"An actual girl, eh? Tell me more."

"Oh ... she's someone I got chatting to once and, amazingly, she took up my invitation. My main aim was to listen to Eric Clapton and the guys – see if I could pick up any tips."

"Pull the other one. How far did you get?"

"Bill, I wasn't trying to get very far – you know me."

"Sorry I spoke."

"She ... let me kiss her ... once, if you must know – when we said goodnight outside her guest house. This is no big romance."

"I'll believe you."

Michael and Bill had just returned from church. Holy Trinity had such history for them and they had gone there for some nostalgia and had nodded "hello" to the ageing choirmen they knew well. The Christmas morning service was little different from the thousands of other services they had attended as choirboys years before; similar except for the hymns that still gave Michael that indefinable thrill. He wondered if it was simply because their melodies and harmonies were the best; perhaps that was why they had been repeated annually, way beyond the memory of anyone living. Along with this sublime music was the receipt by his parents of more than one greetings card depicting country churches with brightly lit windows in deep snow beneath grey skies. Michael never wanted to dismiss all this as sentimentality. He would have been more than content to trudge home through such snow, after carol singing in a sparsely-populated village, and be enclosed in his cosy shelter with parents and Bill. He thought of someone else who might accompany them, but that would have complicated things.

There was now no snow outside and the sky was more blue than grey, but he could at least pursue the conversational ramble that he and his friend had followed so many times. The Christmas holiday, that he now had to call vacation, was already two weeks in, and he knew that study must, before long, be resumed. For today, though, and probably Boxing Day, books would remain closed.

"Played your guitar much recently, Mike?"

"Oh yeah. Well, as much as I can. I'm still trying to get my fingers round a few classical pieces, but I've been trying some folk as well. There's a guy in our guest house who's very good – suggested I make out the chords to songs on my own rather than buy music. He's got some nice Joan Baez records."

"Joan Baez! What a voice."

"I was actually induced to part with some money and buy one of her discs. Mind if I put it on?"

Babe ... ... I'm gonna leave you

"Lovely the way she hangs on that first word for a few bars – haunting in fact," said Michael. "I wouldn't mind having a go at singing some of her songs ... and I don't need an electric guitar for it."

"Wonder what it's about, that song. Is it personal or some ancient folk thing? They say she and Bob Dylan were lovers. Perhaps it's about him."

"Really? Haven't got a clue. There again, if I was to sing it, I wouldn't be thinking about leaving when the summer or any other time comes along. I've yet to join up with anyone."

"What about the girl you took to the dance?"

"I don't think we're joined up ... anyway, I never pay much heed to the words of songs. It's the sound and the melody that's important – for me."

Subsequent tracks on the LP continued the themes of hot passion and jealous violence with undercurrents of menace and evil that emanated from some undefined part of distant history.

"I suppose you'd describe this stuff as dark, eh?" Bill suggested. "They're either about adultery and/or knights and knaves hacking each other to death."

"Don't get much of that around here these days. But then I've always lived a sheltered life."

"There's always some adultery going on."

"You reckon?"

"Well ... things you hear. Not in my family but ... it's not uncommon apparently."

"We must both have very orderly families."

"Yeah, but there's probably a world out there that's not very orderly ... to say the least. I was thinking – there wouldn't be many popular books, films and plays without violence, promiscuity and adultery, or all three. I don't think you and I were designed for drama, Mike."

Michael and Bill didn't agree on everything, but one thing that united them was a distrust of, even disdain for, the human race. Bill maintained that whenever humans meddled with the natural world, something went wrong. They were both content with the conclusion that man's assumed position at the pinnacle of creation was not only undeserved but false. In support of this, Michael quoted Mr Jenkins, his short, fat biology teacher at school, who had said that the rise and fall of homo sapiens would probably just be a little blip on the vast evolutionary timescale of insects. On a personal level, neither found this very comforting, but they had to concede that Jenkins' conjecture did have a certain weight of probability in its favour.

Michael had never been convinced of the supremacy of mankind in anything. He was at one with Bill's view that the achievements of mankind could only be seen within man's narrow perspective. He and Bill considered themselves fortunate to be able to read, write and study in their own ways, but felt that these abilities had arisen by a freak of nature, and that nature could now well do without their species. The last war, that both had escaped by a whisker of history, exemplified, they thought, the indelible, inherent malaise that infected their fellow men and women.

"Ever heard of Buffy Sainte Marie, Bill?"

"Oh yeah – Universal Soldier."

"That's it. This mate of mine at Sussex had one of her records too. That Universal Soldier song has really stuck in my head; the idea that wars are the fault of all the soldiers, not just some nutcase at the top. I mean, if most Germans had thought a bit and said: "wait a minute, this Hitler bloke's a bloody crackpot", then things might have been different."

"You might think that, but I'm told at the time they were desperate – starving even – and they thought he'd rescue them."

"Give me strength! It's the same old story – the new Messiah will save us all if we follow him and do what he tells us. We've got to stop doing that, Bill. People have got to stop following leaders and think for themselves – not start killing people because some raving lunatic says they're undesirable. Why have we got this so-called wonderful brain?"

"Do you always think for yourself, Mike? You know, you read your physics book and say: Einstein said this or that – it must be right."

"Perish the thought! I know it takes me a while to figure out if physics makes sense, and sometimes I can't, but I think I'm being trained not to accept anything until I've thought hard about it. Characters like Einstein work on the assumption that you forget what's gone before and start again. In his case, it led to historically dramatic conclusions. Very few are privileged to have that sort of insight but at least the rest of us don't have to accept everything, or anything, at face value."

"Hate to disillusion you, Mike, but it's never going to be like that. You're going to have to accept it."

"Oh God, I'm not very good at persuading people to change their narrow view of the world. You're the only one who's ever really going to listen to me – and maybe ignore me as well."

Michael had never been completely at ease in the company of young men, other that Bill. A group of more than two schoolboys had, in his experience, rapidly descended into unsubstantiated exaggeration or embarrassing banter. After schooldays, he had not found the situation to be improving. He had some suspicion that a group of young ladies might not be so irksome, but he had no real evidence. Was it, he wondered, concern about his undoubted ignorance of so many things that made him shy of group scrutiny? Bill and he had never mocked each other's innocence and callowness. He had never been able to talk at length about emotions or philosophy or art, in however a halting or under-informed manner, with anyone but Bill.

"So did you pick up any tips from Eric at the dance, Michael my lad?"

"Sort of ... but I need to listen to the records and go through the riffs slowly. I should be able to get there in the end, with a lot of patience. I'd really like to get an electric guitar sometime – even start a group. We might get noticed by some agent or other."

"Bit of a long shot, as always, but you never know ..."

May 1969 Sussex – The Group and The Agent

The ringing, twanging tones of his guitar ground out the dirge-like tune, for want of a better word. The distant Ball, though never to be forgotten, had assumed the guise of a fairy-tale. Michael had then looked on at those wailing into their microphones with an emotion approaching hope. Now, he attempted a groan into his own equipment with some half-heartedness.

Shiny, shiny, shiny boots of leather ...

The notes came together in melodiously banal to harshly discordant groupings. Michael had worked them out to sound like passable imitations of the original, but few of their prospective audiences would know the difference. He just had to be careful that the same discords occurred at the same place in each verse. The harmonious encounter with Caroline that he had sought for in vain, the previous night in the pub, had been dislocated irreparably by the arrival of Rod Wyatt.

... why am I singing and playing this sort of stuff? ... "Venus in Furs" ... huh! ... Jeff instigated this ... seems to like dubious erotic material ... or erratic in our case ... "Venus in Furs" ... does Sarah still wear that fur coat? ... not in this weather I suppose ... haven't seen her for a while ... camped out in Rottingdean apparently ... good place for finals revision ... .I wouldn't have described her as Venus ... more like a prettier version of Hayley Mills ... what am I doing here? ... what have I got myself into? ...

The discords were just about right but the finale of the song suffered different interpretations from the three members of the band.

"Oh c'mon, we've gotta get the ending right. We're always messing this one up." Jeff looked at Michael with his accustomed air of dissatisfaction. He always seemed to be bordering on depression with an over-developed willingness to find fault in something or someone. Michael couldn't help feeling like the target. The problem was, Jeff was a good bass guitarist. Michael had welcomed Jeff's arrival in Brighton the previous year. Jeff was not only someone he knew from school; he had renewed Michael's hopes of his own group, but sometimes he was as bad as Woods. Such old school ties were often in dire need of being loosened. Once, Michael had come close to envying Jeff – up on the stage at that school dance – and envying the others with girlfriends. But now he was lead and Jeff was backing him, so to speak.

The impending discussion of how "Venus In Furs" should be terminated was suddenly postponed as the door opened.

"Hello, boys!" said Rod Wyatt with an exaggerated show of jocularity. The "boys" murmured their greetings. "I waited outside till you finished the number. Sounded polished – really polished."

Michael was unimpressed by Wyatt's enthusiasm or the age range he had placed him in. Song-writer Cliff, who accompanied Rod, merely smiled broadly behind his black glasses and his medallion still glinted.

"Did your friend turn up at the pub last night, Mike?" said Rod.

"Er ... no, I ... don't know what happened to him."

"Funny how we should bump into you like that ... Anyway, I don't want to interrupt you – for a while," Wyatt continued, "I just want you to carry on as if I wasn't here. Just do your own thing, you know."

... Fat chance of that ... why don't you all go away and leave me in peace? ...

"What about running through the Steppenwolf one?" suggested Steve.

"Now you're talkin'," said Jeff almost breaking into a smile. The satisfaction in his features indicated a desire for the bizarre which the Velvet Underground or Steppenwolf music espoused. Michael preferred not to take it so seriously. After a few moments of hesitation, spent trying to ignore Rod Wyatt, he counted them in and methodically ran through the chords, finding it difficult to escape from a feeling of absurdity.

I'm waitin' for my man ...

... It's about drug dealers, Rod ... but, I know, I feel a complete prat singing it ... I've never taken any drugs ... I won't even take an aspirin ... why should I worry about you anyway? ...

This time there should have been little chance of getting any of the three easy chords wrong. The problem was that its simplicity caused Michael's mind to wander yet again onto everything that was bothering him. The repeated lyrics, caused by temporary amnesia, would never have been noticed by anyone, but he twice changed chords in the wrong place and was glad to get to the end and not leave any men waiting any longer.

They waited for Rod Wyatt's pronouncement.

"Yeah ... they're coming on well those two numbers ... 'course, we have to be careful about introducing too much, sort of, way out material into the repertoire. You can't afford to alienate your public. They're the ones who're going to pay hard-earned cash to listen to you. You know what I mean?"

... Our public? Who the hell are they supposed to be? It's our repertoire. Even though I don't wait on street corners for drugs, or fraternise with fourteen-year-old nymphomaniacs in fur coats, we'll decide what we play ...

"Yeah ... the main thing I wanted to discuss was ... we've got to work on your image if we're going to sell you ..."

... The only thing I should be working on now are the mysteries of the universe ...

"... We're all in agreement, I think, that Cliff's written a great song. I think it fits your style very well. OK, it's fine to add a few unconventional ditties, so to speak, but – and correct me if I'm wrong ..."

... You're wrong ...

"... they're not so compatible with your overall image," Wyatt continued to grow in confidence, if that was possible. His speech was a peculiar blend of poor and studiedly correct enunciation but the intermittent display of refined consonants was unable to compensate for the rest. The musicians' response to Wyatt's comments could not have been described as rapid.

"To be honest, Rod, I don't think we've thought much about our image yet," said Jeff, seeming to imply that such a thing would be thought about.

"Well now, that's where I come in. I've given it a lot of thought ..."

... Oh no, you haven't, have you? ...

"... And believe me, I know how important it can be. We need to do a profile on each of you for promotion material. You know, what you eat for breakfast, who your musical influences are, what film stars give you a hard on, you know the sort of stuff ..."

... I don't believe this ...

"... Anyway, about the demo; it sounds really great – I keep on playing it – and Cliff and I are not sitting on our backsides, you know. We've being talkin' to various people at the company and we're trying to get the radio guys interested, BBC and commercial. We're not going to leave a stone unturned, so don't worry ..."

... I'm not ... I mean, I am ...

"... And the other thing for today is that, surprise, surprise, Cliff's got a new number for you. It'd be great if we could get the framework in place this afternoon, so, Cliff, why don't you run through the chords. These three'll pick it up in no time."

Michael handed over his guitar with a smile but more than the usual reticence in his mind. Cliff cleared his throat and spoke falteringly about his latest composition.

"Er ... it's um ... got a more sort of bluesy feel, you know ... called 'That's Easy For You To Say' ..."

"Nice title," interjected Wyatt.

"... and it goes, er, something like this ..."

... the chord sequence is quite nice I suppose ... but his voice is so bloody awful ... anybody must sound better than that ...

In the subsequent two hours, the trio had managed to make "That's Easy For You To Say" sound like a proper song and had been drilled in what Rod Wyatt referred to as the "stage version" of "Nobody's Fool", the demo that they were assured would soon be taking the world by storm. Michael kept on looking at his watch but no one seemed to take any notice.

"You're working hard, lads. I think you deserve a break ..."

... Hallelujah! ... are they going to go at last? ... it can't be true ...

"... so let's go and get a drink or something and then we can concentrate on your other numbers ..."

... it isn't true...oh my God! ... what am I going to do? ...

"Yeah ... OK, Er ..." It was Steve being diplomatic. "Time's pressing a bit. I can make another hour but then I ought to get away. I've got a mountain of revision to do. I know it's a bit of a bore. There's the little matter of exams in less than three weeks."

... Steve, I could kiss you ... why the hell didn't I say it? ...

"Steve, I fully see your point of view. Don't worry, trust your Uncle Rod ..."

... but you're only about 28, Rod! ...

"... I'm not going to lean too heavily on you. After all we've all got our commitments, right Cliff? But having said that, we stand to make a bit of bread out of this – and not a little recognition, believe me."

"I keep reminding them," said Jeff.

"He's only a second-year though," said Michael, still managing to smile.

Two groups formed as they wandered away from the drinks machine in the empty, slightly less tropical, JCR, one composed of Cliff, Steve and Jeff and the other of Rod Wyatt and Michael. The latter's impression of entrapment increased as Wyatt spoke to him in hushed tones.

"You know we're relying on you, Mike. I don't want to pressurise you but you can make or break this whole enterprise. I'm confident you'll make it. You've got the talent. It's your voice, that's what this is all about."

Despite the layers of falsehood, Michael knew that Wyatt was sincere, earnest even. Someone who might, given an ocean of leeway, make him famous, was telling him that he had a great voice. He had always wanted to believe it, he had wanted to sign Rod's dubious contract, but now he wanted to run away and forget. It was not just the exams. It would all go out of his control unless he put a stop to it. The appeal of just being allowed to sit on his bed and strum or let his voice echo into nothing more than a bathroom was overwhelming.

Wyatt raised his voice to the others. "I was just saying how talented all three of these guys are, eh Cliff?"

They had been assured that it would be the final run through of "Nobody's Fool" but Michael fluffed a quick succession of chords which increased the perspiration on his hands and the heat in his face, and then he began to forget the words. He stopped in mid verse.

"It's alright – don't worry," said Rod Wyatt. "Look, Cliff, why don't you take guitar for a bit and let Mike concentrate on the vocals. It's not your voice, Mike, don't get me wrong, but perhaps you could work on your delivery a bit more. Come on, you're heartbroken – really feel the lyrics …"

… *I am bloody heartbroken … every extra five minutes I have to stay here … Look, Wyatt, even Steve's looking at his watch …*

"… You've gotta project, you've gotta make us believe you're sincere about the words, even though you think they're crap …"

… *I think they're crap …*

"… Alright, just once more – bear with me."

Michael forced himself to believe in the lyrics and project his anguish. He was saturated with sweat and Rod Wyatt's patter, but a good performance seemed to be the best form of escape. His relief was enormous as Steve began the unscrewing of his drum kit, and he could even withstand Wyatt's continued background buzz as he switched off the power to his amp.

"Right, well done lads. You've worked like ni… – oh, shouldn't say that – especially in this heat. You're starting to work as a tight unit. As long as you believe in what you're doing, it'll all come right in the end. With Mike's vocals backed by that really solid rhythm, you can't go wrong." His glance rotated around the musicians as he delivered the speech. Their only answer to flattery was to avert their eyes in smiling embarrassment.

… *What does it matter about solid backings if you can get a battery of electronics that'll make Donald Duck sound like Paul Robeson? … And don't lecture me about believing in things … I believe in things that really matter … Old Bamford at school always told us never to be ordinary … but I don't want to be extraordinary in the Rod Wyatt sort of way …*

"For now, just think that 'Nobody's Fool' is the key number. It's original and it's what can make your names. Keep it in your heads – run over it on your own. You can even sing it in the bath, eh Mike? That's if you students still have baths, eh?"

… *The only thing I've got to keep in my head is physics … got it? … PHYSICS … and I've got to forget about Caroline … she's a lost cause …*

if that's the right word ... another hot Sunday afternoon ... what is she doing with that lecturer? ...

The five hesitated by Jeff's van and Rod Wyatt's red sports car. The strength of the sun had been unrelenting but now, the temperature had moderated from unbearable to luxurious. Signs of life outside were rare. There were few individuals bothering to make the arduous journey over the lawns or along hot paths from one scorched red brick building to another. Michael could almost relax in it with the impending departure of Rod and Cliff. With added relief, he inadvertently put a stop to the proceedings by remembering that he had left his microphone in the music room.

"OK we'll be in touch," said Rod. "I'm trying to line up that gig down here for you, so keep practising. Any problems, give us a buzz. Be good, and if you can't, be careful, eh?..."

Rod and Cliff sped away with unnecessary acceleration out towards the Lewes Road while Michael raced back up the stairs. He stood in the now quiet music room for a few seconds, absorbing its welcome emptiness. The people and feelings that had been encountered the very first time he had entered the room momentarily reassembled. The indulgence, although fleeting, could not be encompassed without a degree of caution. It was something else that old Bamford used to say about it not being normal to keep on thinking of the past. Despite the distant warning, he was unable to prevent the lapse.

... It was a dark, foggy evening. The air was like me, raw and fresh ... All was uncertainty, expectancy, excitement, no anguish ... I was going to be an intellectual – and we were rehearsing Mozart! ...

October 1966 Sussex –

The Choral Society

"You tenor or bass?" The thin, affable, clean-cut young man asked Michael as the newly constituted Choral Society assembled in some confusion for the academic year's first practice. Michael had been on the verge of asking somebody something for a few minutes and was grateful for the enquiry.

"Bass as a matter of fact."

"Thank God, I won't have to sing solo then. I'm Chris." He held out his hand and Michael took it. "Are you a newcomer?"

"Yes, in both senses – to the choir and the university."

"Good, that makes two of us. What are you reading?"

"Physics. You?"

"Electronics. Comes about from having spent years taking old radios and TVs to bits. Physics was always a bit esoteric for me."

... esoteric ... good word – I think ...

"Oh ... well I was never any good with radios. I prefer to be theoretical," said Michael.

"You mean you're the sort of person who contemplates whether they exist or not?"

"Not that theoretical." They both laughed, "I'm no philosopher. That sort of stuff really gets you tied up in knots."

"Physics does that to me fairly well," admitted Chris.

Chris's tweed jacket, grey flannels and short hair were an affirmation not only of his practical nature but of his non-conformity. Michael could guess that he wouldn't have dreamt of being apologetic about his dress, even in a roomful of denim, dark glasses and bubble cuts. The ease with which he and Michael had slipped into conversation gave the latter optimism that some form of friendship might develop, but the optimism was always cautious. He would never be guided by first appearances.

"Right, we seem to be a bit short of tenors. Do any of the nominal basses feel they can rouse themselves from the depths to reach a few high notes?" The Greek-looking director of music posed the question, with the mildest of accents and the most penetrating of gazes along the male section. There were no immediate volunteers.

"Come on, we're going to be rather unbalanced with seven basses and two tenors. Just two defectors will be enough."

Michael did not want to change. He was a bass and a bass he wished to stay. When his voice had broken, it had plummeted. His last days in the boys' pews of the church choir had been as an impostor, one proud to reach the lowest of notes. He had held onto his place partly through not wanting to be considered too early a developer. Now he had descended, he was reluctant to go up again.

"Well, I'll pick on the devils I know," said the director. "How about you, Mr Foster? I've always considered you very versatile."

"Flattery will get you anywhere, Stavros," said Foster, undoubtedly not fresh and undoubtedly "in", amid a flutter of laughter. He raised himself from his seat and increased the tenor ranks to three. His confident demeanour was compatible with the unusual combination of curly, unruly hair, Victorian sideburns, flowery waistcoat and tight trousers. He was yet another individual the like of whom Michael had never seen except on television. He was relieved when another would-be bass eventually crossed over.

"Wonderful! ... Right, I fear we have a somewhat similar problem with the ladies."

While an equivalent rearrangement was taking place between sopranos and contraltos, Michael made a quick reconnaissance of their faces and shapes. There appeared to be no one with a combination of both that would keep his eyes constantly wandering from the score or the conductor. His reactions changed quickly from disappointment to resignation and finally rested on mild self-contempt that he had acquired this sort of habit. Chris didn't appear to be performing a similar examination. They discovered that they were both undergoing the agonies and tribulations of learning the classical guitar. On the other hand, Michael guessed they were not destined to be close musical friends when Chris expressed his dismay at Michael wanting to acquire an electric version as well.

"This year we have on our programme, among other things, the Mozart Requiem – that's for a concert at the end of next term." Stavros continued, "Then there's the Tallis Lamentations – all eight parts, ladies and gentlemen ..." he looked around and received the anticipated gasps, "... and we also have to try and cope with a British premiere at the first Brighton Festival which takes place towards the end of the Summer Term." The director's announcement was met with additional mumbles from the chorus indicative of its diffidence at being able to handle such a tough assignment.

"I think for the latter we will be auditioning after this rehearsal," he paused to smile, suggesting that it would be a painful task sorting the sheep that merely followed from those who could read and lead. "It's a piece by Henze. I don't know if any of you are familiar with him …"

The side-burned Mr Foster gave a knowing: "Oh God, yes!"

"… thank you, Mr Foster …"

"Never heard of him," said a whispering Chris to a heartened Michael.

"… It's not particularly easy music, I grant. If we feel we can't manage it we'll have to hand it over to a professional bunch, but I'm sure you're made of sterner stuff. For the present, let's see what we can make of Mozart …"

"You going for the sight-reading audition?" Chris murmured.

"Short-sight reading in my case." Michael was honest. "I can see the notes but I only have a tentative grasp of what frequency to assign them. I've never had any training anyway. If I had, I certainly wouldn't admit it."

"I had a teacher once but I had to sack him for incompetence. That's a lie by the way. The only thing I've ever done is to try and follow everyone else – musically that is."

"Don't worry, they can't do without us."

Chris offered Michael a lift after choir in a rarely-encountered student vehicle. They had both provided volume, if not perfect accuracy, at the rehearsal and they had both bravely staggered through sight-reading, but were resigned to being discarded for the Henze. They made their way up to the car park close to the science buildings. It was around nine but a good proportion of the lights still gleamed. Michael could not help wondering what or whom they were illuminating. It wouldn't be undergraduates – it could only be those who spent their life trying to avoid them. He imagined the lights shining on the first, speculative equations of a new theory, or the oscilloscope trace offering new clues to the secrets of the atom. It was all there waiting for him. His very impatience made him feel that it was all within his grasp. Could he ever doubt himself? Michael Burgess? A few unique ideas, one discovery. That would be enough.

May 1969 – Speaking to Caroline

He might not have been proud, but Mozart could possibly have applauded the efforts of the choir to get through his Requiem that distant frosty evening. The performance had few, easily forgivable, imperfections. For that hour, Michael forgot everything – physics, girls, Woods – as the glorious harmonies echoed around the circle of the Meeting House. The structure aspired, so it was said, to be inclusive of all faiths – and maybe none. Whenever he had wandered, without particular purpose, into the empty building by day, the rays of the sun that passed through the multi-coloured windows might, in earlier times, have prompted ideas about the glory of God. Choirboy Michael had sometimes come close to piety in his church days but obedience to, and love for, an entity that was being imposed on him had eventually failed to capture what he hoped was his questioning mind. Those beams of light penetrating the Meeting House did not come from any Sun God as he might have believed if he had lived in ancient times. They were propelled from the unimaginable furnace of nuclear fusion – or so he had read …

And there were those who were adamant that a being such as Mozart could not have existed without Divine Intervention. Michael had no idea how Mozart had produced all his music but he still wanted to draw on some sort of analytical logic rather than resort to miracles. Michael's observations appeared to have shown him that songs were as fundamental to the musically incompetent as they were to the virtuoso. He could envisage cave dwellers sitting around their fire and suddenly humming rather than grunting, and being rather pleased with the result. Countless thousands of years had transformed this discovery into the intricacies of Bach's B minor Mass and Mozart's Requiem. He was convinced that their works derived from a long history and not a little obsessive struggle, and that the notes were pulled from somewhere in the composers' heads rather than from the hand of God; they were just better at finding the right notes than anyone else.

The word genius worried him. He never felt moved to use it to describe anyone. He wondered if this was because of his belief that no one would ever label him as such. Even if he had produced another theory of gravity, he liked to think that he would have been uncomfortable with elevation to some sort of supernatural status. Those who had been called a genius, he had to admit, had unusual, if not unique, abilities; but he could not ascribe to them any particular admiration or adulation, or feel that they were deserving of great trophies. Any artistic masterpiece or scientific advance, he reasoned, should have been its own reward. To him, any purported paragon was simply human and, from anecdotes he had come across, often fell sadly short in other aspects of life. Michael could neither worship success nor excuse failure. No one knew how the icons of history achieved what they did, but he was certain that they didn't know either, and that their feats were not due to any conventional application of hard work.

This meandering, amateur philosophy floated through his mind as he tried to gear up the machinery of his brain for another assault on quantum mechanics. He sat in the shade on the sloping lawn outside the library. He was attempting to forget the rehearsal with Rod Wyatt and his side-kick the previous day, and instead concentrate on the textbook and the consequences of Schrödinger's Equation in front of him. The sudden postponement of this endeavour, and the nature of the interruption, would take some time for him to recover from.

"Hello ... it ... was you, wasn't it?" Caroline stood looking down at him.

"Oh ..." Michael, thrust into a shocked state, momentarily thought of denying any involvement but he knew he was an incompetent liar and he could do nothing but own up. "I ... it was mad, I know. Why do we do such stupid things?" He said, looking into the distance and trying to suggest that the writing of surreptitious notes to hoped-for admirers was commonplace.

She sat down beside him, making his heart beat faster, but from unease rather than ardour.

"No, you're not mad ... Michael, isn't it?"

"That's right, yes. How did you ... oh, the signature of course ..."

"It's ... it was very flattering ... and I'm sorry I didn't respond."

"No, please don't worry ..."

"I couldn't be ... unfaithful to my ... boyfriend. I mean unfaithful even in the mildest of ways, you know." She smiled and he attempted to.

"Please, you mustn't worry ... I mean, perhaps you don't ... I understand ..." Michael was making his too-frequent demonstration of acceptance of what he thought of as inescapable. He was incapable of saying to Caroline that he knew of her attachment to a lecturer, that it was not right, that it would end badly and that he, Michael, was an infinitely more promising suitor, if that was the right word.

"It was very sweet of you." She continued, "... but ... I'm sorry. I just wanted to explain ..."

"There's no need to explain anything ... when a stranger passes pathetic notes to you, you're hardly likely to drop everything and come running." Even though he could make no reference to "the boyfriend", Michael was suddenly finding it easier to speak like this, now he knew there was nothing to lose. "I ... sort of ... noticed you one day and ... you know, liked the look of you ... oh hell, sounds so trivial ... not just the look ... I felt some sort of connection ... but ... well ..."

"If it's any consolation, I think you're very nice ... although I don't know you. I'm sorry ... I knew all along that you were looking at me, of course I did – those times in the library," she managed a weak, distant smile. "I wanted you to come up to me ... I really did ... but then, as you can see, there was someone else ... But the situation is what it is and ... well ... perhaps ... I'll see you around. I'm sorry I have to go."

She got up, threw the well-known knitted bag over her shoulder, smiled at him briefly, then walked away. Two weeks previously, he might have gazed for a while at her bottom in the tight jeans but now she became a blur that faded into the distance. And Schrödinger's Equation was even more blurred than before this brief, heart-rending conversation.

Is she really a cock-teaser, as Woods so poetically put it? ... what a dreadful expression ... I don't see it in her ... no, I don't mean that ... oh God ... I'm not going to concentrate now ... it's impossible ... there's only one thing I can do ... it will be painful ... but liberatingly painful ... He gathered up his books and sauntered out to the bus-stop.

The intensity of the afternoon sun had moderated but it still forced the eyes to close and the sweat to trickle under the flimsiest of clothing and his garments could not have been more flimsy. The pavement on the side of the road to which he had staggered was now shaded but he felt nonetheless its radiant fierceness piercing the soles of his already baking feet. With each step the ache in his stomach became deeper and more widespread and a small extra weight was added to each leg. The slope of Elm Grove was unmerciful. No horizontal sections existed to lessen the pain. He had measured it on the map – three-quarters of a mile of straight, unrelenting ramp.

... *I'm not going to make it* ...

Michael almost gasped out the disappointed thoughts from his anguished mind. His face burned.

... *yet again, I'm not going to make it, I'm not going to, damn it!* ...

His prediction was agonisingly fulfilled as the already slowing run dissolved into a walk only thirty yards from the top. Turning the corner, his eyes were met by blinding sun and his quivering legs by a more gradual incline that could now be negotiated at a respectable jog after the brief respite. He squinted across at the part-green, part-parched slopes of the racecourse. He had reached the summit of his own circuit and the movements of his body quickened, despite the still-suffering lungs, in relieved anticipation that it was now flat or downhill to home. As he descended, he scanned the glistening sea, his gaze drifting, briefly, eastwards.

... *Sarah's now over the hills down there in Rottingdean, nestling close to the sea ... appropriate surroundings for her ... haven't seen her for a while ... I suppose she's hiding herself away like I wish I could ... just two more weeks to have the details mastered, ready, at-hand ... forget the big picture, the overall scheme, the philosophy ... all that I need now are the practical details ... as many as I can cram in ... I've got to get back to it, but getting back to it just shows me how much more there is to do ... and now the only athletics I do is this – on my own* ...

His uphill fight was now being repaid as his stride quickened and lengthened in the descent through the Kemp Town side streets, his speed and the shade now enough for him to relish the sensation of cooler air rushing past his naked upper body.

... I know that it's juvenile vanity ... but if only Caroline could see me now ... men still need to show off – even me ... we need them to say "wow! look at that – I could eat him!" ... do they say things like that? ... Caroline probably doesn't – but might be moved, be a little bit impressed by my physique ... even by my yellow silk shorts ... but no, I suppose not ... I really don't figure in her mysterious life ...

The strides were made more forceful, almost masochistically, by the thoughts.

... I can't go by Queens Park ... not after the letter ... I don't know if I can ever face her again ... but I know something in me will force me to ...

Upper Rock Gardens was passed with barely a glance to the left. How distant it seemed; its era of hopefulness and endless possibilities had now given way to a rapidly shortening period of resignation to fate, and the desperate longing for questions that he could make a good attempt at answering.

The cover of the side streets was removed as he sped down the steep, wide thoroughfare of Edward Street, almost falling over himself, then turned right into the traffic on Grand Parade and again zig-zagged round the shoppers on the Lewes Road. Now, with self-consciousness rising to the surface and a sudden unwillingness for most of his body to be revealed, he turned left as soon as he could off the main road, but not before becoming the subject of dubious verbal admiration by a passing group of schoolgirls. Escape once more into the side streets and into the shade was welcome but it mattered little. He was nearly there – experiencing the personal triumph, replayed hundreds of times, of the last few hundred yards. The acceleration in response to the sight of the finish was abruptly curtailed by the cruel steepness of Roundhill Crescent which induced the final twist of cramp in his stomach. He bent double outside the house in apparent examination of the cracks in the pavement from which the heat rose and re-fuelled the burning in his face.

"God, what a lovely sweaty body! I could almost fancy you. Aren't you at all concerned about showing your nipples off to the general public?" said Tony who laid aside the latest issue of *Private Eye* as the wet, limp Michael rested his legs over the arm of a chair.

"It's obviously not the general public I've got to worry about. Amorous attentions seem to be closer to home."

"Fear not. Restraint is my watchword – and, as you know, I'm exclusively a girls' boy, if I see what I mean. But I haven't cuddled anything except a pillow for what seems like decades."

"Well, just restrain yourself for a few more minutes. I haven't even got the strength at the moment to knee you in the balls."

"Michael, your language is definitely deteriorating. Such phraseology is atypical, I feel."

"Running up one-in-four inclines tends to make me aggressive. What you see normally is a quiet young lad – someone who never advances when he can retreat. But out there I'm a tiger – woe is he who gets in my way. It's a terrifying sight to behold. Six-feet-two of raging inferno – with nipples blazing! Actually, I don't really like talking about my nipples."

"No, neither do I. Let's talk about someone else's ... did Caroline respond?"

"Oh Christ, I knew you were going to ask eventually. No, no, and no again – is that clear? She didn't appear at the pub but, would you believe it, my self-styled manager did ... And I haven't even thought about her nipples."

"Bet you have – in private."

"Not even in private. Look, this is serious. It's putting me off studying ... I'm sorry to be boring ... just when I need no distractions. It's not a question of tits or bums ..."

"You're still aggressive I see ..."

"It'll fade soon ... This is, to me, an anonymous girl – a woman, no less – who has some sort of halo around her. *I* don't know why. I didn't manufacture it. It was suddenly just there ... Oh hell, who's masterminding all this? I've been planted here with some delusions of academic grandeur in my head – I can now admit it – but it can't be as simple as that, oh no. I have to confront added little difficulties like trying not to think about or look at girls with halos – and trying to avoid would-be managers with their own delusions."

"You poor old thing. It's the dear old probability theory again. Surely a chap like you has been exposed to enough quantum mechanics to know that. It's all chance – all centred around the normal distribution ... Sounds comfortingly benign doesn't it? Pity it can so easily bugger up your aims and aspirations."

"And talking about that, I've held myself up long enough. I think I'll disappear – for a bit."

"I thought I wouldn't be able to detain you for long," said Tony.

Michael descended the stairs and opened his door, devoid of the extreme urgency to study – to cram, even – that had gripped him as he had fought and almost conquered gravity up Elm Grove. The familiar, internally generated, calm after the battle had moderated the anxiety, but the imminent exposure of struggling intellect to the daunting spectrum of physics held him back even more.

... *don't read, just turn the book over and scribble down the steps, then compare ... it's painful, but Rodwell said it's the only way ... Now, let's say we get: "Give a brief (you have to watch the word brief) explanation of the Born Approximation" ... right ...*

He breathed in and out deeply, apprehensively.

... *First, this describes a method given by Born for the approximate calculation of particle collision cross-sections. Schrödinger's equation states that ...*

The treacly flow from his pen dried up after three-quarters of a page but he refused to despair. He reached with some relief for the book.

... *It's not bad. It's not bad! I think I've got the main bits ... I'll read it through once again and then I'll give it another go ...*

The afternoon grew in hopefulness. He satisfied himself that he could give more than passable accounts of atomic fission and fusion, could discuss the widths of spectral lines from gas discharges and almost pontificate about the fine structure of atomic hydrogen. Each time he heard the heavy tread of assorted friends leaping up and down the stairs, he held his breath momentarily in anticipation of being disturbed and of having to refuse invitations to join an excursion to the pub. He was glad that ignorance ruled him out of making up a four at bridge.

The blanket azure splendour of the sky had darkened almost to indigo, seemingly without him noticing. Yet another precious day was being wound up; there were few left. Too few? Certainly, many of its hours still remained but he knew his mental stamina would not allow him to devour them totally in the pursuit of scientific enlightenment. He didn't wish to aim for the top of some intellectual Elm Grove and disappoint himself at the end with threadbare answers from a tired brain. He convinced himself that enough light had been shed – on him and by him.

Noises from elsewhere in the house had ceased some time ago. Despite the earlier desire to be left alone, despondency and loneliness were attempting to creep over him as he looked up from his table through the window of the semi-basement room and over the garden at eye-level, neglected for yet another day in its long history of neglect. The emptiness of the house was confirmed and he returned to his room with a consolatory coffee. Searching the likely bars was now regarded as futile. He sat down on his under-sprung bed and pulled the double LP from the plastic case.

… "Wheels of Fire" … I wonder what they are? … Fancy calling yourself Cream … I could never promote myself like that … but, boastful or not, they've become such a part of my life …

He thought he had earned a listen, although he had no confidence that it would aid in dispelling any feelings of desolation. He placed the stylus, with customary care, onto the edge of the record and waited expectantly for the chords and the emotion that always accompanied them and always would do. Steve, Jeff and he played them but they couldn't reproduce the sustain.

… Well, you can do anything in a recording studio … I don't suppose they can make it sound quite like this on stage …

And then the rap on the drum, the milliseconds of silence, and then the voice – saying something about sad times and sad parties and, as he interpreted it, final parting at some station or other …

In a white room with black curtains is a station …

He was convinced that all the songs now seemed to have been designed to leave a mark of sadness on him. He didn't understand what the White Room was, but it did the same.

… That Leonard Cohen doesn't help much either nowadays … I wish they wouldn't keep playing it upstairs. It's all so bloody mournful … apparently a famous poet … but I never understood poetry … what is this "bird on a wire"? …

Suzanne takes you down to her place by the river …

… and who is this "Suzanne"? … are we supposed to know?

If you knew Peggy Sue …

Buddy Holly! Now we're talking ... I suppose I didn't know who Peggy Sue was either ... but that was simpler ... are we being led to believe that "Suzanne" has some sort of mystical significance? ... Peggy Sue was a better song anyway ...

Michael reverted to his tape recorder and the songs he'd caught on radio over the last couple of weeks.

The Witchita Lineman wants someone for all time ... does this apply to me and Caroline? ... for all time seems like a long time ... Now Badge ... is that shorthand for something? ... Clapton's singing about the times someone drove in his car ... it's going to be a long while before I drive anyone around ... and what's this love laid on the table all about? ... some frantic, impromptu sex session? ... that's a long way off too ... is it something more profound? ... how will I ever know? ... do I care? ... but then he told her about the swans in the park ... reminds me of the ducks in the park when I sat on that stupid bench waiting for Caroline ... all these words are a mystery ... dredged up from some personal, unfathomable thoughts of the song-writer ... I've got to pick myself up and carry on ... I always have ... and the curtain's about to fall ... the only thing I know is that these songs will be with me forever ... constantly conjuring up burning sun on a park and on red-brick university walls ... and gut-tightening exams ... and girls drifting away ...

The Greycliffe year had offered up refrains about girls in colourful clothes, frantic youths crying "gimme some lovin", wild guitarists screeching about abstract entities like "purple hazes". Nothing in those bygone days had tempted him towards prolonged melancholy. Even when he had heard of wounded hearts having "passed this way before" or had been exhorted to "look at all the lonely people" it had held no personal meaning for him; but Eleanor Rigby and the tracks that accompanied her, were an indelible part of that sombre guest house ...

Early 1967 –
Greycliffe Guest House

Michael stood alone in room 6 and looked out of the window to catch that small visible section of sea. He had done well in prelim exams, a distinction no less, but the eager anticipation of great things to come in those first few months and the memory of dancing and drinking with a beautiful girl, and even kissing her once, now seemed so distant. He had met Sarah by chance in the refectory not long after the Ball, and tentatively suggested another date, but her politely expressed refusal was clear; with sinking heart he understood that she did not seek permanent attachment.

Room 6 had, for some unknown reason, become a hub of Greycliffe life. For someone who had hoped for a single room, he was not displeased by this. Con, the mathematician from downstairs, had proved himself much more than capable at physics as well, even though he complained about having to do it for the first couple of terms. Con's room-mate, Gareth, still claimed to be ahead of the maths syllabus due to his public-school experience. Michael was glad that Owen, with whom he shared, did not outwardly boast of any special prowess. Another visitor, Dave Parker, was introducing him to folk music and claimed to be impressed with Michael's attempts with the classical guitar. Dave was himself a very competent guitarist. What was more, while most of the room 6 fraternity skipped lectures from time to time, Dave was always early for breakfast and off to the university on his motorbike. Michael had always been sensitive to competition and he was more keenly so now. He was no longer sure if he could surpass others without trying too hard.

He would attempt to reinvigorate himself with music and took the LP out of its case. He had been reluctant to join in the accolades of praise that had greeted it. Nothing could be that good. He was adamant that he would never subscribe to inane descriptions like "album of the decade". But he liked the first one on side one. Woods didn't like "Taxman", because it was by George Harrison. His disapproval was good enough recommendation for Michael.

It was alright certainly – it was better than he wanted to admit, but he still preferred "Drive My Car". That reminded him of verbal exchanges with Bill as they walked by the Thames on summer evenings; and of watching himself pretend to play the guitar in the mirror in his parents' front room and, for some reason, the biology lab at school. Now, he could play some Frescobaldi – and "Drive My Car" wouldn't be so difficult, would it, if he ever got his electric guitar?

Good day sunshine ...

He looked out at the steadily falling rain.

... Sarah probably, at this moment feels good and, ten to one, she's looking fine (how could she look otherwise?), but as for being proud to be mine ... you can't be serious! ... Do I really want to listen to this next one – For No One? ... does my mind ache when the day breaks ... it's really not quite as bad as that ... is it? ... she always has kind words that linger on, but why should she need me of all people? ... just about the first bloke she comes across ... and what love behind the tears? ... whoever shed any tears? ... emotional involvement, if that's what this is, is never important enough for that ... is it? ... for goodness' sake! Why is everybody looking for someone to love them all the damn time, whatever that means? I'm not going to be dragged down into self-pity by these maudlin – a good word I learnt from Bill – sort of lyrics ...

He lifted the stylus prematurely, put "Revolver" carefully back in its jacket and picked up a 45 he had just bought. He had first heard it during one of his now customary incursions into the basement coffee bar next to the Pool Valley bus terminus. That evening, he had made his usual selection on the juke box ...

I've passed this way before ...
I'll be there ...
Gimme some a-lovin' ...

None of the words neatly encapsulated any of his current emotions or status, but they had already been heard enough to be forever linked with that little basement. In no time at all they had transformed the coffee bar from something to be avoided to somewhere he liked to be. Then, someone had pressed a button for something else. In an instant his ears had been invaded by an unprecedented aural assault. The bass and lead intro had rooted him to the spot. His foot had tapped imperceptibly but something inside him had been leaping. The good vibrations had become great. He knew the electric guitar had suddenly broken free and would never again be constrained to its conventional solo fill-in role or confined to strummed accompaniment. In the empty room 6 he was free to play a make-believe guitar ...

Purple Haze all in my brain ...

... Things are no longer the same! ... whoever this is has chanced on something different ... Eric's solos are good but even they are just blues ... modifications of something else ... no one else lounging about down there in the coffee bar had looked excited about it ... perhaps I didn't either ... but I know it's revolutionary ... I could really have a go at playing this couldn't I? ... given a chance ...

Even back in his sombre Greycliffe bedroom on a day of unending drizzle as far as the eye could see, Purple Haze raised spirits that were on the edge of descending into pointless reflection of perceived loss. But was this, he wondered, a loss of connection to someone that maybe had never really been found in the first place? Purple Haze seemed to have no link with individuals locked in unrequited, or requited, love and, for Michael, this was an added attraction. Its lyrics possessed no clarity of time, place or meaning for him; the girl that "put a spell" on the composer seemed to have been thrown in as an afterthought.

Popular music was always moving on, but again there was a big step-change – as in the arrival of Beatles and Stones, or earlier, of Elvis, Little Richard and Jerry Lee. Only a few months previously, Owen had bumped into him at a university dance and said that "there was a great group on in the refectory". Michael had stood in perplexed amazement as the multi-coloured bubbles of light reflected off the red-brick walls along with the thunderous notes of organ and guitar. No one had heard of Pink Floyd. He wanted to dismiss the light show as a cheap gimmick, but he could not get away from the combined power of sight and sound. A few days later, on yet another trip back home, he caught sight of a poster advertising the said Pink Floyd at the Thames Hotel in Windsor. A sceptical Bill accompanied him on a freezing night, along with some twenty other mortals, to be blasted with a second sound and, much-reduced, light show. Bill did not become a fan. Michael kept an open mind.

For some strange reason, Pink Floyd and particularly Purple Haze prompted him to discard his erstwhile tiresome world of futile pursuits with aggression, and indulge in his quest for scientific distinction unencumbered. He realised that prelims success was but a very small step. With renewed vigour on that dreary day, he left Greycliffe for the bus to Falmer and the library.

May 1969 – The university library

... perhaps I could have been more dedicated ... more obsessed with physics ... spent more time here in this library ... been less distracted by ... guitars ... and girls ... very few girls though ... and self-appointed agents trying to steer me towards another career ... no, I must only blame myself ...

He sat with his book on *Stellar Structure* open. He had liked that course. It interested him and was more straightforward than some others. That Professor Tayler was a jovial sort of chap. One day, he talked about the limits of the observable universe and someone asked what he thought was beyond that. His initial reply of "Oh God!" caused great merriment amongst the students. With his ginger beard and slight limp – the professor reminded Michael of a retired sea captain for some reason. Today, he would forget about atomic physics and project his mind to the cosmos.

Ten o'clock had been an early start for him and, reasonably pleased with his current understanding of the life-cycle of stars, by twelve-thirty he considered heading for the refectory. But such an ostensibly mundane action had not been without its difficulties recently. The spectre of impending examinations had insinuated a fear that some sort of breakdown, whether nervous or not, was about to consume him. He had had to leave crowded places to avoid the embarrassment of imagined imminent physical or mental collapse. Such had not yet occurred – and he had to eat something.

He thought it good fortune that there were no close acquaintances in the dining room that he might be expected to join. But as he sat down, there were two people at a distant table who would presumably not have welcomed him. Caroline Selwyn and Alan Mercer were obviously deep in conversation. They frowned, then they smiled, and he frequently laid his hand on her arm. Michael had not quite finished his lunch when they stood up, but he had an irresistible urge to follow them. He kept a discreet distance and watched them part at the entrance to the Arts Building with a quick but affectionate hug.

... how could they do that so openly? ... surely someone will notice and say something ... perhaps they don't care ... why do I care anymore? ...

May 1969 – Windsor, Bill's kitchen – A week later

"If I was you, Mike, I'd try and forget about this Caroline. You've got other things to concentrate on, haven't you? I thought you'd come back home to study and forget about other distractions." Bill offered his remedy for what Michael had described as his current fixation.

From the viewpoint of his slight seniority, Bill had always tried to dispense some sort of sagacity, but had never approached dogmatic or condescending. He often raised his eyes to heaven in exasperation at Michael's persistent questioning of, and dissatisfaction with, his world. He was more content to accept things the way they were.

"So if I'd told you to do the same with Penny, what would your reaction have been?" asked Michael.

"If she'd decided to abandon me, I couldn't see myself constantly pursuing her, and probably making a complete idiot of myself. I think I'd know when I was defeated. Do you really think you're defeated?"

"Probably ... I had visions of an uncomplicated friendship – of someone who was truly interested in me, who I could go to a dance with and maybe kiss and cuddle occasionally – and who wanted a simple soul like myself ..."

"Simple soul? Do me a favour."

"Well, if I was a lecturer, I wouldn't be trying to get students into bed with me."

"How do you know that's what they're doing?"

"Oh ... alright, I don't ... I don't want to think about what's going on."

"You know, I think what you really want is a girl that's untainted, who's never or hardly ever been kissed or touched in any way. In short a virgin – and a pretty one at that."

"Is that really how you see me? Selecting someone to be with who meets all the right criteria?"

"Doesn't everyone do that in their own way?"

"But I don't expect someone to be perfect."

"I think deep down you do."

"Well if I do, it's not been a very successful strategy. Mind you ... I did know one or two young ladies who come close ... we still pass the time of day ... but they're long gone now ... maybe you're right about me, but the crazy thing is that even I feel I don't want to, you know, seduce these supposedly pure young girls either."

"I'm afraid your idealism isn't going to stand the test of time, Mike. Let's say that this Caroline, despite all her supposed shortcomings, drops her lecturer and says she's always fancied you like crazy and wants to make mad, passionate love. What do you do?"

"Nothing for a while – I'd be paralysed with the shock of it. But ... how can I pretend? I suppose I'd go along with her ... suggestion."

"And then what?"

"How do you mean ... ?"

"Would you stay with her for life if she wanted you to?"

"Life? I've never thought that far ... how do I know? I'm not much more than a child for God's sake ..."

"If you're in love you would have said yes – immediately."

"I don't want to talk about love. It's like discussing religion. You never get anywhere except tied up in knots."

"Well, I'm happy to say that I love Penny and I want to be with her for life."

"If you're content with that, then that's OK. I can't and don't want to argue with you."

"Thank God for that!"

"But ..."

"I knew there would be a but."

"Bill, the thing is – I'm a scientist, or trying to be. I want pure definitions, for love as much as anything else."

"Come off it, Mike, you can't define emotions like this in a few sentences. How about this, though – something I read somewhere, I can't remember. Say you did marry this Caroline and a week after your wedding she was in a car crash. Her face was badly injured and she was paralysed. So there would be no more gazing at her nice features and no more sex. If you stayed with her until the day she died, which could be decades, and looked after all her needs and still be faithful, then that would be love. Anything less wouldn't be."

"So when people say they're in love, it's an empty gesture if they couldn't commit to such a life if they had to?"

"I reckon so. You might be attracted by a pretty face and nice knockers and want to get into bed with the owner of these, but that's not love in the pure sense as far as I can see. We're attracted because it's a basic urge – it's overwhelming sometimes ..."

"It is ..."

"... and it's highly pleasurable ..."

"... I'll let you know ..."

"... but it's a sort of trap. If things change for the worse, then is this proclaimed love going to live up to its name?"

"Then perhaps human beings think they've created something called love but can't really live up to it – or rarely. What's that we sometimes heard in church: "there's no greater love than laying down your life for your friends" – or something. Mm ... dare I ask you if you really love Penny as you say, rather than just lusting after her beauty?"

"I ... don't think of myself as a luster, but ... I feel we have something ... I'll stay with her whatever ... that's all I can say."

"I've never wanted to announce that I'm in love with anyone, because when people say such a thing I'm never convinced. Now I'm even less so from what we've talked about. What you've really said is that true love is nothing to do with physical attraction. The phrase 'in love' should be called something else. God knows what though. Still ... all I can say is that with Caroline there was this immediate ... ooh – there's something about you that attracts me. From a physicist's point of view, I ask myself – is there some sort of mysterious, undetected perfume we're transmitting to each other? If not, so-called 'love at first sight' is purely based on an image. I can't project as far as calling that love. It might be desire but it's not love. Oh, Bill ... does anyone care what I think anyway? I've just got to move on ..."

"You have ... How's the group going then?"

"Sometimes I wish I'd never started it."

"What's wrong with you? Nothing seems to be right."

"It started out OK but it's getting complicated. I've got this so-called agent keeps phoning me up and even visiting me in Brighton. I don't need to think about groups and things at the moment. I'd be happy to just play my guitar on my own in my own room. It was all so simple at the start. My mate Jeff from school came down to Sussex – miserable sod, but he plays a good bass. And we met this drummer Steve – nice chap from Norwich. And we were just going to play some blues ..."

Late 1967 –

Brighton Front

Michael and Jeff left the drab and long uncared for Imperial Hotel and stood for a few seconds of shelter in the shabby entrance. They exchanged brief words of surprise at being faced by a night of heavy rain tossed around by swirling, gusting wind. From the depths of the Imperial the small group had been unable to discern any meteorological disturbance. The name and style of the establishment were reminders that better days had been seen there. Formerly elegant features had been, if at all, poorly re-decorated, but its walls could still provide thick insulation against the worst a seafront had to offer. Michael's fantasy had taken its first step into reality. He had formed a viable blues group. The room of drummer Steve was part of a set which formed a so-called flat in the Imperial. Jeff was, compared with the other two, an experienced musician, one who had trodden, even jumped on, the boards with his bass. Michael had envied him so much at that school dance – the only proper dance he had ever been to. He had envied him much more than he had the small number of boys who were maintaining bodily contact with a girl. In fact, he had refused to recognise this as envy. As he stared at the group on stage, his overwhelming desire was not just to emulate, but to do much better – given time. He could already play some simple Bach – if there was such a thing. And now, in Brighton, it was beginning to happen. He was part of a potential group that had met together for the first time. Their guitars had been brought this evening but had remained effectively silent. The record player volume and Steve's partially-erected drum-kit, some of which looked as though it had been commandeered from the Salvation Army, had overpowered the attempted play-along improvisations. They didn't have the means to convey with convenience their cumbersome speakers and amps to the venue. But there was unspoken agreement that such considerations were a formality. There was no way to go but upwards, was there?

"He's a good drummer, Steve, isn't he?" said Jeff with uncharacteristic enthusiasm.

"Yes, nice bloke too. We could have the makings of a good band."

"There's a lot of work to do though. First we've got to work out a really good set. Then there's all the arranging to do." Jeff was descending to his normal level of practical pessimism.

"Well, you should know well enough."

"Transport's a problem too. But I might be getting some wheels next term."

"Oh great ... I've got a test coming up next vacation. Maybe then I could get something of my own." Michael knew that the projected development in transport was wildly optimistic; two tests had already been failed. Inadequate practice would probably be remedied far sooner than inadequate funding. Still, at the moment they had nowhere to travel to.

"We could do with these wheels now but I think it's easing a bit," said Michael hopefully. "Anyway, I suppose I'll see you before next Friday. Keep practising."

"Yeah, you too."

Michael's demand was directed largely at himself. All he needed was time. There was nothing mysterious in moving your fingers along and across the strings, was there? The stereotyped patterns of the blues could surely be sorted out with patience; it was just a matter of time. He must start cautiously. He would take a riff from one of his favourite records and play it slowly, then quicken it day by day until he had mastered it at speed. That was what Segovia advised. Any set of notes could be analysed. They had all been derived from human minds and fingers; he would admit no reasons why his could not do the same.

With guitar strapped over his shoulder, he started off in the direction of his basement flat in Hove, pausing for a while at the first street corner. He deliberately breathed in deeply the rain-filled air, pulled his meagre coat collar up as far as it would go and crossed to the sea side of the road. Out beyond the promenade railings the delicate curls of foam that intermittently broke the intense blackness belied the heavy roar and hiss of their accompanying waves as they pounded the beach. The rain, caught in gusts, spread across the diffuse, warm reflection of the orange street lamps.

He was far from tiredness but the energy that was welling up within him could find no certain direction. What lay before his eyes and swirled around him was a wet night in a seaside town somewhere on the south coast of a small country whose powers people said were failing. He didn't want to believe it. In its not-so-distant day, that country had, without boast, transformed the world with its innovation and science and encompassed that world within its empire. The builders of that empire were no heroes in Michael's eyes – he had never looked for heroes – and he harboured an exasperation that they had rode roughshod over so many people.

Almost everyone in this small country would have heard of this town, if only for Mods and Rockers or a debauched King who had an exotic taste in architecture, but had poets ever sung its praises? Even he would have laid his money down against it. He could only remember a writer who'd chosen to immortalise its criminal element – a good story though. Michael's dad had said that Max

Miller, a child of the town, would have got the job of Brighton Mayor if he'd wanted it.

... *I found out he died in Burlington Street ... only a few years ago ... only a few doors away from Sarah's old guest house ... would you believe it? ... my God, he was good, wasn't he, old Max? ...*

I like the girls who do,
I like the girls who don't,
I like the girls who say they will,
And then decide they won't.
But the girls I like the most of all,
And I know you'll think I'm right,
Are the girls who say they never will,
But look as though they ... no, Mrs, you'll get me into trouble, you will!

... I know he was before my generation but listening to recordings ... to stand in front of an audience on your own and have them crying with laughter and never wanting to go home – with just a few jokes ... I heard that once, when he was dying, he'd said: this bloke 'ere is nothing – but that Max up there on the stage – gor' blimey, 'e was really something wasn't 'e? ... I'd like to be really something, someday ... transform myself ... put the place back on the map ... who knows? ... with Jeff's and Steve's backing ... they sound really good already ...

No search parties would be sent out, even if he tramped along the front till dawn. As on his first hour walking out into Upper Rock Gardens, he was alone, independent. It was, he liked to think, his most natural and happy and pure state. He could penetrate and study his aspirations without the need to communicate his findings to anyone. He could improvise the blues endlessly – mentally or even vocally along the deserted road. But tonight, there was something else in his head – other music that had been refreshed by a play-through of Cream's Disraeli Gears LP at the evening's meeting.

Dance the night away ...

... Jeff said the words were pretentious ... what does that mean? ... what does he know anyway? ... they suit the night – the mood ... the phrases go

up and down like the waves ... and the waves beat down on the shore like Ginger's drums ... it all goes together! ... what the hell does Jeff know? ...

The notes and phrases in his head induced an excited tension in his stomach. The lights from the hotel windows signified to him havens to which the occupants had been able to run and hide. His first thoughts were of escape but, as in the past, he also had a longing to hold the moment, the place in his mind, in his body – crystallise it, freeze it, not let it escape. Now the need was more intense; there were renewed anxieties of things passing him by. His thoughts were of wrapping it all around him – of losing himself in the back streets that lay, in his short history, unmapped and untrodden behind the rain-swept hotels, flats, pubs and fish 'n' chip shops that presented their best faces to the Channel. Now that perceived wounds had healed, he began to think about all the undiscovered life that remained here – in the known confines of his cloistered world and in the unknown world outside. The songs of Greycliffe days were already coming back to haunt, if gently, and there was no doubt that this one would do the same. The guitars and drums seemed to come from far away – megadecibels from ten miles or so – maybe down near Shoreham. But the long notes of the breathy vocal line dominated – for ever, slowly, slowly rising ...

Dance ... the ... night ... a ... way ...

... The lines encourage me to find an ocean and sail into the blue ... but I don't want to sail away ... I'd rather stay here in Brighton ... I suppose this is some sort of love song – like most of the others ... but that doesn't matter this time ... I've always thought it peculiar though, that love, whatever it is, has got such a monopoly over music ... I'm grateful for the odd Beatles thing that broke away ... don't think I can accept lust either – not with my recent history ... couldn't sing about it! ... Hendrix and The Stones are probably not so much love but rather more writhing, intertwined nakedness ... the phallic guitar – give me strength! ... it's pathetic ... if I have to watch someone, I'd rather he stood still, machine-like ... Eric and Jack aren't so bad ... I like to think of this song as symbolising defiance – my defiance, my anger at human beings who are often pretty bloody awful ... even students ... particularly students ... I suppose I have to assume

that someone, somewhere thinks I'm bloody awful too ... surely not ... I couldn't stand that ...

He couldn't do otherwise than stop and cross the glistening road when he reached the gaping, elegant crescent of Brunswick Square. He passed into its shadows.

... There's the flat, over on the right ... number 20 ... I'd love ... I'd like to see her face right now ... why should I have to dance myself to a shadow though? ... as the song suggests? ... still, if I was a shadow I could hide in a doorway and wait for her ... Michael! Michael! ... what are you doing here? ... just drop it eh? ... just leave it – her – alone ... she's moved on ... and you'll be moved on if you hang around much longer ...

He gave the briefest of glances up to the first floor window of number 20 without stopping. A light was on but the curtains were drawn. He conceived the vision of an interior of good furniture and perfumed bedrooms, where discussions of art and literature were being carried on in the accents of colonels' daughters.

... Or did Sarah say lieutenant-colonel? ... Michael! ... you are a crazy fantasist! ... mind you, if she did look through the curtains now and see me, she wouldn't think it too odd, would she? ... it's a small enough town ... I could just go out with her once a week – that's all I need ... we could go to some disco, far away from other students, or we could dance the night away right here in the gardens of Brunswick Square ... and hold hands, and clasp waists and gaze at each other ... that'd be enough ... once we almost danced the night away to Eric's band ... then I could walk her back here and have a nice long kiss on the doorstep – after checking the coast was clear – and then I could go home ... really happy – delirious ... I wouldn't need anything else ... that would be more intoxicating than any opiate ... that would be infinitely better than ... I don't want to think about it ...

With little hope of communion at the shrine, he followed the circumference of the Square and came out once more onto the front. A gust of wind and spray of rain was thrown into his face, invigorating him and making him sing in his loudest voice in the deserted road ...

Dance ... the ... night ... a ... way ...

... the old cars finish their run on this road ... just up there by the Pier ... that line from "Genevieve" sticks in my mind for some reason ... the Kenneth Moore character said, sadly, that he always dreamed of his trip to

Brighton coinciding with some romantic affair ... I never thought about Brighton coinciding with anything in my life ... now I know how he felt ... now I can't let any part of it go ...

Within a few minutes he was making determined if laboured progress across the shingle to the water's edge as the wind began to subside and he began to take refuge in the distant past. It was strange but he wanted to be strange. He hardly ventured onto the beach these days, now that he lived so near it, but it seemed natural to be there now. The beach and the sea had always been symbols of escape in years gone by. He remembered sitting with Bill on that clifftop in Devon, in the middle of the blissful period of release from the struggle at school to meet his own demands and seek praise.

"Just look at that sea!" Bill had said. "The power! Man is powerless against it!"

With some contentment, they had yet again agreed to dismiss man as a cosmic annoyance, as a nagging pain in the neck of Mother Nature.

"There again, woman is another matter ..." Bill had added.

The turbulence of the dark sea that had pounded the beach was diminishing. The vision of escapism was fading, for the time being. Michael could no longer support the pretence of insulation and isolation.

... the song was good ... is good ... is great ... one of those that helps me explode out of my workaday shell ... and dance the night away ...

The damp side streets of Hove led him, although reluctantly, to his shared haven of rest in a triple bedroom in Norton Road, which might politely be described as musty-smelling.

May 1969 – Caroline's boyfriend

Michael was at least grateful to be heading back to his single bedroom at Roundhill Crescent. Waiting at the bus-stop on the Lewes Road, he thought about bedrooms that had either been compulsory or to which he had been invited. As an only child, he had only ever occupied a private bedroom, until he came to Brighton. He was convinced it had made him what he was. It was a place where he could think, study, listen to or play music without interruption – unless he requested it. The next best thing to being alone was to talk endlessly with Bill in his room. He recalled the Sunday they listened to Bob Dylan for the first time and that song "Bob Dylan's Dream" – apparently about young men sitting and talking – and thinking they could sit around forever and wouldn't get old.

The words had made Michael think about mortality and the infinite, and that he, Bill, his mum and dad, his room, would eventually disappear and be forgotten. He remembered how he had had to fight to overcome the sadness. By the start of university life, such sadness had been discarded. There were by then only endless possibilities and the greatest of expectations.

Room 6 at Greycliffe, with all its limitations, had inadvertently become the hub of a disparate group of students – all of them boys, but it had placed him at the centre of some sort of social life. He had, on occasions, been invited to the bedroom of a girl – Sarah's, but only to take her to the Ball; Angie's – it had not gone well; Cathy's – she was so nice and her room was so sweet-smelling and tidy.

He would go back to his dingy, dusty room now for, he prayed, uninterrupted contemplation of physical science. But as he took his seat on the bus, he stared in unprecedented disbelief at the couple a few seats ahead of him. His daydreaming had been sufficient for him to miss her close presence for a while. Caroline not only sat next to a young man, but one who did not look remotely like Alan Mercer, one who could only be a student. Their lips coalesced for an agonisingly long time. Even when those lips parted, she laid her head lovingly on his shoulder. Michael had been trying to force himself to accept her relationship with the lecturer but this new, horrifying revelation was too much for his mind to accommodate. He wanted to get off the bus at the next stop, or even before, but he could not divert his eyes from her and the boy. He realised that the first glimpse in the library had dazzled him and created a perception of a sweet, kind-hearted girl. Now he could only see her in promiscuous pursuit of sensual pleasures that he did not dare bring to mind.

... Surely she's not like Angie ... or maybe all girls are like Angie ... wanting pleasure ... she was such fun ... and so alluring ... it was impossible for me not to submit, wasn't it? ... even me ... boys seem to

think that there's no problem with multiple girlfriends ... don't biologists say that men have many sexual partners so that their genes get spread around ... sounds like a lame excuse ... I know plenty with no girlfriends at all ... a few with one ... but no one with many ... but maybe I've been blind all along ... I've been blind about Caroline ... and I was blind about Angie ... oh God, they're kissing again ...

Late 1967 –

Angie

"Hello, I'm Angie." She looked proud of the announcement as she and a friend stood outside the door of the Norton Road basement in Hove. She was only three or four inches less than Michael's six feet two and could have been described as well built. Bold, wide-open eyes, in a face framed by a mass of black curls, looked straight at an unsuspecting Michael and she started to giggle. "This is Fiona. We ... er weren't ... actually invited – we came along with our friend there who just came in. Hope you don't mind."

The idea that their intrusion was to be met with any opposition was not to be treated seriously. Michael stood aside and they burst, with more breathy laughter, into the hall to join the already impressive number of first year girls and associates. Second-year students, such as Michael, had been encouraged to hold so-called Freshers Parties, presumably to make naïve or diffident first-years feel more at home. Neither adjective could be applied to Angie. Her preferred drink was beer. Michael poured himself the same and they started to talk. He was surprised how interested she seemed in him but he was careful not to make too many poor jokes or monopolise her.

... She's a bit giggly ... for a mathematician ... but she has got a nice face ... eyes particularly ... Bill always talks about eyes ... hers are big and they really shine ... OK that's enough ... this is an informal get-together ... ah, one of my favourites ... "Drive My Car" ... it's not one of the

fashionable ones but it does something to me ... I suppose we could dance ... is this a dance sort of party? ...

Baby, you can drive my car ...

... It's great ... and I don't often say that ... the lyrics are amusing, not some rubbish about aching hearts and things ... you get too much of that ...

Michael and Tony were proud of their makeshift record player. Tony's turntable and Michael's new guitar amplifier had been connected together and in some miraculous fashion it had worked. Not only was the reproduction reasonable but behind it lurked a storehouse of terrifying power. A careless twist of the volume control would have sent the partygoers reeling and foaming at the mouth.

"I like this one," said Michael. He leant cautiously towards Angie, catching a heady whiff of her perfume as the two of them moved their shoulders in time.

"D'you know ... I wouldn't mind a drink of water," she said as the song ended, "I think I've had too much beer."

"I'll get you some."

"I'll ... come too – give my ears a rest."

The light in the kitchen glared and revealed every detail of its imperfections. Michael carefully checked the glass he had found and poured the water.

"We've got orange squash if you like."

"Ugh, no thanks, too sweet. Just water will be lovely."

They stood leaning against the rickety table. Michael fought for a new topic of conversation.

"Phew, that's better!" Angie finished half the water in one go, smiled momentarily at Michael, then turned to stare at the wall opposite. She took another gulp and, having laid the glass down on the draining board, put her hands behind her neck, and yawned.

"My conversation eh?" he said, making his downward glance below her neckline as rapid as he could.

"No." She laughed. "It's past my bedtime. I think we really must go. Ooh Double Diamond – makes me dizzy."

She pretended to stagger towards him and in a second it had happened. Their mouths met. There was no embrace. They simply stood and kept their lips pressed together for at least five seconds.

... This is crazy! ... These lips are wonderful ... but how on earth did that happen? ... if someone saw, I'd never live it down ... I've only spoken a few sentences to her! ... I can't get away from girls even if I stay at home! ... it's no good ...

"Oh ... I'm sorry," she said looking down, suddenly demure. "Must be the DD ... sorry, that's not very complimentary."

"That's OK ... I ..." He stopped and they moved apart at the sound of approaching voices, looking as though they were uninterested in each other ...

Angie – A week later

When he saw her again, he jumped inwardly, as though she was someone he was trying to avoid. The snack bar was sparsely populated when he walked in. He spotted her and he knew her recognition of him was almost as quick, but her smile was a pale imitation of her beaming face at the party. She continued talking to her two girl companions. The queue was short and he had little time to decide where to sit. There was really no option. He could not place himself at a distant table, although that was his inclination. That would make the kiss a triviality. It was impossible for him to think of it that way even though a part of him would have been happy to deny it had happened. The emptiness of the snack bar enhanced his feeling of vulnerability as he walked towards the table. There was no cover; he felt naked. He couldn't hide, at least from her, behind a facade of quiet indifference. He had not engineered the small bodily contact, but even the modest nature of the kiss was enough to create embarrassment. As he said hello and sat down with the three girls, all he could imagine that Angie had in mind was the memory of his lips against hers.

"Hello, fancy seeing you here!" her kind eyes sparkled. Any fear he had had of being regarded as an intruder was mercifully quickly removed. He was introduced casually to the friends and described as "the one who organised a great party".

No rendezvous had been arranged at the party; there hadn't been even a second of opportunity as coats were donned and banal farewells made. In a way, Michael was glad – he needed time – but the kiss had forced him to reassess his views on hope. He hoped that something would materialise but he received no such impression that Angie had similar intentions. What had it meant? It had just happened – unpremeditated, he was content to believe, in both their cases. Unrequited desires to kiss had started long before he wanted to admit them. The shy girl he had been randomly paired with for doubles in a local tennis tournament; the pretty teenager, perhaps a year or two his senior, he had not been able to take his eyes off in that cafe on an Eastbourne holiday. Helen Shapiro for a time. He sensed an absurd though passing jealousy of the unknown men who would have succeeded in kissing them and perhaps with reciprocated passion. At the very least, he had forbidden himself to divulge such desires to anyone but Bill. The kiss with Sarah had been beautiful but formal. In Angie's case, the kiss had been unsettlingly casual. He felt he was moving from a world of shyness, caution and deliberation into one where kissing, full on the lips, was done on a whim – on the spur of a sensuous moment.

He was thankful that no one knew of the kiss except he and she. At the same time, the idea of cosy, intimate secrets with a girl was still not something he could cherish. The recollection was somehow mildly tainted by the realisation that he had succumbed. He conceded the emotion of gentle relief that it had happened. He conceded the pleasure of the firm contact of her soft, warm mouth with his; but the pleasure was perhaps more rooted in the feeling that *he*, Michael, had been able to attract. A girl, who two hours before the kiss had been unknown to him, had been sufficiently moved to commit herself to a few seconds of what could be called intimacy with *him*.

Her first question took him by surprise. "Michael, what's the Zeeman Effect? Our personal tutor has asked us to find out. I'm supposed to be a mathematician but we've got to do all this physics stuff."

Michael was daunted by the micro-lecture he was suddenly called upon to give but it did take his mind off her lips. Self-respect would not allow him to say he didn't know the answer but his knowledge of Zeeman's pride and joy was not, and never had been, uppermost in his mind. His delivery of its finer points was consequently not what one would call crisp.

"I still don't get it," she said, maintaining her smile.

"Well, if you'll excuse us, we've actually got a lecture." One of the two aspiring sociologists, whose name he already couldn't remember, said as they both got up. Michael was relieved that Angie did not follow their cue and leave as well.

"So what's your personal tutor like?"

"Nice young man, but a little too personal if you ask me. The first time I met him he seemed to be more interested in my chest."

Michael just about stopped himself from suggesting that the tutor couldn't really be blamed, but her observation did help to relax him a little. He knew he had little time in which to act. Soon she would have to go and a second chance, if ever it came, would not be the same. He had to do something. His pulse had accelerated when the two other girls had left because he was then totally exposed. Now, it quickened even more. A number of options were examined mentally in rapid succession.

... dinner's too formal and expensive ... forget the expense ... theatre's a bit pricey too and I don't know what's on ... what does it matter what's on? ... a film, that's it ... I know of something I'd like to see ...

"Er ... there's a film on," he made the dramatic announcement but she intervened before he could put forward the reason for this revelation.

"Really? Quite a few I should think."

He laughed with the triumph of a hopeful ice-breaker who had at last broken through.

"This one's called *Psycho* – I was wondering if you'd like to come?"

"I'd love to! But it does sound scary."

"Don't worry, I'll protect you."

When she had gone, he began to revel in the warm feeling of the aftermath of modest victory, intensified by a steadily reducing pulse rate. He couldn't deny that his pleasure was enhanced by the thought that he had a competitive edge on his new flatmates, although he had never thought of himself as a girl-magnet. Whether or not his friends considered themselves to be competing was of no concern to him. They appeared to be content with collective refuge in whatever public house was considered to be fashionable, and consume as much Double Diamond as possible. The only DD's held close to them were in a pint glass. If there were any hot affairs going on between them and, so far, unidentified girls, they were astoundingly circumspect about them. Could he keep Angie a secret for long? He decided that, until the time was right, if it ever was, he would remain aloof and secretive about the liaison. Any form of advertisement or innuendo about it, he would do his utmost to inhibit. It was his alone to savour.

... Surely she has some finer motive for any desire she might feel for me ... women aren't led by physical form in such a basic way, are they? ... Bill always said so ...

Psycho – A few days later

"Hello, Michael."

"Hello."

Angie's welcome at the door of Perrycourt, her guest house in Charlotte Street, was as effusive as he had hoped or imagined it might be. Her eyes sparkled even brighter than before, her make-up was enhanced and necklace and larger earrings had been added. Even at the party everything about her had been more casual. Her coat was left undone and he glanced, but only when it was safe to do so, at the red knitted dress that held closely to her body. The gratification was potent but he chided his eyes for their trespass. They were taking advantage; the dress just happened by chance to be a close fit he supposed.

... She must see me as being better than some miserable peeping Tom ... she must not see me as being pulled like an insensible magnet towards the trivial thrill of a tight dress ...

She closed the heavy, glass-panelled door and they descended the steep steps to the pavement.

"You don't mind us going straight out, do you? Only I suppose it might take a bit of time for a bus to appear. You're not dying to go to the loo or anything?"

"No, don't worry ... You ... look very nice."

"Oh, thanks," she gave him a mock embarrassed look. "And *you* look very smart ... for a student."

"Thank you too. Some might take that as an insult but I don't like to conform to the average idea of what a student is supposed to be like."

"You're very punctual as well."

"Yes, well Alfred Hitchcock said that we wouldn't be allowed in after the film starts."

"Who's he?"

"Don't tell me you don't know Alfred Hitchcock?" Michael allowed himself some mock astonishment. "He happens to be the director of the film we're going to see. He's known as the master of suspense. Haven't you ever seen his weekly thriller on television?"

"Ooh no, I avoid all that scary stuff – sloppy and romantic is more me."

"You know, perhaps this film isn't suitable for you," said Michael with slight apprehension over his choice.

"Don't worry, I'll just shut my eyes. What's it about anyway?"

"I haven't got a clue, except that some character in it owns a motel and is supposed to be mad."

"What's a motel?"

"A sort of American hotel, with a big car park, I think."

"Oh. And is that American mad or English mad?"

"Pardon?"

"Well, you know, is he bonkers or just annoyed at something?"

"I don't imagine it would be much of a film if he was just annoyed."

They reached the bus stop on Upper St James' Street and stood separated by a respectful and respectable gap. Michael was looking forward to holding her hand but he was undecided about when or even whether it should happen this evening. He felt the responsibility for the decision was all his. The coming of the bus allowed him to put it off temporarily. They both looked out of the window more than at each other as the bus went down the hill, across The Steyne, up North Street and along Western Road. It was as though they had never seen the view before. After the initial exchanges, she was quieter than he had expected.

They got off the bus and walked along still without touching in any way. He was happy about his reticence to do so. Another couple passed close by. Their hands were firmly clasped and the boy was trying to kiss the girl but, at least at that moment, without success. The girl had the look of patient superiority, the boy one of unquestioning adoration. He appeared to be oblivious of the possible attentions of onlookers. Michael was quite sure he would prefer to die rather than stoop to such behaviour. He would always be detached, however much he was urged by dark instincts into grovelling sycophancy of the opposite sex.

Michael and Angie crossed the road and joined a small queue at the entrance of The Ambassador.

"You don't mind if I bury my face in your shoulder from time to time, do you?"

She made a quick, mock-frightened movement towards him, pushing her arm up against his. Within a split second, he knew that his decision had to be made. He considered it a victory that now it was she who had demonstrated first a compulsion to touch him. He clasped her around the waist and held her for no more than a second but as his arm fell, their hands touched and their fingers intertwined. A tension that he had been unaware of until then was suddenly released, but he was still reluctant to move or be moved too quickly. He looked around for possible observers.

Their hands parted as they reached the kiosk.

"You mustn't pay for me," she said in a sincere tone.

"No, please don't worry."

"But we're both students."

"No, come on, I'd rather."

"Alright, but I'll pay next time."

... *Next time? ... she's willing to keep this going ... does she really mean that? ...*

They walked, separately, into the semi-darkness. He experienced an emotion similar to that at an untried funfair ride. He had stepped into the car, been strapped in and knew that there was no getting out and no turning back as the machine started to move. He had never possessed the bravado that provided immunity from the childish fear of horror films or funfair rides. Now, he had been somehow directed onto a path which, without completely realising it, was not transient and which he would find difficult to step off or turn back from.

"Shall we go in here?" He had hesitated momentarily before asking. His suggestion of the back row struck him as excruciatingly obvious but there seemed to be no other option. Recent developments had caused him to hope for a second kiss but not for an audience, even in his anonymity.

The plot moved slowly but with an unmistakable undercurrent of tension and expectation of terror. As the girl drove, in some kind of desperation, out of town, Angie and Michael knew that horror was approaching. As if to protect each other, their shoulders and heads inched closer and closer. It was the drive into Bates Motel that prompted Angie's close whisper. Her voice gave an impression of nervousness and vulnerability but Michael could not believe that she suffered from either. Nevertheless, the arm that he finally placed around her shoulders did possess an element of protection, from what he knew not. The act of moving his arm into this position had not been achieved without some anxiety. There was nothing that could be deemed abnormal about it but he desired at all costs to avoid any hint of disapproval. He had always been led to believe that the overriding objective of such an action was as a prelude to some more base expression of passion; but he was surprised by the warmth of his feeling as his shoulder provided what he thought must have been a poor cushion for her head. His feeling was that if nothing else was to happen between them, that awkward, sideways embrace would have been worth any effort he had to make. The reticence Sarah had exuded in vaguely similar circumstances was a world away from the relaxed comfort that Angie appeared to be experiencing. He knew he was on the threshold of something new and all his old reservations were fighting for his precious independence. But the urge to cuddle was pulling closer and closer until their lips met once more and relaxation was, for the moment, complete. Now there was no need for urgency in the kiss. When the parting came, it also seemed natural, the sideways embrace and their attention to the screen strangely reinforced.

Bates of the Motel had shown the girl her room and she was now undressing and stepping into the shower. Michael had heard rumours of the shower becoming a distinctly bloody and watery grave. He had to contend now with two growing but totally distinct forms of tension; he had to try, with as much equanimity as he could, to remain unflinching during an anticipated murder and, like the starlet, he felt that he was going into something with little hope of escape.

"Good God! It's Bates' mother!" thought Michael as the sinister, shadowy figure tore back the shower curtain, to a background of screeching violin chords, and, within seconds, tore the flesh of the occupant. He prayed that the jerk induced by the magnitude of his surprise had not been noticed, but it was unlikely, as Angie simultaneously buried her head in his shoulder.

As the screen suspense subsided marginally an idea came to him which revived his unease. It had been there, he thought in the far background, and hadn't been considered a possibility on this occasion. Should he even contemplate such an action? It would thrust into stark reality the proclivity that he had wanted to suppress. But the desire was so powerful; he was afraid he could not go back. He was locked into the fairground car and he was forced to ride. The now obvious fullness of her breasts and tightness of the dress that covered them were beginning to pulverise any restraint.

... But she's not deliberately making her breasts stand out and tempting me to touch them, is she? ... she's a guileless, kind-hearted girl whose tits ... sorry ... bosoms just happen to be a bit larger than some other girls ... it would be ludicrous for her to try to hide them anyway ... I can't risk touching them, can I? ...

They kissed once again but this time the quality of the kiss seemed to be telling him that restraint was foolish. Even then his previously bulging storehouse of indecisiveness wasn't exhausted.

... I really shouldn't ... should I? ... her kiss is just the manifestation of a warm personality ... it's not meant to be a signal to commence some kind of physiotherapy, is it? ...

As, this time, she approached him rather than he her, he knew he could not remain content just with lip contact. His hand moved, first covering with as much delicacy as he could manage, her nearest breast and then, with more confidence, holding and squeezing it firmly.

He felt that he had crossed some second great divide and the grizzly events at the Bates Motel had become temporarily a vague background. An electric tingle shot from somewhere down in his shoes and left a satisfying warmth somewhere around his loins as she increased the pressure of her lips in response and let him continue the massage unhindered. He had only expected disapproval. The idea that she was pleased by his attentions was not only novel but unreal. He could not shake off the notion that the lack of objection, on her part, to his temporary invasion of her chest was the natural fortitude of a young woman suffering the mechanical actions of a barely more than adolescent male. Presumably she suffered them in the knowledge that all potential admirers would act in this way. As his right hand returned to a more neutral position, he told himself that it would stray no more that evening. Enough was enough. His first thoughts after the tasting, that, he had to admit to himself gave intense pleasure, were for mouth-washing rather than intoxication. A quick glance to left and right gave him adequate reassurance that he had not been under the gaze of third parties.

"Oh no, I can't look! She's going down into the basement," whispered Angie turning to Michael. "It's the mother in the chair … oh shit … sorry, Michael, oh hell … I bet she's got a knife …"

… I've never heard a girl swear before …

He wasn't sure if it was he or she who had jumped more when the mother's chair had been turned to reveal flesh long since rotted and the dutiful son standing by, with foot-long knife, to claim the next victim.

… am I just Angie's next victim? …

The disturbing thought inevitably came to him only a week later. He had to ask himself the question but he still wanted to resist the temptation to equate her with a predator, even a murderer, of a young man's deepest emotions. A mere few days had passed, after the back-row embrace, before she revealed her nakedness to Michael – and for the exposure to be reciprocated. He had been startled by the ease with which clothes had been shed and astounded at her body, the first time he had gazed on such a sight. Bill had sometimes used the word voluptuous, and he thought that this was a perfect description. She had been firm in her desire for their friendship not to be properly consummated, but they had still given each other pleasure. An excited amazement shot through him when she had used her mouth in the most intimate way. Friends had joked about such an act, but he had never imagined it would ever be performed, especially by a girl who had only just left school.

Michael could not now understand how he had continued to succumb to Angie's charms, despite her confession that there was a boy called Barry "back home" with whom she did "properly" make love. He realised that he had deluded himself into the crazy notion that her apparent eagerness for him would eventually make Barry irrelevant and rejected. It was not to be. She claimed that she could not continue seeing Michael while Barry was still part of her life. Their affair, if it could be so called, was dead within two weeks. But still buried deep inside him was the wish, as on that first Perrycourt evening, that he could now turn round and, when he turned back, she could be dressed in that tight-fitting knitted dress and that they could play with intimacy once more in the safety of the back row.

"Let's not be enemies. We'll see each other ... around, you know," she said, making a fruitless effort to raise his spirits as they parted in her bedroom.

"Maybe," he said without emotion, certain that he could make little impression on her, even though her features had formed themselves into a show of sadness. "It's just that I'd hoped ... it doesn't matter anyway. I'll get going."

No relief came as he descended the steps of Perrycourt for the last time. He should have been taking a deep, thankful, unbelieving breath of the cold air, suffused with drizzle, in response to an evening of unsurpassed, unexpected, unplanned intimacy. He told himself as much, as he denied his lungs their due with short respiratory spasms of his aching diaphragm. There was only one way he dare go; there could be no waiting at bus stops. He had to turn left and go down to the promenade and walk. There would be no nostalgia, no passing of old haunts, no humming of the blues – just walking. That hateful, itching voice that was ready, would always be ready, to remind him of his own ability to discard and then to trawl the sea once more for mermaids, would be strangled unmercifully and with bitter enjoyment.

There, when 1968 was approaching, no revolution had swept him up in its passionate embrace. He had never looked for revolutions. The sexual kind had been proclaimed, debated, glorified, but any new freedoms allotted to him had been severely rationed. Any promises of a new land had not been kept. If there was any war of the sexes, he saw himself as a casualty, never as a willing fighter. Such a revolution could only be seen as a lie in the cold, dark little side street. There had always been, there always would be, victors and vanquished, never the great upheaval where all were fulfilled. Propaganda had tried to convince him that the shortness of a skirt was a mark of its ease of removal but he wasn't falling for that. And though the girls were now apparently free to indulge without restraint, a boy like him who was suspicious of any drug, could never consider a pill to be their gateway to liberty.

If he had wanted to think about it at that moment, there would have been no yearning within him for any other kind of revolution. He paid no heed to what were referred to as the evils of the system. In his mind, no advantage of class had endowed him with his aspirations to superiority and no such advantage would help him solidify them. Either he was special or he was not. No redistribution of wealth, however equitable, was going to make any difference. If he could not bring out the power of intellect, it could only mean that it had never been within him. He brushed aside the undoubted selfishness, but concluded that political rebellion was never going to help him and that revolutions, if they were real, were not for him.

It had not quite ended there with Angie. At risk of humiliation, he had slipped unnoticed one evening into the crowded Charlotte Street corner cafe and watched her smiling, laughing and eating with, he presumed, Barry in the far corner, as his own solitary coffee went cold. It had been a strange coincidence that her home town was not far from Michael's. Barry was a biker, maybe even a Rocker, and he and Angie had frequented the Ace Café by Windsor Bridge. There was gossip in the town of pregnant girls in the Ace fraternity who were uncertain as to which boy had been responsible. Michael had not wished to believe such third-hand tales but, if they existed, he still, more than ever, clung to the belief that Angie could never be one of those girls.

Not long, not long enough, after, that belief had fragmented into an agony of doubt. He had frozen inside when he had seen, from a distance, Angie walking across Stanmer Park holding the hand and kissing the lips of someone who didn't look a bit like Barry.

... perhaps Barry's been ditched ... or has ridden his bike into a ditch ... poor sod ... and she'd been too proud to go back to me ... can't believe a word of that ... Angie, the one I'd pictured, has been destroyed ... the real one just wants a nice, regular supply of different male bodies ... to play with – as far as she wants to go ... is that the truth? ... oh hell, hell! ... I never thought – I don't want to think – any girl could be like that ...

For a while, even Tony's Punjabi accent could not fold Michael's features into a smile. He took some transient refuge in a Wes Montgomery LP that Tony had bought second-hand down Hove High Street. "Never Leave Me" was the track he liked to play. Having already been left, the title didn't mean much, but the snail's-pace, funereal beat suited him down to the lower basement level to which he had descended. In two weeks, he missed even more lectures than Tony. Still, Michael wasn't as breakable as he had thought – or maybe had hoped. At last, and after a shorter time than he wanted to admit, an excruciatingly discordant Chinese medieval song, on one of the records that the Public Library had been desperate to lend to Tony, had provided the final twist in the spiral of recovery. They had laughed uncontrollably. And a heart that Michael could have sworn had been aching, was now ready for running, if nothing else.

... I've got to pull myself back ... yet again ... all for a woman! ... worse, a girl! ... fancy having to copy lecture notes off Tony! ... but there could be a band now ... Tony said he knew of a drummer ...

May 1969 –

Michael and Steve

Steve, the would-be drummer-historian from Norfolk, lounged with Michael in the Junior Common Room and talked about music. Their group of three had got together more than a year back, had then been transformed into a rock 'n' roll band by Declan, the mad Irishman and his eccentric friends, and now they were back to three with a dubious agent and finals only a couple of weeks away.

"I s'ppose old Rod Wyatt's song's not too bad," said Steve in, what Michael considered, a wonderful accent that made him sound like an educated farmer. "Gave us a bit of experience of a recording studio anyway."

"Yeah, but I'm not sure I've got time to spend on all that, Steve. There's only a couple of weeks to go after all."

"Oh, come on, Mike, it's light relief as far as I'm concerned. And, let's face it, we're not snowed under with bookings. Oh yeah, Disco Derek asked me if we could play at a dance after finals."

"I suppose I could manage that – as long as I haven't committed suicide."

"Might increase our future record sales if you do. I can see it now – potential great rock star cut off in his prime."

"I don't think 'Nobody's Fool' has that sort of appeal. It's not 'Purple Haze' is it? Anyway, do I want to be a star?"

"'Course you do. All the adulation, all the money, more girls than you can deal with."

... I can't even deal with the few I've met ...

"I was hoping to do a bit of physics research." Michael felt apologetic in his confession.

"Well, each to his own. But I might jack history in for a while if a big contract came up. I'm not sure what I'm going to do when I leave here anyway."

... I'm not sure I can jack physics in just like that ... how could I ever go back to it? ... I don't want to leave ... I can't leave ...

At last, Steve and Michael agreed that they should both spend more time in some sort of scholarly contemplation and ambled towards the library. Michael sat despondently surrounded by shelves of science books but his inclination, which even he could only describe as idiotic and useless, was to keep watch again in Modern Languages. He had accumulated a series of, in his view and probably anyone else's, demeaning acts – that note placed in Caroline's pocket, that letter of rebuke to Angie about her purported misdemeanours, and that senseless visit to her in the hope that something had changed. He pictured Richard Woods laughing at his actions. Woods, he supposed, would never humiliate himself so. He would drop, or be dropped, and then just pick someone else up.

Caroline was nowhere to be seen but he laid his books down at what he thought was a sufficiently discreet and distant desk from her accustomed place and tried to read.

"What are you doing here?" The continually unwelcome voice of Woods made him start – he hoped not too obviously. "Not many physics books in these parts."

"It's ... quieter here. I thought I might not be interrupted."

"Don't worry yourself, I'm off to the bar for a pint of lunch. You wouldn't be ... you know, looking around for someone?"

"No I wouldn't ... anyway, I've given up on that. I need to study."

"OK, but you might be interested. I happened to see Caroline Selwyn and Alan Mercer the other day in some sort of argument. He was trying to keep his voice down but he seemed to be laying down the law a bit – telling her she shouldn't do this and that. Don't know what it was about. Lovers' tiff I suppose. Anyway ... nothing to do with me."

... or me ... must have been telling her to lay off other boys ...

"I'm really not bothered anymore." Michael hoped that his inadequate dissembling was not obvious.

"Fair enough. See you."

... not if I see you first ... Michael! ... you've got to stop letting Woods unsettle you ... it's about time you put him in his place ... but he doesn't seem vulnerable in any way ... not like me ...

It was true what he had said to Woods. This part of the library was not only quiet but almost empty. He reasoned that conditions were perfect for another foray into nuclear theory, and that there was now little else that should preoccupy him or waste his time. Whoever now or in the past had inspired notions of an idyllic affinity could not be forgotten but, he thought, had to be abandoned. This resolve, at least temporarily, strengthened his concentration and allowed him to shut the world out.

He was satisfied, as far as he would ever let himself be, when he finally surfaced from the depths of his textbook and looked through the window at the sun-scorched lawns. There was still no Caroline, unless she had come and gone, but he did see someone else in a far corner. Cathy and Michael had never really abandoned each other or experienced the slightest hint of acrimony. He understood why she had decided that their intimate friendship should end and a more benign, affectionate one take its place. In the few partings that had happened in his life, whether dispassionate, painful or gentle, he had obeyed some unspoken decree that the girl was in command. He could never impose his will or make demands.

"Hello, Cathy."

"Michael! Hello. You look like I feel."

"Oh, do I?"

"Well, if you don't mind me saying so, you have that slightly anxious expression."

"Is it that obvious?"

"Oh God – two weeks, eh? How are you really feeling?"

"I feel I've still got a lot to learn – again."

"You and me both. Anyway, I know you reasonably well don't I? You're conscientious. You'll do OK. What are your plans when you leave?"

"I was ... actually ... thinking about doing research here if I could. But I think I'm going to need a first and well ... you know ..."

"At least you have ambitions, Michael. I don't really know what I'm going to do, except go back to Ireland for a while. Are you still playing with the rock 'n' roll group? I haven't frequented many dances recently."

"I'm doing a few things, but now with just three of us. I won't bore you with details. Actually I'm trying not to play my guitar too much at the moment. Although we are doing a dance after finals."

"Really? I'll be there. I loved that time when you played in the Pool Coffee Bar." She lowered her voice. "That Declan's a real character. He always makes me laugh when we meet. And that Sam Dangerfield. He's crackers."

"But a great harmonica player."

"It was a great night." She raised her eyebrows and they smiled at each other.

"It was."

March 1968 –

The Rockin' Rs and Cathy

"This is Declan," said Steve, introducing the dark, curly-haired youth at yet another of their practice sessions. His shortness, broad frame and general demeanour made him look older than his years. "I was saying ... er, he had some bookings lined up if he could get a rock 'n' roll band together."

Declan shook hands with, and beamed at, Jeff and Michael in a manner which seemed out of keeping with the standard, studiedly casual student approach.

"Hi there!"

Declan's greeting and Belfast accent made Michael think of The Bachelors but he had a feeling that there was more than chummy good-nature behind the grin and strong handshake.

"Yeah, it's very kind of you to help us out."

Michael wondered who "us" would turn out to be and didn't recall anyone making any promises to help.

"A couple of guys and me've been messing around with some old numbers and I think I can get a booking at the Pool Valley Coffee Bar – if I can get a line-up. I haven't got any equipment of my own ..."

... oh why should you worry? ... a mere detail ... it's all here waiting for you! ...

"... except that I can borrow a guitar and maybe a PA. What d'you think?"

Declan looked quickly at the three of them in turn.

... I don't know – we've already begun to do lots of other things ... blues stuff – that's what they go for these days ... I used to – still do – love rock 'n' roll ... Little Richard ... Elvis ... my older cousins at those family

parties used to play them one after another ... what else could've made mums, dads, uncles, aunts dance in the bloody street? ... my God! ... even my family! ... but that was ten years ago ... still, this could be an isolated event ...

"Yeah, sounds interesting," said Michael, still mentally holding himself back. "Although we don't do any rock 'n' roll."

"Oh come on, Mike. It'd be great if it came off," said Jeff with an unusual show of warmth, "We've been farting around for too long thinking about a gig somewhere."

... I suppose '"we" means "me" ...

"What sort of numbers have you got in mind?" said Steve.

"D'you know any Eddie Cochrane?"

"I know the songs but I've never played any," said Michael not wanting to be outdone as far as rock 'n' roll was concerned.

"Can I borrow your guitar for a mo'? I won't damage it too much."

Declan and Michael smiled at each other – the former more readily.

"Do you know 'Summertime Blues'?" Declan's question could now only be directed at Jeff and Steve who still possessed musical instruments. "I'll just do the intro and you come in when you can, OK?"

Declan's left hand gripped Michael's fretboard like a bunch of bananas, his thumb came over the back and held down the sixth string.

... Look at his bloody thumb! ... How can he use it like that? ... Still, if you're only going to play "Summertime Blues" I suppose it'll do ... Segovia's hand looks like a bunch of bananas ... thumb's always in the right place though ...

Michael sat down on his speaker and looked on. His feeling of redundancy increased as the new lead guitarist got into his stride and the accompanists managed to synchronise. The ending was what might have been politely termed ragged but Jeff's newly found partial exhilaration surfaced again.

"Great! Got any more like that?"

... Jeff dear, there's a whole damn library of them ... what you're really saying is: let's abandon those old blues things we're – I'm – always cocking up, and play rock 'n' roll instead ... you've got no dedication, no tenacity,

Jeff ... you'll just change to fit in with the latest whim ... Jeff, we were trying to do something a bit different! ... I should say they can borrow my guitar but I'm not interested ... that's what I should say! ... mind you, if he can get a booking ... they could do with my voice ... and I've been singing this stuff to myself for as long as I can remember ... and who knows who might be in the audience? ...

Only one clear day stood between Michael and his first public performance. His vision of forging a new path through the jungle of second-hand blues had been submerged in the new all-consuming repertoire of 50's copies. In contrast to what passed for Michael's approach, Declan had secured the booking and had then gone looking for a group. Left to his own devices, Michael would have waited for note-perfection. He wouldn't have wanted to expose any rough edges or bungled chords to his first audience of popular music. Even he, transiently devoid of pressing academic demands, might have gone to the pub this Wednesday evening. Instead he had been left sitting on his bed in the poorly-lit Hove basement trying to plan solos in solitude. In practices, they had been grabbed unthinkingly by Declan more often than not, but Michael didn't feel deprived. They came naturally to Declan's stubby fingers; the rasping, unpolished riffs that he had acquired during his Irish showband apprenticeship were displayed with the enthusiasm of someone who had located another niche where he could play his beloved rock 'n' roll. At this moment, Michael was trying to invent his own finger patterns that might leave their small imprint on the works of Bill Haley or Little Richard. But they were not fitting into place as quickly as he had hoped. Declan's nods to him, at odd times, to take an improvisatory turn had made him feel uncomfortable. Knowing which note would follow which was still far more appealing than starting on a musical journey that, to him, was marked by possible pitfalls rather than freedom.

... I'm going to have to make them simpler ... and play them through slowly until I get used to them ... Oh God! Friday evening's too close! His spine began to tingle. Are the crowd, if it is to be a crowd, at the Pool Valley really going to listen to every note? Most of them'll be drunk by that time anyway ... but the girls won't be drunk ... girls never get drunk ... Sarah won't be there anyway – it's not her sort of place really ... do I even want

her to be? ... And as for Angie ... Still, I'm almost looking forward to the singing ...

Declan left most of the singing to Michael. At least there he had served an apprenticeship – his own private one. As a thirteen-year-old, when the house was empty, bedroom walls had reverberated to his interpretation of Little Richard's or Jerry Lee's latest. Better still, the bathroom echo effect in "Sealed With A Kiss" had sometimes sounded too good to be true. The songs were in his head and heart, waiting to be released.

The small volume of *Social Contract: essays by Locke, Hume and Rousseau* that Declan had put down on the top of an amp at their last rehearsal had seemed an unlikely companion for him. Michael couldn't help associating him more closely with a building site, or with a smoke-filled snooker club with stout in hand. He had introduced smoking and smokers to the band. Sam Dangerfield, piano and harmonica and a polio victim, walked defiantly, supported by his sticks and shrouded in his long fur coat. Michael wondered if Sam's uncompromising nature was rooted in the struggles that life had imposed on him. Even if this were the case, Sam would never admit to it. No one but Declan ever argued with Sam. Declan and Sam swore at each other more often than not, but hardly ever at the others in the band. Their exchanges provided some sort of amusement and, far from being in danger of imminent breakdown, their lop-sided friendship floated along, buoyed up by mutual insult. In common with his view of Declan, Michael couldn't envisage Sam's head buried in Proust or Dostoevsky as he maintained it often was.

Andy Outhwaite, the engineering student, had brought his saxophone fresh, as he had put it, from the working men's clubs of Rotherham, along with his bright eyes, an attempt at a beard and a leather jacket that was effectively stitched permanently to his back. Michael tried to take the tales of his professed precocious showbiz career with as large a pinch of salt as he could, but his good-natured Yorkshire directness was an adequate counterbalance.

Declan had also brought along a name. Whether the "Rockin' Rs" was something derived from personal musical history or whether it had just materialised, Michael never found out and never bothered to.

"It's a great name," Sam had said, unable to suppress totally the increasingly familiar ironic smile that broke out over his prematurely aged and somehow tortured face, but with enough conviction to satisfy the others. Michael felt that if Sam was adamant about something, the others, in some sort of deference to his disability, would go along with it without too much dissent.

"Christ, if I can convince a cynical bastard like Dangerfield, it must be alright," Declan had said.

Declan and Sam would light up with relief after leaving the smoke-prohibited sanctuary of the music rooms. The odd neighbouring pianist, struggling with quiet passages of Chopin or Debussy, and sometimes having the temerity to complain, in vain, was always relieved to see them go.

"Don't you get worried about cancer and things with smoking?" Declan had apparently once asked him.

"Look," Sam had said, "when you've been through what I have – all those bloody operations and that – you don't think about fucking cancer."

Not only close friends, but even distant acquaintances, had been heard to talk about the Friday debut of the Rockin' Rs. Any feelings in Michael of pique at Declan's takeover had now been replaced by an urgency to make his own performance as unforgettable as he could, even though he couldn't quite stretch to gratitude. He could not get used to the idea that the patrons of the Pool Valley, or any coffee bar for that matter, where he had always chosen to sink into obscurity, were about to focus their attention on him, by choice or by chance. The nervousness that still made his fingers shake was slowly giving way to excited imaginings that Saturday morning would even find strangers talking about him, singling him out as someone special.

... a great singer who they would want to hear again ... surely I won't be expected to play great solos as well ... that'll come ... won't it? ...

March 1968 –

The Rockin' Rs at Pool Valley

"Christ, it's too small! How're we all going to get on this fuckin' so-called stage?" said Declan, for once devoid of his customary broad grin, his accent becoming more broad by the minute. Michael hadn't seen him in an agitated state before and began to develop a sense of calm at the sight. But he couldn't do so without a trace of guilt that he was prepared to abdicate responsibility for the practical problems as long as he could shine when things were going well.

"We're not, you bloody idiot," said Sam, "Look, the piano'll have to stay up there, OK, and the drums ..."

"The drums? No, they'll have to go down on the floor at the side. Stevey, you don't mind going down on the floor?" Declan looked slightly desperately towards the drummer.

"Mm ... n ... no, I suppose not," said Steve who had clearly aspired to the stage.

"There y'are, he's ecstatic about it," said Declan, smiling once more, "... But the amps can go on the floor ... we don't need them up there ..." continued Steve still hopeful of elevation.

The Rockin' Rs stood together in the late afternoon sombre emptiness of the Pool Valley Coffee Bar contemplating the boxes that had been assembled and considering them, silently or volubly, as inadequate either to support them or promote their quest for glory.

"Stage looks a bit dubious to me. I'd rather stand on the floor anyway," said Jeff, already looking dejected.

... there again, he never looked as though he wanted to be a star ...

"And the mike stands can go down on the floor just in front of the stage," said Andy with requisite enthusiasm.

"D'you know, he's not as stupid as he looks," said Sam, curving his lips up at the edges.

"Yeah, but some fucking idiot is bound to kick the damn things," said an unimpressed Declan. "OK, now let's sort the power out."

"What about the mike for the piano?" said Sam.

"Look, if we've got no power, there's no point in having a bloody microphone ..."

"I've got an extension lead with a few sockets ..." said Andy.

"The man's a genius. How many sockets?"

"A couple."

"Two! That means we're only four short ... The guy that promised me the PA should be here by now – Jesus Christ!"

"If you'd use your eyes, O'Rourke, you'd see that there are four fucking sockets in the wall already. Don't panic," said the consistently unruffled Sam.

Steadily, amidst recrimination, accusations of incompetence and re-soldering of dry joints, the equipment of the Rockin' Rs began to assume its inelegant, scratched, taped-up, patchwork form. Michael's almost new, silver-fronted amplifier alone seemed to exude professionalism. He stood on the other side of the room to survey the assembly. He was impressed, exhilarated but fearful of being caught up in something of which no one was quite in control. He could have seen it all as trivial, an unknown group of amateurs playing to a restricted, captive audience, but to him this was serious stuff, with the danger of failing to overawe those who knew him.

Like everything else, Declan had borrowed the guitar he was to play but he would have preferred Michael's.

"Hey, this is a great guitar, Mike," said Declan. Michael watched his fingers thudding over the frets with the apprehension of an antique dealer who had handed over a rare vase to the inspection of a bricklayer, "Y' must be proud of it. The Fenders are nice but these Guild's are great – what model is it?"

"Starfire. Yeah, it's very nice," said Michael, who was not sure whether pride adequately described his attitude. Proud individuals were quick to flaunt achievements, normally, he thought, without justification. He liked his guitar, he liked being English and being from Windsor, he liked roaming around the university reading about physics but it was all luck to him, good fortune that had happened to fall his way. He was not proud of himself.

He had been mesmerised by the glittering splendour of the instrument, and amazed when the previous, sad, soon-to-be-married owner had sold it to him for a fraction of its new price – amp and mike included. He had been stunned as the volume, cautiously turned up in his bedroom, had first transformed the tinny feebleness into awesomely deep resonance and piercing ring. His association with it was still in its infancy but he knew he would never recapture those first moments of the encounter. Although still inexperienced the electrified transformation was already commonplace for him.

"Right, let's give something a run through," said Declan, as sockets were plugged and the Rs finally powered up. "One, two, three, testing … Oh Jesus, what's wrong with this fuckin' PA?"

"What about the switch on the mike?" suggested a helpful Andy.

"Oh shi… !" Declan's subsequent phraseology was drowned in a series of painfully aggressive screeches, as the flick of the aforementioned switch released the ferocity of the maligned PA, the volume control of which had been inappropriately wound up.

"O'Rourke, are you trying to fucking kill us or something?"

"Piss off, Dangerfield! Right … Lucille, OK? Come on, Mike, belt it out now!"

Friday night was there; the moment was upon him! The bare floorboards of the afternoon were already disturbingly covered by a crowd that were now scattered but would soon amass around the foot-high stage upon which he was to have a place of prominence. He stood there awkwardly, shyly making an attempt to test microphones through which his voice boomed but without the echo of the afternoon.

"Get y're treble up, Burgess," came the terse comment from the consistently unhelpful Jeff. "All these bodies'll deaden your voice, you know that."

Execution of the suggestion only resulted in more intense screeching from the PA and the unthinking response of spinning round rapidly to wind the volume down. Michael's rotating guitar neck succeeded in knocking a microphone stand off the vertical and into the cushion of amused onlookers. Michael couldn't have been further from being amused but he was incapable, even without an audience, of telling Jeff what he thought – that he was an irritating squirt of dubious parentage who could only stand at the back grumbling so-called orders and thumping away on four strings while he, Michael, was about to play solos on six *and* about to command attention with his vocals! Instead, he backed away with excuses that he might, more often than not, need even Jeff's talents to back him in the future.

Michael knew that there was little point in his trying to appear within anything approaching control. The apology for a spotlight made it still possible to distinguish all the faces below without squinting excessively. Too many of them for his liking stared at him with an air of expectancy.

"Can you guitarists get tuned up?" said Sam, "This is an A, alright?"

"What? E?" shouted Declan, "Stevey, hold on will you, I can't hear a damn thing."

Steve reluctantly ceased the thunderous testing of his kit but sat looking as menacing as he could – as though he wasn't going to be held back for long. The clashing, approximately quarter-tone intervals between Declan and Michael rang round the coffee bar.

"Up a bit, up a bit," said Declan to Michael.

"No! You're not in tune with *me* yet, O'Rourke," said Sam.

"Oh Christ, give us an A again then."

"Hey, turn your volume down when you're tuning up – it's very unprofessional." Jeff wasn't going to let his back-seat-driver mentality lapse without a fight. Michael's longed for edifice of suave sophistication before the public had all but been reduced to rubble, but he strangely found solace in Declan's frustrations.

"Oh Christ, I hate this. As soon as two strings are in tune another bugger is out," said Declan, thankfully ignoring Jeff. "Mike, let's go somewhere quiet and get tuned up properly."

"For God's sake hurry up. Your fans are waiting," said Sam pretending to smile.

"Oh piss off! You want us to play in tune don't you?" said Declan unplugging his guitar with an angry loud crackle.

"And turn the bloody mikes off ..." Jeff's voice faded away as Michael and Declan negotiated a route through the coffee bar patrons who seemed already to be enjoying the proceedings on stage. Michael had long abandoned his vision of gliding unobtrusively into position, with dramatic silence preceding stunning opening bars.

"Miserable sod at times that Jeff – eh? Oh sorry, he's a mate of yours," said Declan whose mood had marginally brightened as they stood together, scrutinised by passing onlookers in the red light of the entrance hall.

"No, don't worry, you're right," said Michael, warming rapidly to Declan's point of view. It reminded him, as he often needed to be, that any personal imperfections didn't always justify irascibility in others and could legitimately be disregarded. "Anyway, he's not a life-long friend. He just happened to go to my school. Don't want to lose him though, he's a good bass."

"It's OK, I'm not going to upset the man. Not tonight at least. Jesus, I still can't hear this fuc ... sorry, madam, damn thing out here."

"Sam's well and truly drunk," said Michael.

"He's not drunk, Mike. He's stoned."

"Right ..." Michael was once more aware of his drug-naïvety.

After what seemed like an age, they mounted the stage once again with guitars that, for the present, were maybe within an eighth of a tone of each other. Whether their pitches would coalesce or part further, with the imminent sweat and strain that they were to be subjected to, remained to be seen.

Declan was for once hesitant in his public introduction, "Alright, we're going to give you a bit of rock 'n' roll tonight, OK? ... Are you ready, lads? ... er ... this is Lucille, OK? ... one ... one, two, three, four ..."

It was happening! They were under way! He was in a group with an audience. Michael felt himself being carried, lifted along – the still makeshift, quarrelsome band were suddenly obliged to pull themselves towards a focus. For once the tempo and tuning were as right as made no difference – just as he had always had in his head. He strummed his chords mechanically but for now he could believe that the others, even Jeff, were playing just for him ...

LUCILLE!! ...

He had never known what most of the lyrics were. He made his own imitation, like an attempt at a foreign language, confident that no one listening would detect misinterpretation; but he relished the bits he did know – about how tight his friends' lips "was" when asked about Lucille – lines that had been imprinted on his brain since he was nine years old.

Anxiety about solos was not only sinking; it had already been submerged in the urgency of being the front man yelling into the microphone. The eyes were now firmly on him! The staccato chords were punched out with all the force that the collective nervous energy of the Rs, just freed from their varying degrees of apprehension, could command. Between those chords, Michael was on his own, almost blissfully conspicuous. The backing of the half-rehearsed crew in their unremarkable seaside venue was enough to make him feel special once again – enough to stem the imagined descent into anonymity among the dense, daily to-and-fro streams of students. At least now those who crowded round him would be able to single him out; he would be recognisable. Declan's take-over could be tolerated for this.

Given these moments and mementos of exposure, he was content to leave solos to others. Andy didn't need to be given any nods. His chance had now come! The, at least temporary, divorce of he and his saxophone from the working men of Yorkshire seemed to have endowed them both with ever greater eccentricity. He could never be described as subdued but now his sax was being swung back and forth as his cheeks billowed and his face achieved an unprecedented redness. The display was only marginally surpassed by Sam, still fur coat clad, who began to resemble, as closely as could be done, a demented orangutan, already hammering unmercifully on the unsuspecting keyboard. As though tired of using his fingers, he occasionally decided that elbows should be given a chance. Michael was afraid that he would soon resort to using his walking sticks.

At last an ending was seen to the solo turns that were being passed round, and to Michael's sometimes thwarted attempts at interspersing them with a vocal line. The final exaggeratedly lengthened chord was met with a startling return display from the mass of bodies that now filled the basement. Any clapping was drowned in cheering and whistling, in some quarters with wild enthusiasm. It was as though a gathering of hard-pressed soldiers in some far-off corner of the British Empire were just being treated to their five-yearly striptease variety show.

Michael's smile covered a surging embarrassment, made worse by his half expecting such a reaction. His head swelled and swam in the warmth of the waves of approval even though he was inclined to see it as the mock adulation of an element largely rented by the gregarious Declan. The first three or four numbers were followed by the same show of apparent ecstasy – unwavering, undiminished in its intensity despite the fact that the Rs slipped out of phase with each other from time to time. Declan's continued monopoly of the guitar solo was even starting to cause Michael to look forward to his own debut. When he finally saw an opening, he tried desperately to remember what he had planned while sitting on his bed. The engineered patterns quickly disintegrated through makeshift improvisation to the safety of a few chord variations but he was just as quickly rescued by more-than-willing saxophone blowing and keyboard thumping. At last, with their meagre repertoire exhausted, the Rs were obliged to repeat themselves but the "Rock Around the Clock" finale, a song that Michael had privately dismissed as embarrassingly outdated, generated yet more passionate energy in the cramped, overheated space.

With applause barely diminishing, he unstrapped his guitar and stepped down into the midst of an unexpected and, he assumed, temporary fan club and received handshakes and back-slapping. He even exchanged congratulatory comments and smiles with Jeff. Then, a voice that was familiar, from someone he had not been aware of while attempting to perform, rang in his ear.

"Michael, that was fantastic! So rock 'n' roll lives again eh?" Cathy exuded her characteristic warmth.

"Cathy! I didn't see you down there. If rock 'n' roll lives, I'm sure we'll do our best to kill it."

"You won't as far as I can see."

"It's great to see you," he said truthfully. "I'm ... glad you liked the group. It was a bit unrehearsed, you know, but ..."

"You must be joking. It sounded so professional."

He dismissed the urge to tell her that it wasn't actually quite the group he had originally envisaged. "Well, there are probably a lot better musicians about …"

"I've yet to see or hear them. I loved your voice. Sorry if I'm embarrassing you but that Little Richard stuff really gets me going."

Michael could only speculate privately on the implication of the last phrase.

"Mm … I don't think anyone could emulate Little Richard – not even me. I'm not even Cliff Richard."

"Don't worry, you've got a unique style."

"I'll remember you said that."

"Look … you might be too exhausted … but a friend's having a party tonight. Why don't you come along … maybe some of the group as well?"

He was not exhausted but there was some unaccountable hesitation in him. Still, he knew that the vacuum-cleaner force of her exuberance was not to be avoided easily. His invitations to the Rockin' Rs were half-hearted. Jeff's acceptance was made more palatable by the existence of his beaten-up van which provided both transport and storage of guitar and amp.

Cathy and The Party –

That same night

Even without an invitation to the party, there would have been no one to bar entry. The open door revealed a crowded hallway through which Cathy, Michael and Jeff threaded, receiving looks that were mostly blank, either from lack of interest or surplus of alcohol. The one show of vivacity came from Cathy's friend.

"Cathy! You made it!"

"I did at last, Jenny. Oh, this is Michael and Jeff. I've just been listening to their fabulous rock 'n' roll group."

"Really? Sorry I couldn't make it, what with all this disorganised party organisation. Grab a drink if you can."

Michael was grateful for the presence of a girl that Jeff knew and who, somehow, was keen to command his attention.

"Let's try a dance," said Cathy. "We haven't had one since that Christmas Ball."

The trial dance, within impossible spatial constraints, gave way to the clasping of hands around waists and the shouting of snatches of trivial comments and attempted jokes into each other's ears. If such attention was to be typical of his new notoriety, he thought it quite likely that he would be powerless to fight against it, but he was not entirely at ease. Even in the modest afterglow of the Rockin' Rs' exposure to the feeble spotlight, part of him still wanted to dump it all and get back to what he saw as normality – the partitioned desk in the library, next week's set of problems. To be whisked away and carried along on a collective wave of intoxication from whatever source could not be accepted simply with good grace.

... Oh God, Burgess, a girl is all but throwing herself at you and you're still not bloody satisfied ... but look what happened before ... I don't want any more of that ... oh please, don't contemplate, question, wonder whether it'll diminish your supposed self-control ... Jesus wept! ... You liked her when you first met her ... you can't deny she always had a certain physical ... presence? ... and she's genuinely interested in you ... perhaps here at last is someone who's willing to ... no, it's heartless to think about it ... but I am in desperate need of some practice ...

"Wow! You're too energetic for me, Cathy. After this jiving and last night I'm beginning to wilt."

"Which part of you?"

"Now, now."

The two were leaving the so-called dance floor in a mock show of nurse supporting wounded soldier when the latter was suddenly brought to shocked attention.

"Well, well, if it isn't the big star! I hear they were rocking in the aisles tonight at the Pool Valley – that's if they had aisles – ha!"

Confrontation with Woods would have been unwelcome under most circumstances but the placement of his arm around Sarah's waist was simultaneously nauseating and appalling. A few seconds earlier, the closeness and touch of a feminine body was beginning to be appreciated once more after a long period of emptiness. Now, Michael only had the guilty urge of trying to distance himself, albeit slightly, from Cathy but she only continued to grasp him more tenaciously, obviously unmoved by the meeting. His startled eyes thought they detected a similar shift in Sarah's position but there was no doubting the colouring of her cheeks. He assumed she hadn't expected to see him and he couldn't believe what he thought she had got herself into. The earth was moving for Michael but not from what was regarded as the conventional stimulus.

"How we've all changed," continued Woods.

"Michael and I just bumped into each other," said Cathy, making it sound, to Michael, like a thing they did a few times a day. "I was just congratulating him."

"Sorry, Michael, we ... I didn't manage to see you tonight," said Sarah. He tried to brush aside thoughts of various options that might have prevented her inclusion in the audience. The possibility of "couldn't care less" was less painful than most.

"Oh, it was only a first try out, you know. We might even be allowed to play again somewhere – if we're lucky." His mouth went into auto-pilot while his brain tried to make sense of the new order of things.

... what did I say once about the sort of girl who would go out with Woods? ... maybe Cathy has more sense? ... she doesn't seem to care too much ... that was so long ago ... this bloody university's too big for me to keep an eye on what's going on ... how long have they been ...?

"It was great – a fantastic band. But Michael was the real driving force on vocals!" said Cathy, giving the driving force an extra hug.

... Sarah, this isn't quite what it looks like ... I know it looks as though Cathy and I are passionate ... or at least she does ... but I haven't seen her for months ... why should you care anyway? ... perhaps you don't ... why must I keep hoping you do? ...

The fame-seeker at that second sought only to remove himself as far as he could from verbal and physical adulation and smiled weakly at Sarah.

"How deprived we must have been," said Woods. "Why don't we drink to it?"

"Just a little wine, if you can find it," said Sarah, still blushing.

"Well, I'm afraid I need a big one," said Cathy. "Give me your glass, Michael. I'll fill you up."

... do you have to phrase it like that, Cathy? – now I'm blushing ... oh hell, for once I don't want to be left alone with Sarah ...

Woods and Cathy left them alone. They began by looking in opposite directions until Michael made an enormous effort at a pleasantry.

"How are things? Haven't seen much of you recently."

"Oh, I've been around, you know. Haven't dropped out yet," she replied, struggling to laugh.

"What bring's you to the party?"

"Dic ... er, Richard's a friend of Jenny's boyfriend Owen. They're both in the rugby club. But Richard's in the thirds while Owen's always in the firsts."

... I'm grateful for small mercies ... how do you know so much about the rugby club? ...

"Really? Owen was my old room-mate. I knew he was good but Richard was never an England possible ... er ... how long – ?"

"Get that down you, Michael," said the currently unstoppable Cathy as the drinks replenishers unknowingly stifled the question that Michael didn't want to, but couldn't help trying to ask.

"Thanks." He took a relieved mouthful. "I didn't know you were such a leading light in the rugby world, Richard."

"Ha bloody ha. You've been discussing me I see."

"No, I just wondered how you came to roll up here."

"Oh, one has to do the rounds. It's the second one we've been to tonight isn't it, sweetheart?"

Sarah frowned and then managed to smile but only at Cathy.

Sweetheart!? You can't call my ... how can you call Sarah sweetheart? ... I might as well become a recluse ... at least I would if Cathy wasn't hanging round my neck ... the only thing is to give myself totally up to physics ... bugger them all ... if you'll excuse the expression ...

"Oh, I love this one! I've got to drag him away for another dance. Excuse us."

The aspiring recluse was thrust once again by Cathy into the mass of squirming, sweat-glistening bodies.

Oh Buddy! ... what's with all this loving and turtle-doving stuff? How can such a wonderful song have such bloody stupid words? ... I will be dead before Sarah ventures in my direction again ... that I do know ...

Michael kept one discreet eye on Sarah and Woods and he thought he caught her looking in his direction, but when they suddenly disappeared, he tried to abandon all in an exaggeratedly jubilant display of dancing.

"Hey, where did all this energy come from?" said Cathy, just about making herself heard.

"Second wind," he shouted back, "You feel like crashing out and then pow! – something injects new life into you."

"You're not on anything are you? If you don't mind me asking?"

"What me? Clean as a whistle. I don't indulge in that sort of thing. No, just rock 'n' roll and a couple of pints."

At last, the dancing slowed and they held each other closer, and then Cathy suddenly announced that she needed some air. Michael was relieved to be cool and removed from the compressed assembly, even in the apology for a garden of Jenny's flat. His tendency was always to look forward to the end of a party rather its beginning.

Their kiss seemed the natural, inevitable thing to do. They were unobserved and it was long and luxurious. When their lips parted, she looked away and spoke in not much more than a whisper.

"Michael, I ... can't quite believe I'm going to say this, but ... well, I've got a sort of proposition ... Oh, God ... what are you going to think of me? ... I'd like to cuddle you – I mean really cuddle. Oh, I can't ... I mustn't go, you know, all the way but ... we could ... please each other somehow ... oh no, I've said it. You can refuse ... and I'm sure it wouldn't satisfy you entirely, you know ... chastity is so ingrained in me, but I do have desires ... and there's no commitment. Oh no, you're going to think of me as some sort of ..."

Michael knew that he could not remain speechless for too long.

"I'm sorry, it was a stupid offer ..." she continued.

"It certainly wasn't. It's been an action-packed evening. I think we both need to lie down somewhere."

"I ... do happen to have a single room. The bed's not big but perhaps we can squeeze in. Oh, and ... maybe you're not worried but ... I don't share a flat with Sarah."

... *I was a bit worried* ...

"I'm not worried. We only went out once or twice – and that was long ago."

It was a short, slow but exciting walk across Queen's Park to Cathy's flat on East Drive. Michael was now relaxed to be held and be holding close.

"Why didn't you think of sharing with Sarah? If you don't mind me asking."

"Oh we got on well, but ... you know ... you make other friends. Anyway, I'm not sure I could afford her place in Brunswick Square. I think mum and dad are subsidising. You ... looked quite shocked when we saw her and Richard."

"Did it show that much? She's free to go out with whoever she likes but Woods ... oh sorry ... I wasn't thinking."

"I don't expect you to see it, but he's a fascinating guy in his own way. Don't worry, I don't think Sarah will be led astray. She might look vulnerable but I know she's quite a strong-willed little thing."

"Look, I mustn't talk about a very ex, very brief girlfriend at a time like this. I do wonder quite what's possessed her though."

"I can see what possessed him. She is rather sweet."

"He's possessed alright."

"Michael, I can see a mental block there."

"The last thing I want to discuss now is Richard Woods." He stopped, turned her to him and in the middle of the park they kissed again.

Her flat was as tidy and fragrant as his was disorderly and stale. He hoped her perfume would mask any odour he might possess after a crowded coffee bar and party. She said she might be thought silly when she requested that they undress in the dark but he reassured her and held her hand and led her to the bed.

"Oh God, I'm trembling," she said, "and I'm not cold."

"So am I ... Let's ... cuddle, like you said. Don't worry, I'm not going to try anything you don't ... want ... you're my guide."

The trembling stopped as soon as they kissed and his body pressed gently against her ample bosom.

The first light of day brought him out of yet another of the brief snatches of sleep they had allowed each other. He was now in a state of exhausted exhilaration.

"I'm awake too," she whispered and wrapped an arm round him.

"Cathy, before anything else ... I must pay a visit."

"It's down the hall on the left."

Even with trousers on, he hoped he would not meet another girl on his short journey. When safely back in the bedroom, he removed them and got back into bed. The night had taken away all thoughts of anyone else in his life, but in the morning, disquiet seeped guiltily back. The idea that Woods and Sarah were at that moment as close and as naked as he and Cathy was impossible to think about without grinding of teeth and knotting of intestines. As a scientist, he had to allow all possibilities and only discount those that fell outside the bounds of reasoned argument. Subjectively, he couldn't imagine any female of his own species, or in fact any other, wanting to get into bed with Woods, an act he deemed somewhat disgusting and fraught with danger. Objectively, it had, agonisingly, to be counted in. He had heard anecdotes of the most beautiful and demure of ladies being obsessively bound to ugly, drunken or violent men. Woods, according to Michael, only fell fractionally short in all categories. The probability had to be faced that Woods' cunning was breaking down even Sarah's God-fearing barriers. Worse still, he wondered if Woods had been given some powers of seduction that he hadn't, even though, unlike Woods, he thought he would have used them discerningly.

When they finally vacated the bed, he was pleased that Cathy was in no hurry to dress, but simply started to brush her hair.

"I don't want to look a mess," she said and turned to face him. "You're a fine figure of a man, Michael. Oh God, I still can't believe I'm saying such things, especially with nothing on myself."

"I've never been called a man before. A boy really."

"Not from where I'm standing."

"And you're certainly a fine figure of a woman. Apart from anything else, you do have lovely ... you know ... you are rather well endowed."

"You noticed?" She looked down at herself. "I've my mother to blame for these."

"Blame?"

"I'm sure you see them as an advantage but, I can tell you, school sprint races with an inadequate bra were a real trial! At least I was at an all-girls school. Any boys would have loved it I suppose. You'll have to believe me when I say I've ... never seen a man naked before. It's a grand sight."

"Surely not that grand ... I'd like to say I've never seen a girl ..."

"Go on with you."

"Just ... once before then."

"Come on ... not Sarah?"

"Good grief! No! ... whoever it was, it didn't end very well. Let's just say that. Cathy, it was so ... nice ... to have somewhere so warm and soft to lay my head." He was no longer embarrassed to gaze at her chest.

"And not just your head, you mischievous lad."

"I hope you didn't mind ..."

"Mind? I certainly did not ... and I'm sure helping each other climax a few times didn't hurt us. That reminds me, I must get some more Kleenex. Oh God, my mother would die of horror if she knew – which she is never going to; but I can see myself in the confessional."

"But, you know ... we didn't go all the way."

"All but the last stop ... I know, but you don't realise what's been drummed into me all my life. I'd only give a priest an edited version. Still ... I'm happy for you to ... come again as it were, if you'll pardon the expression. I know you might want to do this every night, but I do need a lot of sleep. Maybe sometime soonish though?"

"It's up to you to say the word."

She turned to the mirror and he came up and cupped his hands round her.

"You've got a very nice bum as well," he whispered, hoping no flatmate could hear.

"Michael, you are a one for the tit, you know." She leaned back against him.

"Like most boys – well, almost men. My mother would have a fit about all this too. We never spoke about it, of course, but I think she thought of sex as something a little unsavoury. When I was conceived, I think she might have said: 'Oh well, if I must'."

"I can imagine mine saying the same! The thing with sex, I suppose, is that it reduces us to our basic instincts, and people are wary or even frightened by this. Maybe that's why some think of it as dirty and others laugh at jokes in embarrassment. Our mothers would get on well."

"I think my mother's attitude rubbed off on me for quite a while. When I first learnt about ... you know, what you do – and not from parents I might add ... I thought: You can't be serious! Surely people, and particularly parents, don't do that! Now, though, I have to say it's beginning to have some appeal ..."

"I did ... sense that, Michael. I think you'd better remove your hands before I change my mind."

"Oh yes ... sorry."

"I hate to tell you this, but I'm afraid I've got a horrible essay to write for tomorrow and what I'm really dying for now is a shower and some breakfast."

They finally dressed and she left the room. Hearing voices, he hung back in the bedroom until she put her head round the door.

"Come on, you don't need to be shy. Come and join us."

He steeled himself and walked sheepishly into a bright kitchen with clean, uncluttered surfaces, washed-up crockery, a shining floor and two other girls in dressing gowns. He was relieved that he didn't know them. They smiled at him as though he had been a much-loved neighbour coming in to borrow a cup of sugar. He could not lose the notion that behind the smiles lay speculation about the range of his amorous antics, but the unexpected warm reception calmed his unease. If Cathy wasn't embarrassed, and she hardly looked it, he decided that he could relax a little. He was certainly not going to embark on explanations.

At the front door, they placed one last wet kiss, at least for that day, on each other's lips and he strode with a sense of fulfilment down across the park.

June 1969 –

Queen's Park

Michael reclined on the same park bench that had been his secret point of observation for a few weeks. He knew that there was no point in observing anymore, but the location was peaceful and never frequented by anyone he knew, except Caroline – and she had passed into the periphery of his existence, disconnected, immaterial. He could not stay there for long. Finals would start in four days. He had to get back to try to pick up, in desperation, some final crumbs of other people's wisdom.

He looked up the slope to Cathy's old flat and managed to smile. She had been as good as her word. They had met again for pleasure a number of times, going to the pub and cinema as well as bed, but she had finally succumbed to some kind of faithful duty.

She had said: "Michael, every time we go to bed, I get closer to saying 'to hell with it – let's just do it' and it gets more difficult to resist. I've made a mess of things and just led you on, but something still deep in my heart won't allow me to give myself completely, unless I'm a newlywed. And I don't think either of us are thinking about getting married. Let's be friends – if you can accept that."

Michael accepted and reassured her that animosity was not in his vocabulary. He was unabashed to tell her how much he had enjoyed her body, as well as her brain. She left him in no doubt that his had provided reciprocal pleasure. Regarding a particular period of pleasure, though, he remained troubled and confused, but at least had been able to talk to her about it.

"I ... said I didn't want to talk about that other girl that ... you know, I ... saw," he had mumbled.

"Try me."

"Well ... maybe I'm thinking too much about my mother's attitude ... but I've always had this notion that boys are the ones who instigate ... you know ... sex, and that girls, occasionally, grudgingly accept it."

She laughed. "Michael, believe me, girls do like thinking about, talking about and, eventually, having sex. It would be a bizarre world where an integral aspect of life was treated as something to be avoided by half the population. I mean, our own mutual experience should have given you a hint that that wasn't true."

"I know, but ... that was somehow ... different."

"Was it?"

"That girl ... openly demonstrated that she liked sex ..."

"And I didn't?"

"Well ... yes, of course ... I'm not putting this well ... I don't know ... with us it was nicer ... a mutual meeting of bodies, if you like. The very few girls I'd known before her might have had sensual thoughts, but I wouldn't have known. They were very restrained. I mean, this ... other girl ... was getting into bed with a boy at home and with others here in Brighton. On her own admission, she went all the way with the one back home but she chose not to with me ... we didn't consummate ... in the conventional way."

"I think I get the picture. You don't seem to be picking the right girls."

"I don't see myself as a one-man selection committee. People just meet at random, don't they? Sorry, Cathy ... you don't want to hear this ..."

"No, I'm all ears."

"Oh, it sounds pathetic ... but ... why is this girl, a year younger than me, and just out of the classroom, so far ahead of me in ... experience?"

"Only a man could see this as a competition."

"Oh God, is that the way I think?"

"Michael, it's not easy, but you'll come to terms with it all eventually, as we all have to." She smiled: "You know I could be jealous of this apparent seductress, but I'm not. I'll take comfort in the knowledge that our intimacy was, in your words, nicer. You know, pretty well all girls are cautious – even her. Apart from anything else, we've got more to lose if something goes wrong. That's where the restraint comes in. When you're not protected ...

as it were, you have to be careful ... like us, putting it a little crudely, we made sure that your stuff shot in a harmless direction."

"That's another thing I like about you, Cathy – your plain speaking."

With this short exchange, Michael achieved some measure of calm. He was content, as he phrased it, to put the subject to bed and ramble on about other things.

Cathy was not one to lecture, but in their conversations, he had learnt a lot about history and politics. He had always viewed these things as distant or tiresome. It seemed to him that, in the not too remote past, England had seen a succession of gangs beating the hell out of each other for something called power, or torturing and murdering each other for espousing the wrong religion. To him this had all been hideously inexplicable. He had never wanted power over anyone – particularly over girls. Imposing his view of the world, however paltry, on someone else was alien to him. If he ever came up with a new scientific theory, it was for others to praise or discard as they saw fit.

No doubt unwittingly, Cathy had made him see how ignorant he was of the wider world of governments and their often-malicious intent. He had been just barely aware of the incident at the university when a pot of red paint was thrown over an American embassy official and the US flag was burnt. He had never thought of America as some sort of evil force. From his innocent viewpoint, a country that had produced Elvis and Little Richard could not be all bad. He would have been at a complete loss in arguing with those students who seemed to sympathise with Marx, Lenin or Trotsky, but he was sure of one thing. The idea of being lumped together with anyone in any sort of commune by a tiny band of sinister, dictatorial figures in command would have been difficult for him to bear.

One day, she asked: "Did you hear about that Enoch Powell speech yesterday?"

"Oh ... no, sorry..."

"He seems to envisage a war between white and black people in this country. I think he's wrong. I know I go on about the English, but I have to admit they've offered me a nice university to attend and nowadays they're more tolerant and flexible – not like a lot of white Americans."

"Yeah ... at least I did know that Martin Luther King had been shot a couple of weeks ago. Cathy, I've been fed too rosy a view of the USA in my life – lots of comedy shows and cowboy pictures and rock 'n' roll. Seems I need a lot of educating."

Bill had told him that King had been shot at the motel in Memphis where Steve Cropper and Eddie Floyd wrote "Knock On Wood" a couple of years previously ...

... The singer worries about losing the good thing that he's got ... suppose he's singing about some girlfriend ... now it sounds more profound ...

Of his own country, he was reluctant, as ever, to use the word love, but it occasionally occurred to him how much he felt part of it; emigration was unthinkable. It was the only place to be. He thought that no one but a deluded nationalist would be proud of its history, but was grateful that out of the murderous intrigues and oppression of the past he could now say or believe what he wanted to, even though it would often only be to himself. He could even drum up some gratitude to unknown politicians who, by intrigue or design, had made it possible for him to go to the seaside to indulge in what passed for his passion for physics, without having to be the son of a marquis or a magnate.

He had warmed to Cathy's idea, even hope, that the island of Ireland should be one country one day. She was worried that some of her countrymen would resort to any means to secure this, and that things could only get worse. Typically, the topic of Northern Ireland had never exercised Michael's brain, but she made him see that her once casual remark of Ireland's hatred of the English was justified. The English drive for power over the world did not appear to have rubbed off on him.

Now, with only thoughts of mastery over the syllabus, he dragged himself off the bench and trudged back to Roundhill Crescent. At least there was no phone there through which he could be bothered again by Rod Wyatt. That first night at Pool Valley had provided him with an hour or two of local fame and Rod's appearance had made him, temporarily, even hope for wider acclaim. Now, though, he wanted to be left alone and not be bothered by contacts or contracts. The call to Rod the day before would probably be the last time they spoke ...

It had been early evening before he got around to picking up the phone. At least now there would be less chance of competing conversations at adjacent cubicles. The day's buzz of Falmer House had decreased to the sound of a few echoing footsteps. He looked down at the moat, glassily still as it had been for the last few sweltering days, as though it was going to help his call. He held his breath as he dialled.

... what's all the anxiety? ... I don't have to go along with this guy ... anyway, it's out of my hands ...

"Oh ... Rod?"

"Mike. Great to hear you ..."

... Oh God, he's in his usual up-beat mood ...

"You got the note then? You need to get a phone in your house, you know."

"On my grant?"

"Well, when you're a big star you'll have a phone in every room. Look, er ... talking about that. We're still pushing the record this end but, you know how it is in this business ..."

... no, I don't think I do ... or ever will ...

"...things move at their own pace as it were. Anyway, Cliff and myself met with some radio people a couple of days back and they seemed really taken with the song – and the singer of course. That's the way to get in. If the radio producers like you, you're bloody made – no doubt about it ... So, what about the contract, Mike? What d'you think?"

"Yeah, it's ... well, the contract's OK. It's just, you know, my father's got to sign it ..."

"Come on, you can persuade the old man surely. He must know you've got talent."

"I suppose he's a bit cautious. I ... I don't think there's much chance of him signing anything to be honest."

"Oh, Mike, I don't believe I'm hearing this. You've got such a great voice. Everyone says so. Cliff's even got some new songs lined up. Look, have a go at the old chap again ..."

... I don't like you keep referring to him like that, Wyatt ...

"...'Cos without a contract, you know, we're stymied. I mean, we trust each other don't we – but you've got to do things properly in this game ..."

... *You have, have you?* ...

"Anyway, it won't be long before you can sign it yourself."

"Six months or so I suppose."

"OK, but let's not let the grass grow under the old feet, eh? Without the contract ... well, that's that. Think about it, Mike."

Michael replaced the receiver with feelings as well mixed as any Christmas pudding. It seemed everyone had had a go at stirring them up. He was four days away from demanding little short of exam perfection from himself. He was in demand as a vocalist but not, as usual, as a boyfriend. That part of his existence exasperatingly referred to as a love life, had branched off down a few roads that had promised too much only to be stopped short, each at its own version of a dead end. He questioned why he now pursued the vision of yet another sunlit avenue with a girl called Caroline but received no clear answer.

He had tried once to learn about an electronic device called a flip-flop, a thing that went from one state of charge to another without anything in between. Was he expected to believe that something called love was like this? You were out of it, unconnected, switched off, and then you were in. Were there no degrees, no comforting shades of grey? He had never looked towards a future moment when the state of love would be magically flipped into. He still wanted to look at it as the embroidery of a world trying to create an impossibly romantic tapestry. All he could admit to was being spellbound by pretty faces, mesmerised by shapely breasts and that he had found less than a handful of girls that he liked to be around. With excruciating embarrassment, he had also tried to hold on when there was no call. Now he had been distracted, but by none of these things. Caroline's face might get a few second looks, she could boast no cavernous cleavage, he had barely spoken to her, but her mysterious beauty had switched him, from a distance, into a state he still could not label.

His footsteps echoed on the bare, polished boards of the corridor and clicked down the deserted steps. Out in the fading light, his face was bathed in the warm closeness of the still, evening air.

Random windows were already illuminated; the surroundings could still stop him in his tracks and make him want to soak it all up. He would have been at peace with it all if time had not been pressing. It was seven-thirty – he could still spend two more hours in the library.

June 1969 –

The Ultimate Final

It was all nearly over – the last final was upon them. Michael, Jim and Tony sat on the bus in unaccustomed silence as it trundled too quickly along the Lewes Road. A jumble of theorems and equations ran round Michael's head, seemingly trying to escape, but something else occupied a part of his brain. Tony, the evening before, had abandoned revision, he said for ever, and had resorted to a cursory study of the *Evening Argus*.

"Hey, listen to this. The university has finally made the headlines – or at least page 2. 'Lecturer Alan Mercer has been arrested for assault.' Doesn't say who he hit. I didn't know we had violent lecturers. Does anyone know this bloke?"

"What is he – arts?" asked Jim.

"Yeah, says he in Sociology. You ever heard of him, Mike?"

Michael's purported honesty was on the point of divulging his intense interest, but the shock of the announcement elicited few words.

"No ... never heard of him ..."

Whatever Alan Mercer had done, it had to be put aside, at least for a day.

"Right, you can turn the papers over now ... and you've got three hours. That's up to twelve-thirty."

The cheerful voice rang emptily around the gymnasium.

... It's alright for you to smile, Dr Invigilator, you're way past this ... Christ, I've been up for five hours already ... kept waking up thinking it

was all over ... then that dreadful sweating ache when I knew it wasn't ... read through them carefully and don't write anything for a while ... they said ten minutes or so ... but I don't think I can last out that long ... so is this Mr Special? ... already perspiring amongst the massed ranks of desks lined up wall to wall? ... Mr Special should be anticipating an easy ride with time to relax and gather himself between each beautifully executed answer ... not searching for oases in a desert of unintelligibility ... This is the last – the final final – Mathematics 6 / Physics 7- thank God it's only Physics ... although that complex numbers paper was alright ... I did nearly all of it ... then someone had to say it only counts five per cent, bugger it ... after that they decided to turn the screw on me ... The first part of number one's alright ... oh, hell look at the last bit ... in what important aspects would you expect the following reactions to differ? How the hell should I know? Wait, alright – I might be able to say something ... number two's a bit better, thank God ... I'll try that ... no, just have a look at the others first ... I CAN'T BELIEVE IT! ... Bose-Einstein Condensation ... it's gone ... they've just handed it to me on a bloody plate and I know it's gone! ... come on, some of it must be still there ... you delivered a bloody lecture on it once! ... It can't be nearly an hour ... I'm still only on the first one, for Christ's sake ... oh, bliss, bliss! the stellar structure stuff looks OK ... and I'm allowed to do both ... God, my bladder's bursting ... three-quarters of an hour to go ... I'm going to have to go out ... I just can't concentrate ...

The stream spattered forcefully, joyfully against the porcelain; every moment of it that passed, every second that was checked on his watch, was ecstatically well spent. The pleasure neutralised the gloom for that short time.

... there, only a minute and a half ... for once I was decisive ... at least both of the stellar structure ones are complete ... that MUST count for a lot ... but the rest is so bitty, so incomplete ... calm down, just CALM DOWN! ... that relativity thing is almost like a foreign language, God, I spent so long trying to make sense of it all ... thinking about Caroline most likely ... oh, God, ten minutes ... it's a disaster ... no it isn't ... I think I can add a bit more to number three ...

"Right, stop writing please, ladies and gentlemen! Stop writing!"

Michael scribbled a last ungrammatical, despairing sentence, cheating by five seconds, and then rapped his pen down noisily on the desk. The noise was drowned in the collective sigh, the collective loud whisper to adjoining desks.

"Make sure you've got your names on the top of the first page and your reference number – you have all got your reference numbers I hope? ... You can now go and get drunk – shouldn't be too difficult for most of you."

"What's this, the bloody cabaret?" said Jim, suddenly appearing behind Michael, "... Well?"

"Not so dreadful I suppose."

"Don't give me that. You thought it was easy."

"I didn't say that."

"I must admit it could've been worse. Tuesday's took the fucking biscuit as far as that's concerned."

The thought that he didn't have to spend another minute in any library or any lonely bedroom searching for topics that could be fitted inside his brain had yet to come home to Michael. He was taken up in those moments with Jim thinking it could have been worse. Jim would not try to hide things like he would.

... Jim, who spent so much more time than me in the bars of Brighton, has done better, I can tell ... no you can't ... How does anybody know? You haven't got any reference point. You'll just have to wait and see ... just forget about it for now ...

"I looked at that relativity one, number five, and thought, Jesus, didn't I do a course on that, didn't some luminary once drop a few gems about time and space – then it suddenly came to me. It wasn't as bad as it looked. Did you do that one?" said Jim.

"Er, no ... I don't really care much for post-mortems."

"Oh, come on, Mike, it's all over now anyway."

"Yeah, but I couldn't stand thinking of all the things I forgot that I might now suddenly remember."

"I'm the one who should be looking miserable, not you," said a smiling Tony, "The promise of A-levels has not materialised I'm afraid. I did bits of some of them but from my perspective it wasn't a tour de force. Michael, you can no longer refuse a drink."

The three, augmented by a few other unburdened souls, mostly now ex-physicists and ex-mathematicians, sprawled themselves around on the grass outside the open doors of the bar. Michael was half way into his third pint, two and a half more than his normal daily intake, any depression dissolving into resignation. The postmortem that he had been fearing had gradually been abandoned. Why the corpse might have died or whether it could still have life in it were questions that were, for now, losing their appeal. It was then that Michael heard a girl's voice, a voice that could make him forget about almost anything.

"How is it going, Michael? You look sort of relieved." Sarah looked down at him, throwing him into a temporary confusion made worse by the heat and the now completed third pint. He manfully fought back to appear as controlled as he could.

"Sarah! Hi, I've just finished – or am finished. I don't think relieved is quite the word. What about you?"

"I've got one more to do – the worst one probably," she laughed a seemingly unworried laugh. "Then I can just say goodbye to it all."

... *have I got to say goodbye to you, you lovely gorgeous creature?* ...

"Let me buy you a drink," he said looking fixedly into her face and trying desperately to stop his eyes from wandering down the contours occasioned by her T-shirt or alighting on the thigh exposed by the unaccustomed brevity of her skirt.

... *I know it's hot, Sarah, but give a man a break ... seeing your thighs at close quarters for the first time, especially in my present state is not without its dangers* ...

"Well, er ..."

... *oh God, please say yes ... it's only a drink* ...

"... Thanks, that would be nice. Just a tonic water. I must go and do some revision this afternoon. Do you mind if I join you inside. It's a bit hot out here."

... *Yippee! Why do you say all the right things?* ...

He looked back to the bodies strewn on the grass and smilingly raised his eyebrows at them without comment and, he hoped, without letting Sarah see.

"How do you think you've done though?" she said as she perched on her bar stool and attempted in vain to pull the hem of her skirt lower.

"Not as good as I'd hoped, but there again I know it's difficult to tell. I want to do physics research and I'm going to need a two-one, perhaps a first."

"No easy options for you then? I'm sure you'll do well. I'm sure you're conscientious."

"Sometimes needs more than that though. I always make things difficult for myself. Have you got anything lined up for the future?"

... what a stupid question, Michael ...

"Apart from marrying a millionaire that is?"

"What?"

"Joke."

"He'd be a lucky millionaire."

"Michael ... honestly ..." she said and looked down at her thighs, with a blush on her cheeks, while he maintained his horizontal gaze, strengthened by the fourth pint.

... Wait a minute, this IS Sarah who's sitting chatting to me isn't it? ... I am feeling a bit dizzy but I don't think I'm hallucinating yet ... Is this God giving me a little treat after all my labours? ... He suddenly makes her pop up every now and again and we carry on like old friends ... well, at least she does ... I'm dying to give her a cuddle if the truth were known ... which it won't be ...

"Do you ... see much of Richard these days?"

"Which Richard is that?" They both laughed, "Michael, it was only a short aff ... thing."

... she did nearly say affair, didn't she? Perhaps she didn't really mean it ... Sarah doesn't have affairs ... does she?

"And what about Cathy may I ask?"

"Similarly short – but she's a lovely girl, I'm still fond of her."

... Don't make it sound too much like desperate longing ...

"... Are you still playing in your group?"

"You mean you haven't been to see us?"

"Oh dear, I'm afraid not."

"Well, we've got something on tomorrow night believe it or not; you'll be finished by then, won't you?"

"Yes, thank goodness."

... You're interested? ... Please say you'll come along ... I might even be able to impress you ... or something ...

"Someone's organized a post-finals extravaganza at the sports pavilion up the hill."

"Sounds fun – I think. I'll ... see if I'm free."

... oh Sarah, why do you always hesitate? ... we're so alike! ...

"Well, I can't imagine you're short of invitations out but, you know, you could be driven totally wild by our music."

"Is that a threat or a promise? What are you called?"

"Axis ... it's the title of a Jimi Hendrix album. Meaningless and pretentious at the same time I always think. Jellyroll sounds better – you've heard of them – the blues group?"

"Just about."

"Yes, they're actually good – whereas we think we might be one day. They're into blues while we're not sure exactly what we're into."

"You're so conceited, Michael."

"Wish I was sometimes ... Anyway, come and dance the night away. Reminds me of one of my favourite songs. You won't even have to dance with me – I'll be too busy."

... stop rabbiting on ... you won't have to dance with me! You prat! ...

"... I'll definitely think about it ..."

... there, you've put her off ...

"...thanks for the drink, Michael, I'd better be off ..."

... there you go again, dropping into my life and then drifting away ... but you look at me so sweetly ... do you look at everyone like that? ... probably ... but you did come up and speak to me – you needn't have done ...

"I hope the last paper isn't too bad, Sarah."

"Thanks – not as much as I do. Bye bye."

"Yes, bye."

... Well, that's it. Goodbye my quiet, shy, retiring diminutive blonde bombshell. It's been nice talking to you once every six months. Suppose I should be grateful ...

"Well, how did you get on ... MICHAEL, DARLING?" Tony stirred the others into laughter as Michael walked unsteadily back to them across the grass.

"Either you've got it or you haven't," said Michael.

"Looks as though you've lost it again."

"You're just jealous," said Michael, for once devoid of embarrassment.

"I think he could do with a cold shower."

"Or a cold bath."

The water of the moat caught Michael off-guard with its chill as he surfaced, trying not to make the gasps too obvious, but he was content to have been chosen as the first in line for immersion. It didn't sober him up or wash away apprehension about what he might not have achieved and as he hauled himself out he tantalised himself with a thought ...

... If only Sarah would let us throw her in when her exams are done ... especially in that T-shirt! ...

Michael detached himself from the impromptu bathers when the bar doors closed, and squelched his way across the park. He had not quite attained the outer reaches of drunkenness and with the sparkling summit of too few words with Sarah scaled, the descent into an empty ravine, along with throbbing head and stale taste in mouth, was beginning.

... I didn't do enough, did I? ... and now there's nothing more to do ... but how do I know? ... maybe I scraped in ... depends how everyone else did, doesn't it? ... no it doesn't, don't fool yourself ... They're not going to slide the scale for you or anyone else; they know first class when they see it – and when they don't ... Come on, I did the two stellar structure ones completely ... a two-one's alright, maybe I'll get that; it's not asking much ... Jesus, all that bloody work, all those grinding evenings in that fuc- ... in that bloody library – and it still wasn't enough? I didn't plan it right ... too many distractions? What if I'd never come across Caroline? ... I wouldn't have had those pictures of her in my mind all the time ... yet more useless dreams of things that seem impossible to live without but never materialise ... But there's nothing to blame. I wouldn't anyway, would I? ... Don't suppose Ernest Rutherford or Marie Curie were ever in this position ... Suppose their equivalent of finals was brushed aside with derision – physics by day and by night, maths for leisure, physics at weekends ... no time for some juvenile diversion like playing in a blues band ...

He trudged to the edge of the trees at the top of the hill, sat down in the shade and looked back.

... used to look exciting, all that virgin red brick ... the first excitement and fear ... it disturbed me, but I didn't disturb it much in return, did I? ... there it sits, still unweathered, still offering fantasies to the next batch of unsuspecting individuals with their own set of schemes for reaching the unattainable ... I think I must have been a batch of one ... Michael

Burgess? – unique in his ability to credit himself with extraordinary scientific prowess, unequalled in thinking that the world was waiting for his voice to revolutionise rock 'n' roll, unrivalled in his belief that Caroline's heart beat faster every time she saw him ... Michael Burgess, without hesitation should be awarded a first class in self-delusion ... all bloody self, isn't it? ... young intellectuals – ha! – should be concerned about the underprivileged, the downtrodden, the underpaid ... I might just claim to be a soldier in the army of under-achievers who can't take his eyes off the over-endowed ... I can't claim much else can I? ... what happened to the soaring, starry-eyed, celibate schoolboy? ... he became an average, frustrated, technically-celibate ex-student – who might just be able to cope with a career in polythene bag manufacture ... I don't want a career! ... what good is that to me? ... what good is a life of steady progression to me? ... I'm in real peril of ending up with a good job! ... oh, God, why have you done this to me? ...

He took the strain off his elbows and lay down to stare at the unclouded sky before the remnants of the alcohol and the turmoil of the day pushed him down into temporary oblivion. In the middle of a conversation about the finer points of Bose-Einstein Condensation with Sarah and Caroline both, for some reason, rather nonchalantly naked and perched on bar stool and bar respectively, he suddenly realised that he was an hour late for his last exam. The panic made him wake and sit up quicker than was expedient. His head swam and he leaned over and retched into the grass. There was not much to bring up but he was quick to resume a semblance of composure even though nobody was watching. The few distant figures didn't encroach on his solitude. The acres of deserted park and the countless square light years of clear blue sky were sufficient.

He walked again and the nausea began to subside. By the time he had got to the far end of the park and turned back, his socks were dry and he was verging on sobriety. He now felt up to saying hello to the few cows that bothered to stare at him. The ache in his stomach at the thought of finals had at last evaporated but there was another indefinable ache to know what had happened to Caroline. He could think of no way to find out.

... Alan Mercer has been arrested for assault ... who else could he have assaulted but Caroline? ...

He hoped a long walk home might do something to ease his mind, but desperation was setting in. Perhaps he could try to suppress his emotions with a practice for tomorrow's dance.

And Sarah said she might come ... oh, Michael, please! ... you know this is straw-clutching at its worst ... don't! ...

June 1969 –

The Last Dance

Michael's low spirits could not resist being lifted by Henry. He envied Henry's second-year status with a whole twelve months before finals. He envied his apparent vision of life as a series of amusements. There was to be "a happening" – so Henry had told them. First impressions of Henry, and most later ones, marked him out, in Michael's mind, as the sort of character who was fast becoming extinct. His outward demeanour was of a wide-eyed, enthusiastic boy who was not yet, and perhaps never would pretend to be, a man. The members of the aspiring Axis and those of Henry's band, who appeared to be intent on taking unpretentiousness into a new dimension, had come across each other at odd times. Now the dance at the sports pavilion, up the hill in the trees behind Maths, Physics and Biology, had brought them together on the same makeshift, unstable-looking stage. The glimmers of worldliness that Michael saw in Henry were tinged with a refusal to take anything seriously, but whether he felt himself so, Henry could not help appearing to be keen. That head boy who had towered over the first year Michael at grammar school had been keen. He too formed part of Michael's mental image of dying breeds – he would practically commit suicide to get the ball out of the ruck, he would paint impressively for the house art competition, he would speak with flowing eloquence, he would, and did, secure a place at Cambridge. But Henry's keenness was the kind that was undoubtedly directed elsewhere; it would try to avoid the frenzy of competition and the pursuit of glory and instead follow some eccentric path purely because an idea had suddenly struck it as pleasingly outlandish. Finding himself at university probably came as a total and profoundly whimsical surprise. The present project was to culminate in the demolition of a 1950's radiogram to the tune, for want of a better word, of "Wild Thing".

"I say, it's a splendid thing isn't it? Just the job," said Henry with evident pride; his voice would not have been out of place on the Home Service. The two trios stood by the stage in the empty hall looking at the outdated piece of furniture that had just been lifted onto the stage, or rather, in its case, the scaffold. "George and I found it in this junk shop in Kemp Town and as soon as I saw it I said: My God, that could do with a bit of reorganisation! Ha ... ! And I think George might push his drums off the stage at the climax as well, eh George?"

"Hang on a minute, those drums cost me ten quid," said George, his dour Yorkshire accent clashing with the home counties of Henry.

"Gosh, ten quid, eh, George?" said Henry. "You didn't tell me. That's more than the rest of our equipment put together. Perhaps you can just throw yourself off the stage, eh? ... Into the clutches of all those screaming women! By the way, have you met Dick? Treat him with respect; his bass probably cost eight quid."

"You should know, it's bloody priceless – I made it myself," said Dick.

"Ah yes, I wondered where that unique sound emanated from. I ask you, fancy a chap called Henry teaming up with two cats called George and Richard. We just had to call ourselves 'The Three Queens' eh?"

"You mean *you* had to call us that – we didn't find out until the tickets were printed," said Dick, looking as philosophical as George about his new-found name and doing his best to counter Henry's exuberance.

"I think this band ought to have a different name every gig," Henry continued. "That way we might avoid detection."

As far as Michael could see, Henry talked about cats going to gigs in the spirit of someone who had been asked to try out a new vocabulary, which he found totally absurd, but was happy to continue with to provide others with entertainment.

"Hey, I hear you guys were appearing at Jimmy's last week. I'm impressed – that's a great club!" said Henry.

"Yeah, but it wasn't the regular blues night – we weren't exactly a star feature. It was just that a mate organised his birthday there," said Jeff doing his best to stifle the attempted promotion but without success.

"Still, it's a start, eh? The only way is up now!"

"And your careers can't fail to take off tonight with us as the support," said the more thoughtful George. "Whatever you're like, the contrast'll be stunning. I'll get my drums off as quick as I can when we've finished but I can't promise at the moment to throw them into t' crowd."

"Yeah, you'll know it's time to get ready when the chords of 'Wild Thing' ring out and I begin to dismantle the woodwork," added Henry with renewed vigour, "Actually, I think I'll take a surreptitious screw-driver to it in a minute so that the whole performance looks more impressive. We don't want the thing to remain unscratched while my guitar falls apart. That wouldn't do at all – make me look silly, what?"

Wild Thing! You make my fart sing!

The Three Queens were about to reach the promised climax. The "Post-Finals Extravaganza" was not short of punters. Even The Queens could boast that they had performed to an almost packed house. Jellyroll probably had some bigger, more sophisticated audience somewhere else. But the sports pavilion already had a population density of pretty well one per square yard. Michael knew it wasn't going to stop there, and that by the time he was due to climb onto the stage, little of the dance floor would be visible. He was always nervous. He felt that it all hung on him.

Henry, in contrast, was parody personified. He was useless at pretending that he or anyone associated with him was anything near wild, even though The Queens sweated and grimaced menacingly at each other. Even when a space was made for Henry's run-up onto the stage to kick in the radiogram speaker, disbelief could not be suspended. Still, there was no doubting his enthusiasm as the wood splintered, the ends fell sideways and the turntable was removed and stamped on with both feet. The partners not only kept the beat going while Henry was otherwise employed, but their efforts in doing so resulted in the awesome rupture of a bass guitar string and the overturning of a high-hat, both, by the look of it, unscheduled. Having tried, unsuccessfully, to bounce his guitar a few times, the following chords strummed by Henry confirmed that the tuning was now in terminal decline as opposed to merely critical.

> *Wild Thing!*
> *Christ, I could do with a pint!*
> *But I wanna know for sure …!*
> *Come on, girl, stiffen my resolve!*
> *WILD THING! …*

Michael's thoughts still rambled as the wood flew across the stage but Henry's feigned impressive collapse on the final, excruciatingly discordant coda forced him to break into a laugh. Michael could never imagine someone like Henry brooding about something the way he did.

… *The Queens can play the fool but I've got to impress, haven't I? Steve's great … and I suppose I have to say the same about Jeff, but it's my singing and playing that are going to be listened to … I've always wanted that but it makes my guts ache every time I'm faced with it … and now I've got to forget about … everything else …*

"Ouch, sugar! I'm going to have to get these splinters out of my fingers," said Henry as the two bands mingled on stage in the process of equipment shifting and refuse collection, "I'll probably never play again."

"Thank Christ for that!" said George.

"Ha! Ha! He doesn't really mean it you know," said Henry. "He always gets very moody after a gig. Hey, Dick, why is your drum kit still on the stage? It's supposed to be scattered over the floor by now?"

"We do need one sane member of this band," said Dick, just about raising a Yorkshire smile. "And it's about time a star like you bought me a drink."

"Mean bugger. Anyone got any tweezers?"

Jeff did his best not to laugh. Instead, he set about the intricate task of plugging one end of the curly lead into his guitar and the other into the amp.

... *He's always bloody ready before anyone else ... doesn't have anything to do does he though? ... I've got the mikes, Steve's got all that ironmongery ... one day Jeff's precious bloody amp will blow up, with any luck ... not tonight though ... please ... I didn't mean it ...*

There was an interval before they had to start. A friend who had come to be known as Disco Derek had already launched smoothly and suavely into his pile of 45s. Derek was only associated with good memories. Last year, he had managed to book Jimi Hendrix and Michael had gone with him and Steve to see their beloved Aretha at Hammersmith Odeon. His inter-record comments had acquired the honed edge of the professional DJ, but no one seemed to hold that against him. Not even the normal sight of the flower-patterned shirt and tight white trousers, and one or two girls leaning on his equipment, ever caused those who knew him to bristle with undue envy.

... *If Woods tried it on like that it would drive me bloody mad ... where the hell is he these days? ... why should I care? ... God, I hope he doesn't get a first – even in sociology! ... Derek sends himself up ... that's the difference ... or nobody takes him seriously – why do you take Woods so seriously? ... I hope Derek avoids playing Jumping Jack Flash ... we did give him a list ... still, most of our stuff is a bit obscure ... oh no, not this one ... Jethro Tull ... "Living In The Past" ... wish I'd seen them when they first played at Jimmy's ... everyone seemed to be astounded ... yet more lyrics to give the mental anguish a little boost ... Jethro's walking miles to drink your water ... sexual innuendo I suppose ... I need that like a hole in the head ... I'm always living in the past ... is there anywhere else to live? ... just now I don't see a bright future ...*

"The great Ian Anderson and Jethro Tull there, good people," Derek purred into his microphone. "But we're not living in the past are we? We just wanna 'Breakaway' to the future with the Beach Boys ..."

... *What is this? Some conspiracy? Did you have to play this, Derek? ... Why did I have to start listening to lyrics? ... Time is my destiny? ... what's that supposed to mean? ... One or two lines make sense I suppose ... everything's passing me by, and now every day is part of a long* drawn-out goodbye ... I suppose I have to view the world as new but I'm not sure I'll ever do what I want to do ... These Beach Boys seem to be reminding me of everything I've lost ... but why should I listen to them – again? ... What happened to those days when she wore colourful clothes and the sunlight played upon her hair – and they made you think you were on the brink of something momentous? ... those distant good vibrations mixed up with a one-time Sarah-kiss in the warm glow from a hallway lamp ... an etching from history ... the only acid imprint my brain'll ever get ... why couldn't they leave it at that? ... What's the point of thinking of her – or of anyone? ...

"What're we starting with then?" said Jeff making his words sound like an oral exam question and wrenching Michael from his reverie.

"I've actually written down a list for a change. 'White Room' first?"

"Can't we have something else for a change?"

... Trust you to bloody alter things, dear Jeff ...

"... What about 'Born To Be Wild'? Get 'em rocking a bit to start with – and follow it up with 'Can You See Me'."

"I don't mind," said Michael not giving nearly full rein to the apathy within him, "What do you think, Steve?"

"Yeah, might be the best thing tonight. 'White Room' is a bit sedate. We need a bit of impact."

Michael knew he was in the right place. At the moment he was not interested in impact or making them rock, but he had some vague gratitude for the circumstances that had forced him to the sports pavilion and away from the potential downward spiral of wondering what might have been. Those few minutes between the signal from Disco Derek that his last disc was spinning and the first chord did their usual job of blanking everything, even Caroline, out of his mind – except worries about amplifiers blowing, feedback or remembering words. Having the expectant eyes upon him was still not easy to accept as he placed the strap over his shoulder, cautiously turned the volume up and tentatively tested string and mike. Improvisation could now just about be handled but there was nothing to hide behind. It made him almost long for the days with the Rockin' Rs.

Derek gave Axis the benefit of a silken-tongued introduction which was followed by what Michael regarded as unnerving applause and an even worse silence as Steve realised he had to tighten yet another screw.

Michael was relieved to get his version of Steppenwolf's motor running and head out on the highway even though he could never be confident about where the motor would lead him. For several bars he could only look at the fingerboard, despite the simple chords, or squint into the microphone. Then gradually, out of the corner of his eye, he glanced at the mass of bodies moving in time to his strumming. Even then, any sense of power was dispelled by the sight of those who stood alone or in their small groups just looking on.

Born to be wi ... i ... ild!

He was now called on to make a show of wildness but, unlike Henry's, this was somehow meant to be convincing.

... Born to be wild? Do me a favour! ... I don't want to be wild, I don't need to be wild ... wild is what adolescents — am I still an adolescent? — are expected to be ... I don't want to do or be the expected — but I feel I keep slipping down into normality ... maybe I was born that way ... that sample of the top two per cent, so I heard, down there, jigging around to my guitar — they were never that wild were they? — maybe Sam Danger-field occasionally ... The centre of rebellious youth? A couple of sit-ins, a pot of paint over some American, the Chunder club — the association of those with the intention of regurgitating beer rather than savouring it — I ask you! ... and no one has ever offered me a drug ... not that I ever wanted one ... and now there's only a few useless, empty days left ...

As Axis advanced into their repertoire, Caroline began to seep back into Michael's consciousness. He tried to commiserate remotely with her, to force his imagination to share whatever predicament she might be in. As the last deliberate discord of "Venus in Furs" faded away, Michael was almost stunned to see even the static onlookers shouting and whistling their appreciation.

... Must be doing something right ... perhaps the beer's helping ...

He reached over to take another gulp from the glass resting on his amp.

... is this the third already? ... Henry bought me one – or was it two? Then Steve – and I definitely got this one. That makes four doesn't it. Better watch it. I might begin to think I sound better than I do ...

"You sounded a bit flat then, Mike." It was Jeff again.

"What do you mean? Flat musically – which is unlikely – or flat emotionally?" said Michael as they began the impromptu discussion about the next number.

"Well, it was, you know ..."

"No, I don't bloody know. They liked it. What more do you want? You're never satisfied ..."

"Hey, keep it down a bit, Mike," Steve was, as ever, the calming influence.

"Right, now it's going to be 'White Room'. Why? Because I bloody like it!"

In a few seconds Jeff backed away with what amounted to an embarrassed smile and Michael had to overcome the roughly ten-yearly self-imposed shock of losing his temper and wishing he hadn't. He retained just enough anger to bring the fire back into his voice and to count them in without warning with his volume turned way up. This time the chords rang out with just enough feedback to sustain them. It was all an accident but it sounded right – it sounded like it had never sounded before! Steve's drum rap was perfection and Jeff was obedience personified.

... I'm in that White Room again ... where the curtains are black ... apparently ... where ... what is that station? ...

The beat rolled on, loud and heavy. It wasn't good for dancing but Michael didn't want them to dance. He wanted for once to give them a blast, to deafen them; "White Room" allowed him, for a few minutes, to break down the sources of his anger and anguish. He still didn't know what the words meant but he sang them as if he did. It seemed to be yet another song of hopelessness, restlessness, nostalgia, goodbye – just up Michael's street – and he was performing it with unprecedented conviction.

... My God, that's Sarah! ...

With another couple of pints generously donated, he was now able to scan the assembly with what felt like professional aplomb and the sighting of Sarah came just in time for his "White Room" solo. A Burgess blues solo never sounded to him quite like that chap's from Jellyroll, but consolatory thoughts that Jellyroll only ever played blues were always brought to mind, together with belief that there was no physical obstacle that prevented his fingers moving like that. He used to be able to blame preoccupation with the nucleus or the life-cycle of stars. Now he wondered whether he had ever been preoccupied enough.

There were four or five chords to go. As usual he had no patterns in mind, no carefully planned route map. The chord sequence was simple, endlessly repeated; not like the complexity of jazz. He had bought the wah-wah peddle from a little shop in deepest Kemp Town. The proprietor looked honest enough and knew a lot about guitars – Michael had almost made friends with him.

As he clicked the machine on with his foot, fears of malfunction were pushed into the background. There were suddenly no drawbacks. There was nothing more to lose. His fingers wanted to anchor themselves in familiar territory but he bent the strings and pressed his foot up and down without co-ordination.

... You can do anything with this collection of valves and transistors and it still sounds OK ...

Playing safe for once had to be put aside. He moved up the fingerboard pulling out untried chords and discords, anything that before he would have called a mistake being swallowed up in an amalgam of frustration and passion. He was not going to be confined to his normal, conservative couple of minutes. This was going to be a proper solo – and Steve and Jeff, particularly Jeff, would wait and be led – just this once at least. For a few seconds they thought he had given up but it was only to allow his already sore finger tips to wind up the volume control once more before they came back to twist and turn about little-used frets. There was no time to look up or around.

... I can show off ... this is show-business, isn't it? ... For once I don't feel awkward about showing off ... it sounds so good ... better than ever ... but who is there really to show off to? ... just get angry with the lot of them ... that's the way to make a solo go! ... Who are you trying to fool? You can't stay angry for long – even with Jeff. Stick to showing off ... show off to Sarah ... she's long past being interested in you but just pretend she is ... like you've always done ...

Finally he was as satisfied as he could be that he had done enough, that his fingers had suffered enough and that enough of his sweat had been driven off into the steamy, half-light above the heads of the dancers and the onlookers who had swayed and tapped feet in time to him. He nodded in a concluding verse.

... it talks about a party and a hard crowd ... there was a party once ... and she was kind – but was it just for show? ... I'm singing about a sad time at that station again ... without knowing why ...

Listening to the words in his bedroom had and would again conjure up some mythical town, a town that looked a bit like the one he lived in but which was permeated by countless pockets, turnings, corners of sadness. Passing into and out of the station at night and seeing all those points of light stretching away up and down the Brighton hills had made him hope for or even dread many things in three years, but now the songs turned the lights into a host of people and places that he had been merely allowed to glimpse before they were extinguished for good.

The applause at the end of the number could never be as good as the Rockin' Rs' debut but it was still impressive. He could still fool himself into thoughts of being at the centre of this party, this mass of mostly apprehensive souls wondering "how they had done", with maybe one or two scattered around who were either triumphant or resigned because they knew full well how they had done. Michael was only too concerned about being in the centre. He might be making a show of fame now but couldn't shake off the notion that his rightful place was down there in the middle, lost in the mêlée where anonymity beckoned.

... All these stupid songs talk about extremes, don't they ... My life never goes to extremes ... I'm Mr Moderate, part of 1969's batch of temporary academics – a hard crowd at times, but not that often. And I suppose Sarah's kind ... still, just now I feel I deserve some kindness ...

"Well there, everyone, another great set from Axis and they'll be back in a little while but in the meantime do I have some sounds for you – yes indeed!" Disco Derek was once more in his element. For once Michael hoped his interlude would be short. He sat on the edge of the stage with Steve.

"Got any more solos like that up your sleeve before we finish, Mike?" said Steve.

"Shouldn't think so. Unless someone gets me annoyed again."

"Yeah ... I could tell Jeff was getting you wound up, so to speak."

"Well, you know, he's such a critical bugger at times. I never take criticism too easily but I don't normally say anything," said Michael in a rare revelation of his feelings. "Still, I mustn't be too hard on him since he's gone to get me another pint."

Michael looked across the room and was relieved to see that Sarah was still around. She was in mixed company but his mood no longer made him too anxious about how well mixed it was. His hormonal reserves had been depleted. He was not about to chase someone who was lost and had never been property.

"How do you think you did?" said Steve, bringing Michael's increasingly blurred focus back from the other side of the dance floor.

"Not bad I think – difficult to say. How about you?"

"Yeah, it was alright. I'm placing no bets but quite honestly, I feel I did enough for a two-one."

Steve had that streak of confidence that stopped Michael just short of being totally at one with him. Jim could easily get a two-one but he never convinced anyone that it was even a remote possibility – that was the difference. And as for Bill – there was a true unbeliever in his own abilities. He was better than a brother. There was never any question of competition. Soon, he would get back and tell Bill all about this. As for now though, Steve and he rambled on together about staying on, and Michael's usual quota of pints had been sufficiently surpassed to make it seem again something that would soon materialise. He longed even more to wedge himself into the physics library and never come out – not until his PhD was finished.

Another sighting of Sarah at the bar gave him an excuse for saying something to her under the guise of buying a return, animosity-reducing drink for the now subdued Jeff.

"Hello, Michael," she said as he manoeuvred himself as close as he dared.

"Sarah! You did come after all ... I mean, it's nice to see you." He was pleased that he had made it look as though she hadn't been targeted.

"I like your shirt."

"Oh ... thanks. I've had it nearly a couple of years now. Saw it in the window of a nice little shop in Western Road. Red silk, I thought, that's for me! I even wore it to tutorials. Must have been mad."

"It's good to be a little mad sometimes, isn't it? We are students after all ... or were. We've now thrown off the shackles. Might as well let our hair down." Her smile and voice still succeeded in making it sound as though this was something that should not be carried too far.

"I like your group ... you are quite loud though."

"Ah, yes, sorry ... I was a bit heavy on the jolly old volume control in the last one – got a bit carried away – not like me at all. I'll be back down to earth tomorrow."

"Yes, we'll all be that – and wondering what the future holds. What plans have you got?"

"Oh, you know, rock star, great physicist. I do hope I'm not going to be a great disappointment."

"Do shut up!" she said giving him a broad smile.

... You certainly have a nice way of saying that ...

"So you wouldn't want to stay on here in any way?" he said with an attempt at nonchalance.

"Oh, it's been so fantastic, so wonderful. But even if we ... I did, it wouldn't be the same. It's a bit of a dream world you must admit. Now if you became a professor, or even a humble lecturer, you'd suddenly have responsibilities that you haven't got now. Things would change. I'm quite happy to call it a day and get away. I might even go abroad – there must be something around for an art historian – say in Italy. There, is that unrealistic enough for you?"

"Sounds pretty good."

... sounds bloody awful! Don't go too far away! ... I mean, I know I'm not your boyfriend or anything but, you know, I'd like to say hello occasionally ...

"Look ... I think I'm going to have to get back on stage in a minute." He had been sinking into a state of timelessness, not helped by watching her kissable lips utter words for his ears alone, but a horrible reality now seized him.

... I might not see you again, at least not like this ... and you'll be gone before Axis are finished ...

"Let's exchange addresses," he blurted out, "You know, you could send me a postcard from Italy, occasionally."

"I was going to say the same."

Addresses were scribbled, smiles were exchanged and, with much less than enthusiasm, he headed once more towards the stage.

... everyone says they'll keep in touch ... no one ever does ... not even Sarah ... I've got an address ... but how can I really keep in touch? ... and I'm not one to chase ...

With yet another triumph of will over inclination he pulled the strap over his shoulder and prepared to set Jack Flash jumping again, at least as nimbly as he was able to at that moment. He could afford again to be a little wild but it didn't last. He didn't want to watch the dancers. He simply wanted to keep the chords going in the right order, to get through, without any more heroic solos. He even had to endure a couple of encores, and when he did at last look around, he saw, as he had thought, that there was no longer anyone to show off to.

June 1969 –

The Final Result

A number, repeated in quick succession, would have held no meaning for the bus conductor who took his all-the-way fare, or the workers whose hole in the road obstructed the progress of the bus and his distraught, directionless journey for a little while. Two-two would have meant nothing to pretty well all those already walking their slow holiday walk along the promenade. They might have been suffering mild disappointment at the cloud that had descended on them but the forecast was of a clear sky before the day was out. At that moment he could only see that the cloud that had covered him would never be lifted. To him a two-two, a lower-second, a might-as-well-have-been-rock-bottom second was a blight, a stigma – that's what a two-two was.

Nobody had yet tried, but nobody would have been able to make him see it all as being out of proportion. He was once, not that long ago, one of the slow-moving holiday-makers in a nearby town, happy to be released from the school tests, even though they used to be easy for him. He could only see himself as part of the insidious conspiracy since that time that had made him crave for more, much more, than a two-two – that had made him believe it was assured. It seemed that in a flash he was down and out; crying was dismissed as the most futile of gestures. The imagined infinity before him had now contracted to an infinitesimal fragment of past history. The town was growing smaller in the back window of the bus but there were no crumbs of comfort in leaving it, however transiently and impulsively. No roots had been put down, no great marks left. He had been confirmed as one of those just passing through. He would be easy to forget.

His translation of two-two was exclusion – the severing of the chord. Protection from that so-called outside world was still needed. He hadn't finished feeding; he hadn't finished growing into what he wanted to be, but his intellectual dyspepsia had been judged too severe, his growth too slow. No more could he settle into a corner of the physics library and be allowed to go on unravelling the equations or attempt to understand the shapes of the curves. He could not be a part of whatever went on behind the brightly lit windows in the evening. Two-two was no kind of beginning for him; it was the end of the line. Success and failure were not the imposters. He was the imposter – trying to pretend to those around him, and worst of all to himself, that he could become any sort of physicist, let alone a noteworthy one whose name would be noted down by future generations. He knew he would have to face, and bid farewell, to a disappointed, but probably politely encouraging, personal tutor.

The bus bumped and rumbled along the front, leaving behind the dwellings that tagged themselves on randomly to the outskirts, and soon the foreboding greyness of Roedean loomed up.

... *Huh! That's what I call a Greycliffe! Those girls up there aren't bothered yet by firsts, seconds or thirds. But – ha! – some of them will be – someday. They're being fitted out – the best, the brightest of them, that is – for their spells of dreaming among the dreaming spires or around some ancient quadrangle ... Some of them'll even be pretty – even with nice bodies ... It's not fair is it? You shouldn't have such a range of gifts bestowed on you ... What about Sarah then, come on, what about Sarah? She's been given this delicious face and slim figure and how do you know she won't get a first? Even two-one, two-two or three-something, I bet she won't fail ... that's not fair either. There must be loads of girls who aren't pretty and who can't even pass O-levels ... they must, at least secretly, think that life is not fair ... and what about the men? ... what about them? ... what about the men who only associate with fashion models and also get firsts? ... Thankfully, I've yet to meet or even hear about one ... Christ, I wonder what Woods got! ... How can you think about Woods at a time like this? ... I can't bear to think about anything ... I'm bloody finished. I'm bloody finished! What am I going to do? What am I going to bloody do? ...*

He alighted from the green-yellow bus at a stop that he thought was probably as far from habitation as any along the route. He crossed the road and found himself meandering only yards from the fenced-off cliff face. There could have been many worse places for committing the ultimate act – the one that terminated rather than started life. It would have finished things off rather neatly, he thought. But, of course, Michael Burgess was never destined for such an end. Even a two-two would not send him over the edge. At that moment he convinced himself that he would never persevere with anything ever again; but, of course, he was mistaken.

He doubled back from his journey to nowhere and looked up without enthusiasm at the town, more colourless and featureless than clouds could bestow. Somewhere up in the middle of it was an empty bench in a dull park. It might be regarded at some time in the distant future as a poignant memento but it had lost forever its treasured role as the secret, exciting vantage point – the place from where he could use wishful-thinking to transport him to a land that he had promised himself would not be far off. So many walks had been planned with Caroline down the roads that led from the park, those walks on which he could have surveyed it all not as a migrant but as one who could stay and be embraced by it and hold her hand.

It struck him that the easiest course was back to town, up to the station and onto the train and away – right away – right there and then. It was impossible. Roundhill Crescent was completely out of coffee and bread and Tony had mentioned a dangerous shortage of sausages and baked beans. When Michael had said he was going out for a while, he had thought of it in the spirit of Captain Oates, not as a chance to take a basket round Sainsbury's; but he couldn't let anyone down.

... Tony can afford to dwell on practicalities ... he actually got through. A scraped pass was the supreme climax for him ... and Jim ... I knew it would be a two-one ... he can get into research ... somewhere ... I could never be annoyed at Jim ... oh God, I don't want to go back to Roundhill Crescent ... but I have to ... to that first floor so-called lounge ... infamous for being the location where the news was broken to me by overjoyed Jim and Tony ... infamous for endless Leonard Cohen ... memorable for the Beatles Gently Weeping Guitar ... and infamous for being the place where today life, as I have come to know it, has ended! ...

Michael, of course, forced his way back to Roundhill Crescent and then, with an even heavier heart and soul, to Falmer House. He had to look at the list pinned to the notice board, in case, in some bizarre way, Tony had been mistaken. There was no mistake.

"I ... didn't really want to come and see you, but I thought I should." Michael sat on the edge of his chair in Jack Rodwell's office.

"I'm sorry you didn't get what you wanted ... and you won't want to hear this, but all I can say is don't give up. You mustn't see this as the end of the road. When I first met you, I saw someone with a real enthusiasm for physics. Even with that, life doesn't always go smoothly, particularly at your age."

"I could say that I got too distracted by other things, but perhaps I just ... you know, haven't got it."

"Michael, it's no use wondering about what you have or haven't got. Just plough on. I'm not suggesting it's going to be easy, but you must. And you must keep in touch. I want to know what happens to you."

"I will."

Until now, there had been few significant sorrows in his life, and he was not one for drowning them, but, with a glimmer of hopefulness from Jack, and a face as brave as he could muster, he sipped a pint of Newcastle Amber and circulated in a bar full of congratulations and commiserations. There were the expected firsts – for Con and Dave. There were many who were satisfied and even mystified at exceeding expectations, but few, like Michael, who admitted falling below them.

He bumped into Chris, of early Choral Society days, who, unlike Michael, was reasonably content with his two-two. His question to Michael about progress with the classical guitar received a hesitant reply about other things getting in the way. Michael's currently sombre mood was a little increased by the realisation of how he had neglected the instrument. At least now, he could lift it onto his knee again without distraction. He was about to seek solitude again when a bright voice arrested him.

"Hello, Michael. So tell me …" It was an ever-smiling Cathy.

… You look as sweet and cuddlesome as ever, dear Cathy … if anyone can cheer me up …

"Two-two I'm afraid. Not quite what I wanted. I've … got to review my options – to put it euphemistically."

"Oh, I'm sorry – really. But … you know, Michael … it's not going to be any sort of end even though you think so – not for someone like you. I always knew you had determination and … well, I know it's not easy, but … for what it's worth, I've got faith that you'll do well in … whatever comes along …"

"You always say the right things and I wish I had your confidence. But let's not dwell on me. Come on …"

"I got a two-one," she said, trying to subdue an apologetic tone. "I really can't believe it."

"That's marvellous. I'm honestly pleased for you. Come here." He put his arms round her and held her for as long as he thought appropriate. He would never have begrudged Cathy anything. "Do you know … what Sarah got."

"Mmm … two-one as well. She's very happy."

"I'm envious – but pleased for you both. Apart from this, how's life with you at the moment?"

"If I catch your drift, the answer is manless. I just decided to bury myself in books over the last year."

"Mm ... I tried to do the same. Either I just haven't got it, or I get distracted too easily ... No, no, I'm not going to make excuses – particularly to you."

"Well, we distracted each other for a while, and ... well, if you want to know, no one has distracted me in nearly the same way since. But ... I don't think either of us are ready for domestication, if I can put it that way."

"You're right. You're always right."

"If you believe that, you'll believe anything. Now, address please, young man. Ireland's not so far. And I can't see myself moving to California or anything just yet."

The addresses were exchanged and tucked safely away. She made her excuses but before leaving they planted a kiss on each other. Michael was revived by it being not a peck on the cheek but a wet two or three seconds on the lips.

"So when's the wedding?"

As on his first visit to the Students' Union Bar, his last was punctuated by a voice and presence that he hadn't succeeded in avoiding.

"I didn't know you two were still ... you know ..." said a cheerful sounding Woods.

"I'm not ... we're not ... it was a goodbye kiss."

"Some goodbye, eh? So, break it gently."

"Break what gently?" said Michael, jolted out of his daydream as he stood looking at the continuously hard-pressed barmen.

"What did you get for Christ sake, you dummy?"

"A two-two if you must know."

"What! Michael Burgess? Jesus, time's a great leveller so they say. We tied!"

"Yeah but I was doing physics," said Michael trying his best to be humorous.

'Oh God, you're not still trying that old joke. What happened?"

"Nothing ... happened. It just worked out that way."

"Huh! Well, I'm sorry if you fell short of expectations but this bucks me up no end."

"It would do ... Dick, why do you revel in other's misfortunes?"

"What me? I just say what I think too openly perhaps."

"Why don't you moderate yourself for once?"

"You know, you're improving, Mike?"

"Improving?"

"Yes, you're developing a less diplomatic tone. Look, let's celebrate or commiserate – whichever one applies."

"I'll get you one," said Michael without enthusiasm.

"No, come on, my shout."

"Look, you're always bloody shouting. I'll get you a drink. Alright?"

"My God, you are the boss – for a change."

"What do you mean, for a change?"

"Don't take offence. I didn't mean anything. It's just that you don't have a reputation for ordering people about."

"Oh yes, and what else don't I have a reputation for?"

"Yes, sir?" The barman eventually spotted a somewhat indifferent Michael.

"What are you having?" said Michael.

"What about a scotch?"

"Double scotch please."

"I'll drink with you more often I think," said Woods. "So, come on, Mike, I'm interested. The bloody brain box must've been distracted by something. Sex, drugs and rock 'n' roll come to mind ..."

"They would."

"And I've a sneaky suspicion I know which one it was."

"Why are you so interested – as you claim?" said Michael feeling a tension building within him unlike anything he had ever experienced.

"I am a sociologist, with a psychology option, after all – now a qualified one, sort of – and tying with Michael Burgess. Would you believe it?"

"You're not interested in my psychology – you're just pleased to see me cut down to size ... Just as you were overjoyed to take Sarah off my hands ..."

"Ah-ha! I wondered when she would come up. Don't tell me you're still hankering after that ..."

"That? You mean that beautiful woman – girl. Look, I'd rather go outside and talk about this ..."

"Mike, what is this?" Woods looked around him with a puzzled smile, "You're not going to hit me or anything are you?"

"Don't tempt me."

"Well, I'll try anything once – you know me."

Michael breathed what passed for a sigh of relief as they sat on the grass, bathed in what seemed like continual sunshine.

"I wanted to get out of there. We were beginning to draw an audience," said Michael.

"You mean *you* were. Michael Burgess, I know you hate my guts, to use a quaint expression, but come on, we've got so much in common – same school, same university, same degree – although yours was in an inferior subject – and Good God, we've even been seen with the same women."

"'Been seen with' sounds a bit tame from you."

"Please tell me you suffered severe obstruction too."

"What?"

"You didn't get it, dummy. And being the honest chap that I am, I can announce that I didn't either. Don't spill the beans – wouldn't do my reputation any good. It was like trying to get into the proverbial bloody Fort Knox wasn't it? – with both of them it has to be said. Wasn't it ... Mike?"

Michael tried his best to conceal his relief at this confession. "Yeah ... same for me," he lied.

"Even though that last kiss looked a bit juicy? Oh, what the fuck. It's all academic now, so they say."

Michael could never reveal the truth about Cathy. "I think you probably tried harder than I did. I was always more withdrawn than you, Dick."

"Wish I'd had the chance to withdraw, if you see what I mean. Listen, you know me enough to realise I'm not going to lie to you. You always seem to be so clean and pure and untouched and studying physics and things. D'you know, years back at school I even stooped to really loathing you – can you imagine? A sensible chap like me? My dad, before he went off with his girlfriend, the old bastard, used to compare me with you – rather unfavourably of course. I couldn't give a toss now what degree you got, to be honest, but failing at something, if you call this failure, will do you the world of good. Most of us are used to it."

"What's this, practical psychology? Anyway, I haven't been a roaring success ... er ... socially shall we say."

"Or shall we say sexually – just to be devilish? You know, even though I kept a stiff upper lip I couldn't believe my bloody eyes when I met you in Sarah's and Cathy's room that time. I thought: It can't be Burgess! It cannot be Burgess!! With his success rate he'll be shagging her before long. Course I couldn't let on how competitive I felt about it ... I'm not the bastard you think I am, Mike. Even I have feelings but maybe I'm better at handling the knocks that our short lives have dished out – I don't know. I don't make excuses for myself but it affects you when your mum gets knocked about by a so-called father. I'll bet yours didn't do that."

"Most trustworthy man on the planet. I've been lucky."

"You have, so be pleased. And talking about pleasure ..."

"Here we go ..."

"Now listen, don't tell me that the great Burgess isn't excited by the concept of frequent union. If our Sarah had offered it to you every night don't tell me you wouldn't have taken it. Just imagine!"

"Don't worry – even I've imagined ... maybe ..."

"Maybe my arse, you would've. And if that'd been the case, two-two nothing, you might not even have got to the bloody exams! Stuff all this psychology and physics, how successful we are with the opposite sex – and I do mean in the broad sense for a change – is going to make or break us. You'd better believe it. And I do want someone who means something to me – even nasty old Dick Woods. Mind you, I think several practice runs first is a damn good idea."

"I'm actually listening to you for once."

"I'm beginning to like you. And your glass looks empty. I'll get you another."

Parting on more than good terms with Richard Woods was a strange phenomenon for Michael. Three or four pints assisted this rapprochement and they agreed to meet and continue drinking when back in Windsor. He could no longer face the bar and turned to walk, in no specific direction, across Stanmer Park. It was all over. Those days that had stretched out endlessly and hopefully at the start were over. There was no longer a place for him here in a mini-world that had once or twice come close to paradise. Some unknown teenager would take that place next year and go through her or his range of anguish, exhilaration, despair and triumph. He could not despair. He must not despair. He did not want to admit this but the fresh smell of grass and the gentle tree-covered slopes and the stunning blue of the sky sowed some small seeds of optimism in him.

Then, he stopped dead in his tracks. Thirty yards away there was a bench by two trees. On the bench sat a girl with blonde, back-combed hair, wearing jeans and a leather waistcoat. She appeared to be looking into the distance and did not notice him approach.

"Er ... hello ..." he ventured.

She turned in surprise at the sound of his voice. His breath was taken by the state in which he saw her – the stony face, the arm in a sling and the bruise around her eye.

"Caro ... what on earth has happened to you?"

She shook her head and got up to leave. He knew that this was his last chance to talk. He had no other considerations that needed his attention and for once he was adamant, as well as desperate.

"Please ... Caroline ... don't go. I ... don't know you ... perhaps never will, nor you me, but for some strange reason I care about you and what happens to you. Please tell me. Whatever you say will stay only with me."

He held his breath while she stood still and speechless. His lungs filled once more with blessed relief as she sat down again, and he joined her.

"I heard about ... Alan Mercer ..."

"How do you know him? ... Oh, it doesn't matter ..." She shook her head again.

There was a long pause before she continued. "Alan Mercer is my brother."

"What?"

"Yes, my brother. He's ten years older than me. He was at Oxford but was very keen to get a job here. I wanted to be near him and I was so fortunate to get a place. You're wondering about our names? He has a different surname because our father died and my mother re-married. I kept the name of my step-father. God, how I hate that name!"

Michael could only remain silent.

"Alan is a wonderful brother. I treasure his protection and guidance."

"But ..."

"But my step-father is a very unpleasant man, and always was. Would you believe his name is Rupert. A friendly cartoon bear in my childhood. What a misnomer! My poor mother was taken in by him – by the usual superficial charm of his type. She was so vulnerable when our father died. At first it seemed that my step-father was providing what she wanted – companionship and someone to lean on. But as time wore on his deep desire to control everything in her life slowly came to the surface. For years she suffered this ..."

She stopped and took a few breaths to regain her composure.

"... but at last when she began to resist he started to become violent. I never saw anything, and my mother tried to hide it, but I knew it was going on."

"Didn't she ... go to the police, or something?"

"Oh, if only ... I was too young at the time to know how to help. And Alan had gone off to university. One day Mum got me to pack a suitcase and we left and stayed with my aunt for a while. You don't need to know the details, but at last Mum succeeded in getting a divorce. Alan helped all he could but it wasn't easy for him, being at a distance and trying to do a research degree."

"But ... you've been hurt ... I mean physically."

She managed a short, ironic laugh and didn't speak for a while.

"Recently, Rupert has been contacting my mother – only by letter, but with a semblance of apology. What a bastard! So I did something very foolish. I knew where he lived and went to tell him to leave my mother alone. I used words I would never think of using normally. Of course, being Rupert, the only responses he came up with were anger and violence. He grabbed my arm and hit me round the face. I stopped him by kicking his shin – well-aimed I might say ..."

She managed to smile.

"And he was incapacitated long enough for me to leave."

"So ... what about Alan?"

"You can imagine what his reaction was when he saw me. The confrontation was swift, believe me. He threatened Rupert with the police. Alan would never fight anyone but, apparently, a little more than altercation took place and ... Rupert was pushed to the floor and ... hit his head. I just know it was an accident ... he's in intensive care. Alan called ambulance and police and, well ... they had to arrest him I suppose. Oh God, I don't know what's going to happen, Michael ..."

"But surely ... he won't ..."

"Go to prison? Who can say?"

"When the full story comes out surely people will realise ... and they've got to see what happened to you."

"You're saying the right things, but life doesn't always follow the right path."

"What about your exams?"

"Oh, I'm a second year, Michael. Didn't you realise? Next I'm off to France for a year's study if I can face it."

"You must – if you don't mind me saying."

"You're right, of course."

"You ... have a boyfriend ..."

"I do. I'm very fond ... perhaps we're in love. He's not going to France so he's depressed about that ... but we will be in touch a lot."

"Caroline, I can only say that I sincerely hope justice prevails. You and your brother deserve it. Is it ... oh should I say this? ... is it possible, sometime, in the future, whenever, to write to me and tell me how things turned out for you? I will never try to contact you, but maybe ... ?"

"Write down your address, Michael."

In one sense, Michael had found Caroline and discovered something about her, but in another he knew she was lost to him. The three girls he had kissed were also lost, each leaving him with different emotions – in their turn with quiet resignation, heart-rending vexation and only slightly imperfect fulfilment. His lips never touched Caroline's nor did his arms enfold her, and he wanted to be sad, but he knew that it would only be a selfish sadness. They walked off in different directions, both looking back at the same time for a last brief smile. He had gained experience at carrying on and he would continue to do so. It was not going to be easy.

Catching the bus was a bad idea. After all, he had so much time. He turned homeward across the park. The panorama of overt pastoral perfection, dazzling in the mid-afternoon heat, which had put new strength into him, now became a little blurred. It did provide him with an open space in which he could sing a few lines of blues with gusto, but the song gradually faded in his throat.

July 1969 –

Windsor, Reflections and Bill

Nothing would ever be like this time. Nothing had been like this before, or would be after. It was gone. Those thousand days had been reduced to none. This little period, devoid of responsibility for anything or anyone else, was over. The duty he owed to himself had sometimes descended into irresponsibility, but he had never hurt anyone.

His view of time was a conventional, continuous sequence of unrepeatable cause and effect. He had read that some physicists pictured time as an infinite matrix of pigeon holes that, in some unexplained way, might be occupied back and forth at will. Who's "will" this might be was anyone's guess. Would he go back to any of these, if offered the chance by some supernatural being? Would he go back to try to alter his destiny? He had no counter-explanation, but he could only think of such time-wandering as nonsense, and changing others' minds to suit his purposes as against his nature, and ultimately futile. He was sure he had had no influence on the young men he had met, not that he wanted any. They might have, temporarily, been moved to tap their feet, or even dance, to the sound of his guitar, but he could not remember any words of wisdom that changed their minds. The same went for the young ladies, except that one or two might have been amused by his jokes and mild banter; and one had occasionally revealed more than her dance steps after she had seen him up on that stage. No – if he went back, he would still not be able to change anyone.

In the absence of any known route to a past pigeon-hole, Michael was compelled to go only in one direction. The employment he had been offered had come about under circumstances that could deservedly be called fortuitous. He was about to throw the Sunday paper in the bin when his mother asked to look at it again. She spotted a job for a physicist in medical research, with the supposed added attraction of possible study for a higher degree. Reluctantly, he attended an interview and, within a week and with enormous surprise, was given the job. He should have been grateful but remained reluctant. He still craved a position in life where he could delve, undisturbed, into the mysteries of the atom or subatomic particles, even if paid a pittance.

The inevitable consequence of his failure to secure the best of qualifications was imminent entry to a new life called work. As a schoolboy, people would say that he worked hard, but he never applied such a term to himself. Students would ask him if he was working in the library, and he would say yes, but never regarded trying to understand the mechanics of the universe, whether successful or not, whether useful to anyone or not, as work. He didn't want to work – he still wanted to study. He was worried that this might only be partially possible in his new occupation.

Nevertheless, he admitted that there was more to life than work or study. In the past, there had been holidays and playing football and tennis, and running in the park or along the seafront, and talking endlessly with Bill. In recent history, his attention had been diverted by the suddenly more regular encounter with females. He had previously resisted being swept up in collective obsessions, particularly the juvenile attitude of boys towards the girls. Then, resistance very quickly subsided and he found himself constantly looking at faces and bodies that fascinated him. Attempts to discover more about those who sported these superficial charms had given him pleasure and pain. He was told that it would be so, but he discovered that this was not in equal measure. At this moment, pain seemed to have won out. He questioned whether pain was the appropriate word; there had been acute mental pains, but now they had subsided into a rather dull ache when he allowed himself to think back. However his feelings could be described, he was left with a mood of resignation to a life where association with girls, now young women, had to be envisaged as a road strewn with unexpected pot-holes rather than a smooth path of mutual pleasure and respect. His largely uncomplicated life as a schoolboy could not last and the vagaries of involvement with the opposite sex had been made plain, with precious time spent in futile longing, and the inability to make sense of something uncontrollable. Some said that an all-boys school was unnatural, but, in the alternative, he could only see a life of greatly increased embarrassment and even less control.

Like most of his own age, if pressed, he would have had to admit to a large measure of self-absorption. Now it was all over, and he could contemplate with some honesty, he realised that he had made little attempt to understand the feelings and motivation of those around him. The boys had sometimes been friendly and amusing but often an irritation. Three years in Brighton had produced no one who came close to Bill. He had tried to please, in his modest way, the girls within whose circle he had found himself; but save perhaps for Cathy, he had never really discovered a lot about them. Cathy could have been his female Bill, but mutual sexual desires might have taken hold and made the relationship something different. As they had agreed, they were nowhere near marriage, to each other or anyone else. Marrying had, for Michael, always been what older people did. A boy, some two years older from his school, had preceded him at Sussex. In a euphemism of the time, he had got a fellow student "into trouble" and they had married. Michael once saw them with pushchair, and nodded hello, and thought how thankful he was not to be, and had no vision of ever being, in their position.

His teenage years had been spent in an environment of friends and family who appeared to live lives free of endemic conflict. With entrance to university, he carried with him the notion that the wider world was similar. There were students he found abrasive, but they were few and far between. It was only in the last few months that it had been made plain to him that some lives were blighted by more than the odd argument. The rapprochement with Richard Woods had been aided by the revelation of a father who cared little for either him or his mother. Whatever love was, this was not, and never had been, love, as far as he could see. Caroline, perhaps in a more dramatic way, had had to endure schooldays tainted by domestic fear when there should have been refuge and calm. He had to conclude, reluctantly, that these were not just two extreme situations that were rarely experienced. He knew that a world was gradually being revealed to him, where more men than he wished to contemplate were not humane, had no concept of empathy and only wanted to control. This view only served to reinforce the idea, that he and Bill shared, of a malign species. He wondered if it had always been thus; did hunter-gatherer men resort to domestic abuse? The inevitable judgement of his, admittedly unscientific, musings was that the growth of this alleged wonderful human brain had been accompanied by ever greater contamination and distortion. If man was made in the image of God then, he thought, God help him.

Michael was back home once more and in one of his favourite locations – the kitchen of the terraced house that Bill shared with his dour Scottish uncle. With Bill he was always hopeful that the deepest of anxiety or dejection could be shared, if not resolved. In previous days he had tried to make plain to his parents the desolation that kept creeping back at not gaining his first. This was not a situation they had ever had to face. Michael's schooldays had been replete with continuous, at times towering, achievements, but he had to confess that these had occurred in a small, enclosed world. He had a suspicion that they could never last when he ventured further. Mother and father, each in their own ways, had attempted to reignite the notion that, eventually, all would be well and that it was of no use to dwell on one supposed failure. He wanted to dismiss their logic but inwardly had to accept it. Parents had never wavered in their faith in Michael and in their constant devotion, but he had always stopped short of revealing emotions to them. He seemed to want to show them calm self-control, despite infrequent adolescent lapses, and that he was untouched by the trivial vagaries of existence or, perish the thought, sexual desires. With Bill, and with time, he had been able to expose these and other impulses.

"Congratulations, Michael my lad! So you're a Bachelor of Science. Your Mum and Dad told me." Bill, as always, meant what he said and was overtly happy about saying it. Michael had never understood such excitement at someone else's triumphs, however meagre.

"Yeah ... I was going to try and hide it for as long as I could – the grade that is."

"Miserable bugger. Only you could turn your nose up at a thing like this. Your parents did say you were disappointed. I hope you didn't make yourself out to be too cut up about it. They take it very personally. I know them."

"OK ... I should have been more grateful ... It's just that I had something in mind and it didn't happen. In fact, I had quite a few things in mind and none of them happened."

"What d'you mean none of them happened? What the hell do you want?" Bill was still smiling. "You've been swanning around at the seaside for three years, mingling with beautiful, intelligent women – I saw one of them once – and you've made a record, and you've got a degree in physics or whatever it was – and you're still miserable!"

"With respect, as they say, you're seeing things as an outsider. For a start the girls have gone for good ..."

"There'll be others ..."

"... and there weren't that many. I should have followed my boyhood inclinations and ignored them ..."

"Don't give me that..."

"... and the record was only a demo. The whole thing was engineered, and not very well, by wide boys as far as I could see. It'll never get into the shops."

"Did the Beatles first efforts ever get into a shop?"

"I'm not worried about them. I don't base my life on any sort of idol. I don't think I ever have. Maybe I used to think that, with a good wind behind me, I might emulate Einstein, but the world's not like that. I used to create my own little environment from which all roads led to supremacy. Being supreme in something does happen to some, but it's supremely unlikely ... and won't just come from hard work and perseverance ... and dreaming about it will not make it happen either. It's literally an illusion. Maybe most people are resigned to second or third best, or they just don't care, but I'm finding it hard."

"Why do you think about supremacy? I mean, your professors or whatever at university are very good at their subjects but are they supreme? They might be well-known in their own circle but few of us will ever hear of them or care about them."

"OK let's shelve supremacy, but it's being in that circle that I aimed at. Now I'm excluded from the club, if you like, that I wanted to join. This is my version of failing the 11-plus. I'm out. I'm not good enough. I've been told, metaphorically, that I really ought to go and do something else, something that suits my slightly lower intellect."

"But nobody's saying you can't study physics or whatever you want to study."

"It's not something you can do in isolation, Bill. Gone are the days when pioneers worked alone in freezing attics. You've got to be accepted into the system. Otherwise you're nobody. That's just the way things are. As far as nuclear physics is concerned, I'm nobody. At best I'll be a damn technician with a clip-board filling in the little scientific details. No thanks! It's best that I drop all thoughts of carrying on with science. I'm a non-starter. In these so-called privileged sixties, I can't blame money or class. I had a friend at Brighton – Dave Parker. His dad's a bricklayer. Dave got a bloody first-class degree in physics and there weren't many of them. He completely crushed most of the public-school lot. No, after three years of banging away, science has finally given me up as a lost cause. You can aim for a so-called good job, a three-piece suite, central heating and a TV but if you shoot for physics research be prepared for disappointment ... Sorry, Bill. You're unfortunately the only one who would listen to me moaning about myself."

"Can I say something you might not want to hear?"

"Probably not ... but go on."

"These guys that we hear about – you know, Einstein and Segovia, and Charles Atlas – I used to want to emulate him and not be the skinny weakling I've always been. I reckon they were all obsessed, or driven or however you want to describe it. I'll bet they spent every waking minute thinking, or playing the guitar or weight training. Have you ever been like that, Mike?"

"I've tried my best ..."

"That's not good enough. You're not obsessive enough. Your desires might smoulder but they don't ignite. I mean would you lie on your back for days without eating to paint the Sistine Chapel ceiling? Did you blot everything else out of your mind and just devour physics books?"

"Look I'm enthusiastic, not bloody mad. Nobody can do that."

"Some can and do. Your mate Dave – what about him? Did he immerse himself?"

"Well ... maybe. He never missed lectures – ever. And he had one steady girlfriend as far as I could see."

"There you go then. Perhaps somehow he blotted most things out and just concentrated."

"Oh God, Bill ... I did try."

"I know you did, but look, from an ignorant outsider's viewpoint, you lived a pretty good life down in Brighton. You were distracted by music and girls – but who isn't? And you didn't bloody fail your exams anyway. You might convince yourself but you're not convincing me. You're not at the end of any road, however much you like to think you are. Anyway, try and be like me – be grateful for what you've got and leave it at that. It's a lot less painful."

"Why does everyone I talk to have such common sense? And why is it something I just don't want to accept? I don't want to be average – in statistical terms to be close to the centre of the normal distribution. I'm not an outlier. I'm not a shooting star. And all the logic in the world will not stop it nagging at me."

"Coffee?"

"Does it help insuperable problems?"

"Do you have any? Can we change the subject? Whatever you think you've lost, we've still got the music eh, Mike? Nothing can take that away. And even though you're not a great recording star ... yet, you must've had some good times with your band."

"Like everything else it was a struggle sometimes, but the first night is still an amazing memory. I'm sure you could get addicted to applause. Even I got enough to make me tipsy. Maybe I'll start a group up in time. You're right, we've still got the music. Give me a hit song over the last ten years and I'll come up with a place, a person, a picture to complement. All very neat. It amazes me what music does. You can try to think back to a time or place and it's sort of grey and indistinct, but just listen to a record that was being played at the time and it all jumps out in full colour and sound and feeling. Weird ... Bernard Cribbins' 'Hole In The Ground' always makes me realise how much in love, I use the term loosely of course as always, I was with Helen Shapiro for a time. At the moment though I'd rather not be nostalgic – leave that for when I'm old. I was always told it was unhealthy to be too nostalgic."

"Who said that, Mike? Keeps me going – the sounds of the 60s. At least the 70s might herald the end of flower power. We have that to hope for at least. I'm always suspicious of these mass rebellions, telling us that we're on the verge of some new era. I don't think sticking flowers in my hair or soaking up LSD is going to help anyone much, especially me."

"I'm with you there, Bill. Now they're telling us all we need is love ... oh my God – and free love at that. Just sounds like an excuse for shagging anyone who's willing."

"Michael, language! You don't normally talk like this."

"My standards appear to be slipping. Anyway ... forgetting about that, Brighton's got so many musical high spots. Seeing Fairport Convention in a side room at a dance, before anyone knew who they were; standing a couple of feet away from John Lee Hooker singing 'Groundhog Blues' in a pub. What a voice! Jumping around to Peter Green and that slide guitar at the King and Queen. Being blasted away by Jimi Hendrix. I suppose it was interesting to see him, but I've never aspired to any heights of adulation. 'Purple Haze' did sound just like the record – but why shouldn't it have done? I mean it would be idiotic to be amazed that a Berlin Philharmonic concert sounded just like the record."

"Yeah but Mike, people like Hendrix are trying to improvise. His concerts would be a bit sterile if he just stuck note-for-note to what he recorded."

"You're right. Maybe I'm not a fan of improvisation. That's why I've never got along with jazz. I like to hear the notes, the pauses, the inflections that I've got used to. Live concerts just don't do it for me. I like to sit in a low-lit room and listen to a disc. I don't need to see someone jumping around on a stage or, God forbid, setting light to his guitar. Sitting in that cold, uninviting basement flat in Hove listening to 'Fixin' a Hole' sticks in my mind ... Sergeant Pepper, you know? I've no idea what the words mean but I've been known to cry along with it. It didn't 'stop my mind from wandering' though – and wondering where I was going wrong."

"You didn't go wrong, Mike, for God's sake. What about something loud – 'Gimme Some Lovin' – what does that remind you of?"

"Hobbling down a deserted Brighton promenade after seeing Spencer Davis. I had a verruca – bloody painful it was ..."

"Romantic eh?"

"... and talking to a girl in a coffee bar ..."

"*A* girl?"

"She was called Sarah ... I did take her out three times. We went to Brighton Theatre once; and we chatted and laughed, and I kissed her again on her doorstep, and then that was ... it, again. Then there was that time when you gave me tickets for a ballet at Covent Garden – and you even lent me your suit for God's sake!"

"Yeah I remember."

"I didn't know much about him, but there was this guy Christopher Gable and it was his last performance. Sarah wanted to wait outside the stage door to catch a glimpse – nearly missed the last train home, but it was worth it to please her ... Waterloo Sunset ... why do I think of that? We did part that evening at Waterloo Station ... We didn't, of course, meet at Waterloo every Friday night as the song says, but the music pulls that particular meeting ... or parting ... back ... like 'Good Vibrations' ... I can't get it out of my head ... a red glow from her hallway on a misty night – not that sort of red glow mind ... taking her out to see Eric Clapton ... and she letting me kiss her ... God though, what is it about a song like that? The words didn't mean much to me and they still don't. But it's just the whole sound – like 'Purple Haze' or Cream's 'Politician' with that marvellous guitar duet. How can a few bars of them reach right down into me, Bill, and make me want to cry or even scream for some indefinable reason? It seems to be more than just thinking back to a girl I knew. Perhaps even for us it's a reminder that time is passing ... that we're being given another little glimpse of something that we'll never experience again no matter how vivid our memories are ... that we'll never really recapture how we felt when we first heard the music or first kissed the girl ... that even *we* are getting older."

"Oh God, I think I've reached philosophical saturation – I know what you mean though – even me. What about playing a few things and just pretending we're eighteen again?"

"'Reach Out, I'll Be There'. That's another of the stomach churning ones. Have you got that?"

"No, it never grabbed me really."

"Am I really hearing this, Bill? It was central to the first weeks in Brighton for me."

"Thank God we don't agree on everything, Mike."

"Three years back this was just an uncomplicated song of total fantasy ... now the damn thing begins to mean something! ... I really can't find that peace of mind."

"Oh, Mike, give me strength!"

"What about 'You Keep Running Away'? ... one of the greatest Four Tops records – and I don't often say things like that."

"Now there you're talking. I'll give it a spin, even though we're in danger of a nostalgia overdose."

They waited in tense expectation before the record started.

You keep runnin' away

... I never did any begging for Sarah to stay ... and a heart full of sorrow is surely putting it a bit strongly ... Sarah would never hurt anyone deliberately ... but she did seem to keep running away ...

February 1970 –

Ealing and Epilogue

The hallway in Eaton Rise, Ealing was as cold as ice on that Tuesday morning in February despite the sun glaring dazzlingly through the frosted glass of the front door. He never expected post on his way down from the attic room that he was now almost pleased to call home. He shared with two young models who wore nothing but unchanging smiles for him on the life-size posters. A few weeks before, he had found a re-directed letter on the mat from a girl who told him that all charges against her brother had been dropped. She had thanked him for his support, although he couldn't think of any he had given. He knew that his relief was as nothing in comparison with Caroline's. There was no address for any reply, which he had to admit was right.

On this particular day, though, the receipt of a postcard, adorned by an old Master and from an old friend, would have been a pleasant enough surprise for anyone. The signature on the reverse, however, made him stop and study the card in a manner of which Sherlock Holmes would have been proud.

> Dear Michael, I'm having a party to "warm" the new flat that I have to share with my dreadful sister (joke!). I've managed to get a few friends from Sussex to come. Hope you can make it. By the way, I now have an actual job with something called the Medici Society. Hence the postcard.
> Sarah.

He rapidly circulated through disbelief, neck-tightening excitement, thoughts of a Woods hoax, thoughts of Fort Knox and finally settled on cautious pessimism.

... Sarah? Here in London? ... employed in fine arts ... that's her ... Do I want to see her again? ... Dick Woods' advice was to forget and move on ... she's bound to have a new fan club of annoyingly handsome bores and boors ... I couldn't stand it ... I can't go ... Leave it at Good Vibrations ... Why is she inviting me? ... she'll have fallen in love with someone else – else? ... what do you mean else? ... but she is a good Catholic girl ... I can't go ... I've ... made my mind up ...

Michael looked up nervously at the Georgian mansions around Manchester Square, not far from Selfridges, and located the front door.

... honestly ... how does she do it? ... nowhere she has ever lived has been sub-standard ... I thought Brunswick Square in Brighton was good ... but this! ... parents' money has helped I suppose ...

He breathed deeply and pushed the bell marked Rimington, starting as usual at its aggressive tone. An unfamiliar, tinny voice came from the small speaker by the bell. He gave his name hesitantly and, after a pause, a buzzer signalled permission to push open the door. With unusually rapid breathing, given his ever more regular cross-country running, he climbed the gloomy stairs to the second floor and approached the half-opened door behind which were sounds of an unmistakable party. He stopped dead as the girl opened the door wide and looked out from the half-light.

"Hello, Michael, glad you could come."

"Hello."

... Sarah! ... That voice! ... but something's different ... you've put on weight ... a bit ... don't you put on weight when you're pregnant? ...

"Oh, Michael, is my sister keeping you standing out there in the cold. Let him in, Vicky, for goodness' sake." The even more familiar voice of the real Sarah, who showed no outward signs of pregnancy, came from behind her sister.

"Oh ... thanks. I was rather struck by your similarity," he said.

"Yes, but she always keeps going on about how much younger she is," said Sarah, putting her tongue out at her sister in, for Michael, the most uncharacteristically delightful way.

He shook hands with Vicky and planted a regulation kiss on Sarah's cheek.

... That's your lot, Mike ... It's more than you deserve ... don't get carried away ... If you behave yourself, there might be another when you leave ...

Having thrown his coat on the enormous pile that burdened someone's bed and with drink in hand he drifted, with renewed tension, into the large, comfortably full lounge. Yet more comfort arrived when his comprehensive scan of the gathering failed to detect, as yet, a specific male putting an arm round a specific waist.

... The night is young though ... some of them are bound to get warmed up before too long...

"So what are you doing now?" said the girl that Michael vaguely recognised from his to-ings and fro-ings across the Great Court at Sussex.

"I've got a job in medical research – really wanted to do pure physics but ... er, it was difficult to get a grant," replied Michael with as much gloss as he dared put on his failure.

"How fascinating," she said, actually sounding fascinated, "Sounds much more exciting than what I'm doing. I did sociology and ended up in a merchant bank."

"Oh sociology? You knew Dick Woods then?"

"Oh yes, I knew young Dick alright – outspoken, but a bit of a laugh really."

... Woods? ... a laugh? ... oh well, perhaps at least I can laugh with the old sod now ...

"We were at school together."

"Really? They weren't all like him at your school were they?" she said looking at him intently.

"No, he was a one off ... A bit more lucrative than medical research though – merchant banking that is," suggested Michael. "And research isn't all wonderful discoveries you know. Ninety-nine per cent perspiration and one per cent inspiration, or probably point one per cent in my case."

"I'm sure you're exaggerating,"

Under normal circumstances, whatever they were, he would have been more than happy to be told by a nice girl that his job was exciting and that he wasn't exaggerating, but at that moment, he was finding it difficult to concentrate. He tried as hard as he could to make his glances towards Sarah, and the continued look-out for her fans, as surreptitious as conditions would allow. He was not surprised when, as time wore on, what appeared to be an increasing number of young men seemed to want to engage her in facile chatter, if not in marriage.

... Where have they all come from? ... I never saw any of them in Brighton ... all good Catholic boys I suppose ...

"Hello. I'm sorry I haven't got round to you until now, but I've heard all about you." Vicky confronted Michael as he stood in the kitchen topping himself up with another beer.

... Heard all about me? ...

"All good I hope?"

"That would be telling ..."

Despite looks, Vicky was very different from her sister. She looked as though she would come forward where Sarah would retire, or tell rude jokes where Sarah would only be able to tell clean ones.

"... no, I don't want to embarrass you. But I remember you were the first boy to take Sarah out at Sussex. She was quite excited – don't tell her I told you."

"Oh, that was a long time ago," said Michael, thinking he sounded like a retired general talking about some distant military campaign.

That distance increased immeasurably when Michael caught sight of Sarah's waist being held very firmly and of her planting a prolonged kiss on the waist-holder. Michael wished he could have described the young man as ugly but that would have been uncharitable and wide of the mark. He was annoyingly good-looking. Then, there came the announcement to the gathering that the entwined couple were engaged to be married.

... Oh, Michael ... you can't say this isn't typical of the way things go ... one or two girls come along ... and then they go ... they always go ... I can't claim to have been rejected ... anyway, feeling rejected is pathetic ... it's self-pitying ... and, Michael, that will never do ... so ... kind, pretty, demure, virginal Sarah's going to be a wife ... she'll be the proverbial blushing, stunning bride ... she's going to lose her ... you know ... she's going to be a woman, as it were ... perhaps already is ... on the current schedule probably way before I become a man, as it were ... who would have thought it? ... I know this thought is graceless and unworthy of me but ... he's going to see her with nothing on ... perhaps already has ... no, she's a good Catholic girl! ... oh dear, so was Cathy ... but one day they will have passionate ... you know, sex ... after all, Michael, she is an adult ... she is allowed to ... I know ... I know! ... but I mustn't think about it ... I can't think about it ... Michael doesn't get jealous does he? ... does he? ... and he'll keep her only unto him as long as they live ... I just can't think that far ... I'm still a lad, a kid, a boy aren't I? ... I'd like to walk hand-in-hand with her down a leafy lane ... and go to see Eric Clapton together again ... and I suppose eventually have that naked cuddle ... but then? ...

The congratulations of the party-goers was effusive. He smiled at the couple, shook a hand and planted the proverbial cheek-kiss and, having bid farewell to half-known ex-students, strode, with as much determination as his melancholy would allow, out into the freshness of the elegant Square.

Sarah was about to, or already had, descended from the pedestal that Michael's youthful idealism had created. His reason and experience told him that she had never viewed herself as being on such a superior plane – that she was a girl with expected desires, normal pleasures and pains, and one whose kindness, although seemingly constant, was probably sometimes marred by anger, irritation or antipathy. He always saw himself as discarding fantasy and clinging to reality, and now he had to try to see a real Sarah. He could dwell on her sympathetic, warm-hearted disposition and her lively conversation; but he could not deny his head had first been turned by her face and form. He could not be surprised that other boys' heads had spun similarly, and that reciprocal emotions might have arisen in her.

Now, she had come down in his mind, she would inevitably, from time to time, shed her clothes, wrap herself with eagerness around the young fiancée and sigh and moan with the pleasure of penetration, along with peripheral amusements. What else could he expect when his Cinderella and her Prince Charming were at last alone? They would be said to be "making love", but Michael could only see this as, at best, manufacturing some sort of transient rapture – not as love. He could not maintain, to Woods or anyone else, that he would have resisted being enfolded thus with her, and sigh and moan together. There would have been no shame in their supposed shared animal craving; but he still would not have seen such invasion as any pinnacle of success.

Sex – the great horizontal leveller. He had tried, in his no doubt imperfect way, to immerse himself in the discipline of physics. He felt comfort in its dispassionate pursuit of the secrets of the world around him. The subatomic particles and the stars obeyed physical laws, but however much he thought of being resistant, he also had to obey biology. He knew he could not be set apart, and escape its grip. He had, sometimes, willingly succumbed, and had to admit to feelings of occasional delight bordering on euphoria; but this subservience had also revealed how easily it could make him feel pain and humiliation. He viewed biology as messy and unruly.

The concept of that small, but purportedly momentous, penetration had, years ago, seemed distasteful and remote. Then, it had not generated in him any feelings of desire or romance or humour, as it seemed to do for others. Even gradual acceptance at the dawn of student life had not convinced him that any girl would agree to this apparently sought-after union with him. His prediction had been fulfilled, and even *he* felt discontent. Now, something that was probably commonplace, even routine, a right for many, remained beyond his ineffectual grasp. The supposition that consummation was regular and easily obtained in his world by those outside was, he had discovered, yet another myth. Above all, a Michael and Sarah union, let alone reunion, was never destined to happen. He did not believe in destiny anyway.

Love still troubled him – the way the word was used and abused to conveniently suit too many circumstances. He could apply it unquestioningly to mother or father and their child, and even to brothers and sisters, but to little else. In any case, he had known nothing of these. If asked whether he was in love with Sarah, he would hesitate to give a straight answer. There was no doubt that he desired her, but he knew that that was a selfish motive. He could easily see himself being with her for a long period – laughing with her, being kind to her, looking after and protecting her. But the leap from this to thinking of her as the most revered being on earth, for whom his protection would extend to the ultimate sacrifice of giving his life, was something he could not contemplate with honesty. Now, however, these thoughts were of no relevance. She had drifted away – another passing passion in his life.

The earth had moved, the universe was constantly changing – it was obvious, he didn't need physics to tell him so; but the quantum world had introduced him to the step-change, and his own little world was now undergoing much the same. He believed he had dismissed fantasy and dreams in his life with a vengeance, but he wondered if he had blindly succumbed to them. If so, his new resolution was to step up and meet whatever came along with as much fortitude as he could muster. He had been dangerously close to viewing the last three years as peppered with failures, but even he had to admit now that this was a gross distortion. Still, one certainty that lifted him was that he had a voice, he could play guitar, and now he could escape to his attic bed-sit with more than one excuse to sing the blues!

October 1970 – A new dawn

If not the perfect spot, it was one in which he felt entirely at home, and happy that he had re-started on that familiar road. He sat on his bench looking down at the gentleman delivering the first lecture on quantum mechanics to the eager-looking MSc students. Michael had written to every university in the country, except of course Sussex – and even some abroad. Of the very few hopeful replies, one succeeded in making his heart beat faster. Nuclear and Particle Physics – the title of the part-time, evening course at Birkbeck College in London had seemed to him like something heaven-sent, pulling him like a wasp to some deep honeypot. It involved a short train ride after work and, with his vastly increased, although in reality modest, income he could afford to pay for it. His letter of progress to Jack Rodwell had received a swift reply full of unrestrained encouragement.

Work was turning out to be not too work-like. He had been admitted to the staff of an institution known as the Cyclotron Unit at the, apparently, prestigious Hammersmith Hospital. Gradually, he had come to learn of its fame – the first place in the world to make radioactive isotopes for medical research. He was being paid to study the interaction of neutrons with biological tissue. He would not have hoped for or foreseen such an outcome, but he could see that it was certainly not without merit. All colleagues were older than him, and knew much more physics and chemistry. Far from looking forward to tedious work, he was conscious that he would have to study to keep up, let alone forge ahead. Even then, he still thought that the further degree that had been mentioned was not beyond him.

... a doctorate, Michael ... just think of that! ... no, don't dream ... dreams don't materialise into anything substantial ... you've got to study ... and, would you believe it, there are quite a few girls around the site ... and a bar fifty yards away ... but don't get too distracted ... you know what happens ... still ... there is that pretty girl I've made up a tennis doubles with sometimes ... why shouldn't I ask her out? ... one or two of my offers have been accepted in the distant past ... probably won't lead anywhere ... where do you want it to lead? ... not sure, as usual ... but I'm used to being, if gently, dropped and moving on ... passing through to something, maybe someone else ... still I'll ask ... you never know ...

Details of Songs

Title	Artist	Composer	Year
Reach Out, I'll Be There	The Four Tops	Holland, Dozier, Holland	1966
Gimme Some Lovin'	The Spencer Davis Group	Winwood, Davis, Winwood	1966
Good Vibrations	The Beach Boys	Wilson, Love	1966
How Sweet It Is (To Be Loved By You)	Marvin Gaye	Holland, Dozier, Holland	1964
N.S.U.	Cream	Bruce	1966
Babe I'm Gonna Leave You	Joan Baez	Bredon	~1960
Venus In Furs	The Velvet Underground	Reed	1967
I'm Waiting For The Man	The Velvet Underground	Reed	1967
White Room	Cream	Bruce, Brown	1968
Wichita Lineman	Glen Campbell	Webb	1968
Badge	Cream	Clapton, Harrison	1969
Taxman	The Beatles	Harrison, Lennon	1966
Good Day Sunshine	The Beatles	Lennon, McCartney	1966
For No One	The Beatles	Lennon, McCartney	1966
I've Passed This Way Before	Jimmy Ruffin	Dean, Weatherspoon	1967
Al Capone	Prince Buster	Prince Buster	1964
Purple Haze	The Jimi Hendrix Experience	Hendrix	1967

Title	Artist	Composer	Year
Dance The Night Away	Cream	Bruce, Brown	1968
Bob Dylan's Dream	Bob Dylan	Dylan	1963
Drive My Car	The Beatles	Lennon, McCartney	1965
Lucille	Little Richard	Collins	1957
That'll Be The Day	Buddy Holly & The Crickets	Allison, Holly, Petty	1957
Knock On Wood	Eddie Floyd	Cropper, Floyd	1967
Wild Thing	The Troggs	Taylor	1965
Living In The Past	Jethro Tull	Anderson	1969
Break Away	The Beach Boys	Wilson, Wilson	1969
Born To Be Wild	Steppenwolf	Bonfire	1968
Waterloo Sunset	The Kinks	Davies	1967
Politician	Cream	Bruce, Brown	1968
You Keep Running Away	The Four Tops	Holland, Dozier, Holland	1968
Jumping Jack Flash	The Rolling Stones	Jagger, Richards	1968

Apologies to Max Miller for the quote of his little rhyme (p.105-6)

Lightning Source UK Ltd.
Milton Keynes UK
UKHW050329060121
376457UK00012BA/571